Born

OF

Dreams

LOUIS VILLALBA

GADES BOOKS

PUBLISHER: GADES BOOK

The story narrated here was created by the author's imagination and should not be considered as real. Any resemblance to events or persons, living or dead, is purely coincidental.

Copyright © 2021 Louis Villalba
Email: Louis@LouisVillalba.com
Website: www.LouisVilllalba.com
Blog: www.TheClassicWriter.com
Publisher: www.GadesBooks.com

ISBN13: 978-0-9996677-2-9

Editors: Hildi Goldstein and Cynthia Kegel, Ph.D.

To my granddaughter Andrea

Acknowledgement

I am grateful to my editors, Hildi Goldstein and Cynthia Kegel, Ph.D., for their invaluable contribution.

In the drowsy dark caves of the mind

Dreams build their nest with fragments

Dropped from day's caravan

Spring scatters the petals of flowers

That are not for the fruits of the future,

But for the moment's whim.

From *Firefly* by Rabindranath Tagore

Preface

*B*orn of Dreams may be read as a sequel to *The Stranger's Enigma* or as its own. The first novel features Dr. Daniel Brandon, a successful neurologist who falls victim of marital discord and job stress. An unfair and torturous malpractice suit compounds his problems. The situation threatens his sanity, and nightly dreams become his only getaway. He discovers Sonie, the protagonist of his nocturnal escapades. He resembles Daniel physically but always looks young and happy. Daniel Brandon is convinced that Sonie holds the secret of eternal bliss—never-ending youth and joy. The doctor decides to study his dreams and unveil the mystery. He envisages cryptic messages embedded in the nightly scenes. They should steer him through a maze of trails and lead to the resolution of his quest. In a dream, Daniel enjoys a torrid encounter with Julie. She does not look like anyone he has ever met in real life. He falls head over heels for her. The new love catapults his research to an unprecedented height. Daniel must find the secret. He hopes its discovery will let him enter the world of dreams and share eternal bliss with Julie.

One

THE BIRTH

I lie under a white sheet that rests on my face and quivers with my breathing. I kick off the linen and sit in bed. A portentous silence looms over this semidark windowless intensive-care room. Next to me, a monstrous apparatus sits on four wheels and towers over me. An octopus-like tentacle hangs from it with a cup large enough to cover both the mouth and nose of any human. This apparatus and the rest of the surrounding paraphernalia reveal the persistent attempts to save the body I now own. There are turned-off monitors, clinging tubes of the ventilator, metallic stands with limp lines of intravenous infusions, and shrunken plastic bags almost empty of their colorless fluids. Medical personnel certified its death a moment ago. My stark nakedness matches the whiteness and coldness of the marble floor. I wear a white wristband with the name of my donor, Dr. Daniel Brandon; his admission date two days ago, July 13, 2009; his age, 54; date of birth, 04/15/1955, and name of the attending physician, Michael Rosen M.D.

An armchair leans against a wall where a small picture shows a solitary beach with sand dunes and bent reeds. The images don't ease my claustrophobic enclosure. I take a deep breath and bask in odorless and tasteless air. I feel free. My eyes welcome the light that ricochets inside my retina and cheers me up. I am a lucky guy. I am alive in a real world and endured neither imprisonment in the belly of a woman nor crushing through the narrow bony pelvic channel. Nor did I have to bawl a loud cry to let the air rush into my lungs.

My thoughts drift to Daniel Brandon. A few minutes earlier, his spirit split from his body and entered the Other Dimension where dreamland lay. In front of him stretched out a world wrapped in kaleidoscopic colors, scintillating stars, geometrical figures, zigzag bright lights, flower fragrance, and a honey taste. There, he joined Julie and me, Sonie. She was the gorgeous woman whose green eyes had captivated him since he met her in one of his dreams and fell head over heels for her. I was his handsome look-alike in nightly dreams, someone who enjoyed everlasting youth and joy that Daniel wished for himself. He longed to remain in that paradise with us. No wonder he regarded with resentment his abandoned vacant body on the bed I now occupy. His anatomy lingered in a near-death state. It awaited his imminent return from the transdimensional jaunt. Two monitors flashed flat tracings and wailed. Daniel had to come back to the earthly world and reclaim it, or all his cells would perish forever. Time was almost up. I stayed away from his sight and left him alone so that he would enjoy his tryst with his beloved. During their brief meeting, Daniel asked about my whereabouts and soon watched in awe how I slipped into his body—softly and slowly as though I were tucking myself under a beautiful quilt. Julie explained to him how I took possession of his physical frame,

"Sonie left, Daniel. Love works miracles."

Until that instant, Daniel failed to realize how much I had grown to care for him since I had lived in his dreams all his life. He realized I had transferred to him my immortal existence in the Other Dimension in exchange for his ephemeral corporal life on earth, full of uncertainties.

"Now a new man better than me walks upon the face of the earth,"

Daniel said, praising me.

Daniel's words of accolade carry an implicit message: he wants me to improve his image in his terrestrial abode and right his wrongdoings. Medical-practice woes, aloof children, an angry mother, and his main screwup—unhappy Marlene, his wife of twenty-six years he has just divorced. I must live up to his expectations but don't know what life on earth has in store for me. If what I observe around me shows the vicissitudes to come, my sacrifice will be bigger than I anticipated. The plaintive weeping of nearby moribund patients reveals the suffering needed to leave this mortal existence. I now understand the reason that man's secret of eternal bliss in the Other Dimension is the persistence of immortality with which God blessed humanity at its inception. There, humans never lost their eternal existence to original sin. I wonder what kind of gift He bestowed upon life on earth.

A copy of the Chicago Tribune lies on a chair next to my bed. Someone must have forgotten it. The world is in upheaval. War rages in Afghanistan, a recession foreshadows a bleak future for workers, and next to it Goldman boasts a $ 3.4 billion profit. Humanity has a lot of work to do. I take a pause from the observation of my surroundings and notice that no one has welcomed me. Perhaps, it is not such a good idea to be born a grownup. For one thing, you go through the birth procedure alone and don't have the benefit of a mother's warmth.

I shouldn't complain because the exchange was successful. It worked like the installation of a new operating system into an old computer. The transfer of my personal specifications deleted Daniel's cerebral data of vices and virtues he had acquired or kept over the years. His memory files were preserved to allow me to continue his medical career as a neurologist and assume his identity. I need not start from scratch. There is a caveat. I inherited his memories without the emotion attached to each of them. This reaction defines the essence of an individual and sets him apart from others. My situation resembles that of a spectator in a movie theater who watches scenes and gathers some inkling of the involved feelings from associated images. If Daniel cries, he was sad when the event occurred. But as the moviegoer, I might be indifferent or respond my own way, smiling, laughing, or weeping.

I skipped the usual development from babyhood to adulthood. This omission spared me both damaging and constructive molding influence of parents, teachers, peer groups, and society that besieged Daniel. The exchange procedure put me through the paces. It reenacted his difficult life, divorce, estrangement from family and friends, career failure, and a suicidal episode. I don't know the reason humans can screw up so badly and end up threatening their own lives, their most precious possession.

A small mirror inside the nightstand reflects my face for the first time. My young physical appearance didn't survive the exchange filter and failed to transform the anatomy of Daniel into a younger one. I own new brown eyes, a small mustache, and salt-and-pepper hair that confer me a distinguished look. My mature body, however, gained strength, following the Latin dictum *"mens sana in corpore sano"*—a sound mind makes a body healthier.

I utter my name, and my voice surprises me when the sound bursts from deep in my throat for the first time. The air squeezes through the respiratory passages and issues understandable sounds. The feeling must be like that of a newborn during its first cry. I move my fingers and toes. The obedience of these body parts amazes me, and so does the crispy sensation of rubbing them against each other, which causes a ticklish sensation.

I examine my body from head to toe. The earlobes render an inhuman shape to my head, and the folds and holes feel weird to the touch. My fingers crawl down to the chest where little teats lie flat, senseless, and useless for the human male. They are surrounded by bushy hair that has become unfashionable. In prehistoric time, men might have exhibited it to disguise themselves among monkeys. What in the heck is the belly button for? What possible function could this rugged structure have except for nesting fluff or piercing it with a ring? Down a midline hairy path, my male organ stands at attention. The resilient organ has aroused much mayhem in mankind. Palpation evokes pleasure and, as if ordered by high military command, the private part fills up, grows with pride, and turns bluish red in the face.

I sit to contemplate my manhood and watch a nurse peeking into my room. Her eyes open wide and seem to come out of her orbits as she freaks out and screams over and over,

"He is alive! He's resurrected!"

Soon, I am surrounded by a crowd of white uniforms. Everyone looks at me like a wild animal that has escaped from the zoo. I hear hospital personnel rush in and out of the intensive care unit, abandoning the care of their patients and the monitors in the nurses' station. In the room across from mine, an old man moans some indistinct words and attempts to stand up. His overweight wife in a red T-shirt grimaces with anger and scrambles to force him down to his bed, yelling at him,

"Stay put, Stan, where do you think you're going?"

Covered in white sheets, patients from neighboring rooms get on their feet and lumber in my direction. The alarms from their disconnected machines shout deafening noises. The approaching ghost-like figures hold their intravenous stands and drag the connecting tubes. One slips and falls and raises a cry as pitiful as that of a wounded animal. Another stops, uproots a catheter from his or her forearm, and shuffles on, leaving a trail of blood. A thin and tall phantom slips by the wall of nurses and upsets the chair and the respirator next to my bed. The machine hits the floor and makes a big racket. The lanky trespasser stops in front of me and stares me in the face with pleading eyes. An elderly woman sits in a wheelchair, yelling,

"What's going on?"

A black nurse with an ivory complexion runs toward the senior to calm her down. I feel as though afflicted with leprosy because no one dares touch me. The crowd of puzzled personnel attracts more witnesses. Those in green scrub shirts walk in from the surgical suites, wearing expressions of skepticism. Michael Rosen MD, my attending physician, rushes in and invades my space. Marlene assigned her ex-husband to the colleague he had disliked the most. Tall and muscular, he looks like a movie actor and flaunts a full head of dark hair, gray sideburns, a dimpled chin, and a virile smile. No nurse has ever resisted the charm of this conceited jerk. He wears a blue jacket with brassy buttons, gray pants with perfect creases, and a flashy red tie. His face reveals bewilderment and fear.

Father Ruston, the hospital chaplain, ambles into my room, crosses himself twice, and lifts his eyes to heaven. His lips and small gray mustache quiver as he issues benedictions with his hand. It seems that what has happened here can be considered a miracle on earth. I focus my gaze on the cleric and bystanders but cannot make out their thoughts. I frown, clench my teeth, take deep breaths, and tighten my fists. Nothing works. I lost the power I had in the Other Dimension. The exchange filter got rid of it. I wonder what other qualities I have lost. My disappointment makes me waste precious time, for I need to make a statement before they grab me and stick me into one the niches at the altars of a nearby church,

"What is wrong with you guys? Have you never seen a cataleptic patient wake up? You should be ashamed of yourselves!"

The word catalepsy popped in my mind—a trance-like state of unresponsiveness and unconsciousness that is often confused with death. Some victims sat up in the hearse on the way to the cemetery, prompting stampedes in funeral corteges. Everyone knows about this condition because it hit the news a few days ago. A guard found a young man dead in his jail cell. Three physicians certified his demise, the first at the prison facility, the second at the emergency room, and the third at the morgue. The inmate woke up on an autopsy table of cold marble when he was about to have his body opened.

At my mentioning the diagnosis, everyone freezes and frowns as anger grows on their faces. This witticism works because everyone realizes that Daniel Brandon—the person they believe I am—is still the same blockhead he has always been. He never qualified as a saint. I regret the way I must treat them, but otherwise, I don't know what they would have done.

Dr. Rosen performs a cursory exam and auscultates me. The light touch of his fingertips on my chest gives me the creeps. His hand conveys hatred for me as a mother's arms would her anxiety or joy to her baby. He stays silent, but his body speaks through his tight mouth, subtle quivering of his lips, flaming eyes under knitted brows, and a fist's clawing grip on a suffocated pen. I still can't read his mind. Yet, his thoughts issue vibes that rush through the distance between us. My brain captures them, and a malicious message rings deep inside: Dr. Rosen wishes me dead. I wonder why some humans can harbor such terrible evil in their hearts. A wry smile and the disappointment in his tone of voice corroborate my unexpected intuition.

"You may go home tomorrow if your EKG monitoring shows no arrythmia and the blood glucose and serum electrolytes remain normal. Please, make an appointment to get a 48-hour ambulatory electroencephalogram and see me afterward as soon as possible," he says.

The next morning, a house physician orders a 24-hour ambulatory electroencephalogram and an ultrasound of the carotid and vertebral arteries. I won't comply. I am healthy. A nurse hands me a yellow paper with my discharge instructions and addresses me,

"Dr. Brandon, put on your clothes. People are not in the habit of walking nude on the streets of Chicago. You may go home. Here are your watch and onyx ring. Do you want me to call Marlene?"

"No."

Two

I TOLD YOU SO

*D*aniel owns apartment 1122 in Marina Towers, the twin buildings shaped like corn cobs at 300 N. State Street in downtown Chicago. I get to my new home and open the door. A stale stench slaps me because it must have accumulated over the few days he stayed in the hospital. A small lobby abuts a living-room-kitchenette. Lights are on, sofa cushions in disarray, rotten pieces of cake and a half-emptied coffee cup atop a table, a white robe and two slippers on the floor, and the blinds shut. In the kitchenette, the counter bristles with dirty wine glasses, a half-full bottle of cabernet, an uncorked Rhine white wine, and an intact decanter with cognac. Food-stained cookware and silverware spill from the kitchen sink. A wide rectangular entrance leads to the master bedroom. The king-size bed rests undone with wrinkled sheets, and a red-and-blue, square-quilted cover lies on a vanilla carpet. On the main wall hangs a tilted copy of a painting by Frida Kahlo. The Mexican artist boasts a mustache, long eyebrows meeting above the bridge of her nose, two parrots in her arms and two on her shoulders. Towels languish crumpled and scattered on the bathroom floor. The toilet bowl stares at me since its lid stands unfolded. The tub drowns on soapy water rimmed with hair and dirt. The chaotic state reveals my donor's mental condition the day of his admission into intensive care.

I sit on a magenta velvet sofa in his living room, sensing the silence around me like crashing thunder in a deserted valley. My feet land on the coffee table. In front of me loom gilded framed pictures of everyone important in the life of Daniel on earth, loved ones that, along with his possessions, I have inherited. The borders link one another like those of a collage. In the upper corner, a photo features his parents in their early thirties before their divorce. Lorna, his mother, exhibits a skeptical expression that accentuates a sardonic smile. Her incipient frown doesn't suppress her beauty but reveals fastidiousness, a shortcoming that ended her marriage when Daniel was nine. His father, Victor Brandon, has a head full of dark hair and sparkling eyes that render him a joyful and carefree appearance. His corpulence contrasts with his spouse's petite figure. Photographs of Daniel's grown-up children flank the sides of the arrangement. Twenty-five-year-old Ana with her sleek dark hair and pale white skin. A year her junior, blond Emmanuelle with gorgeous blue eyes. And 23-year-old poster hunk Steve with his physical assets on display. The picture of an attractive and young Marlene sits inclined at the bottom as if Daniel had wished its fall and crash against the floor. Or perhaps, he removed it, changed his mind, and carelessly hung it back.

In the center of the arrangement lies the photo of Daniel in a black doctoral cap and gown at his graduation from Northwestern Medical School. His conceit shows up in the pursing of his lips and stern gaze. The image also conveys sternness and stoicism. It makes me reminisce about the events that led to my existence on earth. Over the years, a course of repeated mistakes ended up in Daniel's midlife crisis. The trap of unhappiness besieged him until an escape opened before him—his dreams. There, he discovered me as the stranger endowed with eternal joy and youth, someone who resembled him physically and came alive in nightly scenes. He wished he were me and set to study his dreams and unveil the secret of eternal bliss that accounted for my blessings. His research escalated when Daniel met Julie in a dream and fell so much in love with her that he became obsessed with joining her in the Other Dimension. Through scientific self-experimentation, Daniel discovered the secret of eternal bliss. It led him to the world where his beloved Julie and I lived. But he never envisioned that, in the process, he would bump into an exchange procedure that would grant him an eternal existence in dreamland and me a life on earth.

So here I am. I will dedicate the first three days of my life on this planet to getting used to my new body. Sensations call my attention. I notice the tread of my footsteps on the tiles and its soft counterpart on the carpet. Intermittent blinking hammers my eyelids. Saliva flows in my mouth, and my arms swing as I walk. What are these involuntary motions for? Is man born with the instinct of flying like a bird? I feel the pressure of socks and shoes on my imprisoned feet and the weight and rubbing of clothes on my skin. A watch strangles my left wrist, and a black onyx ring my left finger. Other suppressed perceptions bombard my brain. The touch of glass on my skin, the coldness of water in my mouth, the swallowing of this tasteless fluid without choking. It rushes down my esophagus. My gut worms in the belly with a hollow grumble. I might be hungry or just bloated from the respirator. My gas stinks. What a humbling experience. The biological machine of man needs refinement. I never heard these noises, felt these sensations, or smelled these odors in the Other Dimension. There, even human excrement lacks smell.

In the fridge, there are slices of cheese and smoked salmon inside a drawer, lettuce and tomato in another, and a full gallon of two-percent milk. The skeleton of a pizza lies on the upper shelf. A few eggs and a plastic cup of nonfat yogurt rest in their assigned compartments. Pre-prepared dishes sit crammed in the freezer. I throw the pizza into the garbage can and serve myself a glass of milk, a cup of yogurt, and two slices of cheese. Everything has a different taste—the white liquid exhibits a creamy texture, yogurt a soft acidity, and cheese a pleasant aroma. I pee in the privacy of the bathroom. The warm and narrow stream and fruity scent don't match what I experienced in my previous world.

There, I would disregard adults and children, open my zipper, bring my saluting soldier out, and walk swinging it like a baton on my way to a convenient place. There, exposing your male member was as common as uncovering a finger or a toe.

This place bears a muggy atmosphere and makes me feel like taking a shower. I lift the plug to empty the bathtub, pull the shower head out, and rinse the white porcelain clean. These strands of hair contain my DNA. In the Other Dimension, we didn't bother to remove our clothes before stepping into an enormous hot tub. But here, I strip down and then hear the quiet noise of ejected liquid that evokes a new desire to urinate. Why should I? I did it a minute ago. I hope I haven't inherited the obsessions of Daniel, and that pathology has succumbed to the filter of the exchange procedure. The open window in the living room lets the warm air of this summer morning waft through the apartment. A remarkable view bursts forth before me. A river of metallic blue water meanders in the center of the cityscape. Like giant mirrors, glass high-rises of avant-garde architecture reflect pedestrians and moving cars, images jumping from building to building like Olympic contestants. In the background, the never-ending blue water of Lake Michigan stretches out onto a clear horizon.

It is 3:00 AM on my third day on earth, and I am fatigued. Frida's parrots tremble, and their feathers have turned brown and spread beyond the frame. Lizards crawl on the walls, and frogs croak. My brain can no longer function. Daniel used to fall asleep before midnight every day, but I have no idea how he accomplished it. I have reviewed the files in the memory stores and encountered none with the information. A mechanism must exist to reach the state of suspension of vigil. Or has this crucial function been assigned to unforeseeable luck and chance in humans? The more I search for it in my brain, the further away I find myself from achieving the necessary rest. Another defect in the human machine. How many are they? A long way to go in evolution. Should humans not be able to catch a wink at will as I did in the Other Dimension? If hungry, they grab food; if cold, they cover themselves with a blanket; if tired, they lie down. Why should they not be able to instruct their brains to fall asleep?

I go to bed and wait for slumber to take hold of me, but nothing happens. My eyes are open wider than an owl's. I plop down on the sofa and turn the TV on, and the next thing I know, daylight seeps through the window, and the clock chimes 12:00 noon. This trick must be the answer. Sleep overtook me without warning. It surprises me as if humans were subjected to a daily drill of death in preparation for their inevitable end.

Tomorrow morning, I intend to visit the woman who bore the ultimate responsibility for my donor's upbringing—his mother, Lorna Brandon. I review my memory stores and come up with a summary file:

Lorna Brandon-Shields, 75- year-old mother of Daniel and ex-wife of Victor Brandon. Retired social worker and amateur psychologist. Enjoys card games and meddles in the lives of everyone. Fiercely independent. Sharp tongue. Daniel was nine when his parents divorced. He visited his dad every other weekend until his death twelve years later. Their son felt a devoted filial love for Lorna, which was combined with resentment because of her controlling nature. A few months ago, Daniel informed Lorna that Julie and I existed in the Other Dimension. That I retained all the virtues and qualities her son was born with. But many of those attributes disappeared from Daniel's personality with the passage of time and the malign influence of society. He described my dream world as one of eternity, fantasy, and music, where one could travel to the future or back in time or read people's minds. His mother concluded his deranged mind created everything."

I ring the bell with a bouquet of roses in my hand, and Lorna hollers, "Come in... you've got the key!"

She must have been waiting for me, but the hugs and kisses humans are so fond of never materialize. My donor was an only son, so I expected a warm welcome. The place lies in semidarkness. Kaleidoscopic geometrical paintings and absence of family pictures on the hall walls render the abode an emotionless futuristic air. Daniel felt love and intimidating respect for his mother because she subjected him to constant nagging: "pick up your room," "clean your bathroom after washing up," "throw your dirty clothes down the chute." Anything he did was wrong. Lorna had infused him with some questionable moral vices that made him a successful man before his midlife crisis hit him: money hunger without greed, power without conceit, pride without vanity, jealousy without envy, hypocrisy without pretension, and sex without lust. Not all took root in the youngster since he never controlled conceit. Lorna made him shy and insecure and turned him into an individual who depended on her to anchor himself to the family and society.

Lorna sits at her desk, reviewing bills. Her slim figure and complexion shine with a youthful air, her hair shows streaks of gray, her eyes sparkle with a pale blue color, and her face bears a few wrinkles around the lips. She lifts her head from the paper to address me,

"I told you so."

I say I have come over to say hello and let her know about my return to good health, not to hear any recriminations.

"What's wrong with you? Why do you bring me flowers?" she asked in a perplexed tone. "I am not dead yet."

I have read that flower soften women's hearts, but not Lorna's. She doesn't look angry but lambasts me with a barrage of her son's wrongdoings, erratic behavior, failed marriage, bankrupt office, lost medical malpractice suit. Her tone bristles with anger and resignation, and she doesn't let me insert a word in edgewise. I feel like a Chinese gentleman upbraided in German. At least, she hides no bad thought and levels every criticism brewing in her mind. I wonder whether moms are entitled to ranting. Human relationships seem complicated. Is a son supposed to endure peremptory words because she is a mother? I might have missed nothing by not being born into a family. If it were up to me, I would tell her off, but instead I say,

"My good lady, I've changed."

"What? My good lady, I've changed? You've turned into a weirdo. Is this the way you talk to your mother?"

I don't understand why she gets so upset. I have correctly called her, "lady" as it applies to "a refined, polite, and well-spoken woman." I am tempted to withdraw the qualification since her dilated nostrils and fiery look show otherwise. But good sense tells me I should shut my mouth when my chances to prevail are nil. Her onslaught continues,

"You have changed? What is wrong with you? You should be under psychiatric care before you commit another stupidity."

According to her, I am crazy. But I know my donor's brain was de-bugged of illogical contaminants before the exchange procedure. Why would my healthy brain need a retrograde management like psychiatric care? Here on earth, people with a propensity to suicide or mental mis-perception seek help from professionals who use chemicals to fix their intellect. Do they heal any mind? These crude methods curtail the most dangerous aspects threatening the individual but sacrifice some of the soundest qualities such as initiative, planning, and creativity. It is often a poor trade. I tell her that I need not undergo such raw treatments. I have clear perception, logical thoughts, and excellent decision-making abilities.

"You don't sound like my son. What have they done to you in the hospital? Electroshock? Frontal lobotomy?"

I tell her that she knows everything about my stay because she con-ferred with Dr. Michael Rosen. Besides, the incident somehow filtered into the newspapers, and I am sure she has a cutout somewhere on her desk. It displays the picture of Michael Rosen. I don't understand why women on this planet fall for these dupes with gigantic conceit, dry brains, and a penchant for nonsensical beauty. The photo exhibits the halo of a movie star, his hair eases down the left temple, and his eyes' glitter spills out of a pair of silver-framed glasses. But his attempt at an impression of superior intelligence backfires and turns his portrait into that of an irreverent faker. I have read it,

"Michael Rosen, MD, chief of neurology at Riverfront Hospital, de-scribed the recovery of one of his colleagues, Dr. Daniel Brandon, as a miracle of science. The patient was pronounced dead based on the strict criteria of the American Neurological Association, but the applied well-devised medical intervention..."

The paper praises his present and past accomplishments as though he were worthy of the Nobel Prize.

"He doesn't know how you woke up. He swore you were dead, as he put it, 'absolutely dead,'" Lorna says.

She continues her description of what Dr. Rosen wrote, reading from the newspaper. The doctor mentions a few neurological conditions that seem to split the mind from the body. He acknowledges his inability to explain what happened to his fellow neurologist Daniel Brandon, MD. I remark that doctors don't know everything. A lot of science awaits discovery. A miracle today can become an everyday event tomorrow. The word discovery makes me drift the conversation toward the mess she made in my condo, which I found when I arrived from the hospital,

"I don't understand why you opened my safe and left all the papers in disarray, including the will."

Lorna dislikes my objection and resents her arrangements for Daniel's burial whose down payment cost her one thousand dollars. The funeral home kept the amount because of the wasted time. The upset director informed her that the incident marked the first time someone had played such a cruel prank on him. No word could convince him. Lorna went on about how she had to riffle through the documents looking for the life insurance policy that would cover the expenses. She found out the beneficiary was Daniel's neighbor, Allen Roach, at apartment 1121. So were all Daniel's assets in the will: two condos in Puerto Vallarta, Mexico, a country home in Lake Geneva, Wisconsin, a two-million-dollar pension at Schwab. She wonders what the old man did to deserve such a reward, adding,

"What about your children? What about your mother?"

I didn't think that it would be so challenging to impersonate my donor. He committed many wrongdoings late in his life. Daniel took the term "next of kin" literally and applied it to the gentleman who lived next door. His hellos, goodbyes, and "*how-are-yous*" could have been the reason. The old neighbor's greetings have been consistent acts of kindness. Daniel's children never called, and his attempts on the phone to reach them prompted the same recorded response: "Your call has been forwarded to an automatic voice message system." He left his number numerous times but seldom heard from them. Besides, his mother had enough money, and Daniel discovered what I am about to unveil,

"Why are you surprised? You are bequeathing your assets to the Chimpanzee's Behavioral Research Institute."

"How do you know? Did you wrest this confidence from my attorney?"

I don't want to reveal how Daniel found out. It happened at the Totem Pole in Lincoln Park. A guy who worked at the nearby zoo watched Daniel climb the Indian pole in search of the carved face of his beloved Julie, which his imagination had spotted at the tip. When a disappointed Daniel came down, the onlooker remarked,

"I now understand why your mother left her money to the monkeys."

Her will was common knowledge among employees at the facility. In a conciliatory tone, I avoid this explanation and address the issue from a different angle. One may dispose of one's money as one pleases. I hold no grudge against monkeys or against the creator of the program, Professor Proskish, may his soul rest in peace. My Attorney Samuel Goldstein has already changed my testament in favor of Ana, Emmanuelle, and Steve. I now expect Lorna to follow suit. She often goes out with an assistant of the late professor who happens to be twenty years younger than her. Daniel stayed away from her group of friends. She ignores my words and asks,

"Where have you been since you left the hospital three days ago?"

"Perhaps you believe I went to heaven and came back since some people swear that I was resurrected."

Lorna says she knows better than that because Daniel is neither a saint nor a believer, just a prig. Then, she wonders what I have in the bag that hangs from my shoulder. I show her shaving utensils, a pair of pajamas, and a bottle of cologne. She stares at me and waits for my explanation,

"I want to correct my shortcomings. You always complain I don't spend enough time with you. From now on, I'll stay at your condo every Monday."

Lorna jumps up out of the chair as if a spring thrust her into the air. Her eyes were wide-open, her neck erect like a peacock's, and her words pound my ears,

"Oh, no! You won't be another divorcee returning home. I know what is going on out there. I have a life. I need my privacy."

She continues about Daniel's chaos. The insufferable dirt he collected in the bathroom along with the toilet lid left up. The dirty dishes that he expected her to wash. His lack of initiative in taking the garbage out. She felt liberated when he left home for college. Nothing changes her mind. She turns a deaf ear to my promises to keep everything neat and assurances of my different disposition since my cataleptic attack. Before I leave, she issues a last request,

"If you want to make me happy, behave... call your ex. Marlene was a good wife. Get back together with her. Fix your marriage."

I don't reply. But I know that is one of my major challenges on earth.

Tonight, at home, I realize my oneiric propensity, the ability to generate vivid dreams, must be part of my donor's genes. It remains immersed in the intact neurons and nerve fibers in his brain, unscathed by the exchange procedure. The night scenes I remember in the morning feature Daniel engaged in the bliss of his new existence. He enjoys his surroundings where thousands of paths cross fields awash with yellow, brown, and purple flowers. He is always near Julie, basking in their love.

According to Daniel, an event that occurred the previous day triggers a dream. It spurs unconscious and subconscious desires or forbidden wishes that set off an electrical discharge in the brain. The individual's mood steers the nervous impulse through a specific pathway in the temporal lobe. Here, it collects images from the memory stores and composes scenes with them. Apprehension gives rise to situations of being lost in strange places. Depression and anxiety, embarrassing nude scenes. Self-criticism and self-deprecation, shameful foul scenes, Anxiety and fear, horrifying accidents such as never-ending falls or devastating car crashes. Indifference, images of daily routine. Sexual arousal, erotic scenes. And happiness, pleasant dreams. Daniel believed a dream works as a thermometer of the person's emotional state at the time of its occurrence. It reveals clues about conscious and subconscious issues, wishes the individual is dealing with, and sometimes messages about an unforeseen future event.

I hope Daniel extends me the same courtesy I granted him and lets me be the protagonist of some of my dreams. The question arises of how I will recognize myself. Time will make it easier. The appearance of Daniel will remain the same since the inhabitants of the Other Dimension don't get old. Mine, however, will age. In the meantime, I am making some changes. I have shaved the mustache and sprayed Minoxidil on my receding hairline. Daily exercises and weightlifting should widen my chest and enlarge my biceps and deltoids. Optimism and self-confidence should light up my facial features and smooth the usual creases of a man in his fifties. It takes two weeks for me to have my first dream:

I am in a coffee shop alone. A young Latino waitress serves me some tacos. I explain to her that I saw her shop a while ago and looked forward to coming in. A Mexican-looking diva in her late fifties sings Mariachi songs as I rejoice in the pleasant dream, a gift from my happy mood. But soon I am no longer by myself because Daniel sits next to me. His radiant face shows the same bliss I enjoyed in the Other Dimension. He wears a white-linen, collarless shirt, perfectly white Chino pants, light-blue loafers, a well-trimmed mustache, and sweet cologne like a model at a Pierre Cardin fashion show. The scent drowns the strong odor of burnt coffee and *huevos rancheros.* Julie must be nearby because they are always together. I wonder why he came alone, but he doesn't let me wait too long for an answer and criticizes my handling of his mother, blaming it on my lack of readiness. When I complain that I am trying to correct the mess that he left in this world, he gets angry,

"You are not doing that. You are making things worse."

"I haven't called you, Daniel. When I was in the Other Dimension, I respected your privacy. I never jumped into one of your dreams.

Anyway, didn't you give me an assignment and trust me with it?"

"You make mistakes."

"We all make mistakes. One must hope they are correctable and learn from them."

"It is my legacy that it is at stake."

"I leave you alone to enjoy your blissful existence with Julie. Wasn't that the reason for the exchange?"

"I have also freed myself from the terrible nightmares you subjected me to, Sonie."

"Your mind created them whenever I assigned you a dream."

"So, you believe Sigmund Freud?"

"Oh, leave him alone. Let his soul rest in peace."

"You'll learn, Sonie. You think I was schizophrenic. That my conversations with Sigmund Freud were all figments created by my sick brain."

"What is the point? It was what it was. Now, I've got a sound mind to keep and a tough job to do."

I tell Daniel he shows the same ungratefulness of most people on earth who only think about themselves. They cram the air with carbon dioxide from polluting cars and factories without any regard for others, overheating the planet. They build walls to separate the poor from the rich so that selfishness prevails. The me-and-me-only philosophy rules. Daniel ignores me and says,

"Beware! My mother won't swallow your cataleptic lie. If she finds out the truth, she will have you jailed or committed to an asylum."

I reply I hope that he cooperates with me in improving his legacy. Some areas require attention because, as he knows, everything reflects on me. Besides, he still bristles with the earthly vice called criticism. Here, people have mouths on their faces just to open them and lash out at one another with a bunch of stupidities, no one aware they are highlighting their own deficiencies. Daniel takes umbrage and counters,

"You should have handed my mother a one-thousand-dollar check and gotten the hell out of her apartment."

Three

NAKED TUESDAY

I am on the highest floor of a building crowded with visitors. With an expression of indifference, a young woman walks away from a baby boy who, wrapped in a white blanket, lies inside a cradle. He remains immobile, and this makes me wonder whether the child is alive. I pick him up in my arms. He opens his eyes, and I hand him over to the aloof mother, who holds him and stands stock-still. Everyone tries to leave through an exit, but the long queue barely moves. The public must be fleeing from some danger.

Hidden by a wall behind me, I find another way out, beckon the mother with the child, and usher them to a deserted back passage. A thick cloud of dust enwraps us as we struggle down a snail-shaped, windowless tunnel. The woman's eyes still shine with indifference in the gray penumbra and sepulchral silence that set in. Motionless in the mother's arms, the boy utters no sound, and the blanket now engulfs his body and head. Dust cakes our clothes and faces, whitening our eyelids and eyelashes. We rush down the long spiral without masks or handkerchiefs to protect us. I become concerned about the polluted air that could lead to severe pulmonary illness. Yet, our breathing suffers no ill effect. The respiratory noises remain soft, and the ashy material on our lips, tongues, and nostrils does not distort our taste and smell. The discrepancies make me realize that I am dreaming. The sudden opening of a door that spits us out into a swimming pool confirms this conclusion. This ending shows another characteristic of the dream world: when you least expect it, the most unusual device might emerge for your protection and guard you against a horrible accident.

My dream has a clear message. The scenes smoke me out of my comfort zone, where I have dawdled for three weeks and get me out to help others. Saving mother and child means that. The woman might be Marlene; the boy, Daniel's offspring; and the dusty spiral passage, the vicissitudes I must endure in the real world. The last images seem to augur a happy finale, or do they? Falling into a swimming pool with a baby and a woman who does not know how to swim can portend a disaster.

The backdoor of Marina Towers leads to Kinzie Street, where plenty of signs of social illness and decay loom before me. A young man in a red-and-white checker shirt and blue jeans proffers his hand and solicits money for a sandwich. Next to him stands an overweight, buxom woman in a white T-shirt with a red slogan written on the chest, "TOUCH THEM AND I'LL KILL YOU."

I hand them a twenty-dollar bill, and they rush into a small restaurant with a humongous donut sign. At a street corner, a bunch of hobos huddle over supermarket carts with all their possessions and dig food from garbage cans. No one pays attention to them. They witness my act of generosity and rush toward me with their palms open, their rugged faces contorting and their tattered clothes fluttering in the lake breeze. A heavy stench of humanity follows them like a dog. I run out of money except for a fifty- dollar bill.

We must be kind to others. There are quite a few people who are less fortunate than we are because they had no chance to succeed, or adversities overwhelmed them. We should not misjudge or distrust them. In the Other Dimension, Daniel admired my generosity and readiness to help others. Stinginess plagued him his entire life on earth.

21

He tried to overcome it through psychotherapy but achieved only a little success.

A few blocks away from Kinzie, I am in a different country—Michigan Avenue. The broad thoroughfare bustles with pedestrians and crawling vehicles. Waves of people cram before the traffic lights and stare straight ahead. They act as if afraid to be waylaid lest their thoughts should be halted and the arrival at their destination delayed or missed altogether.

As I walk on the streets of Chicago this late afternoon, I feel like Christopher Columbus when he stepped onto a new continent for the first time. Cities in the Other Dimension show similarities to this reality except for some distinct differences. You might roam into a colossal metropolis of metallic skyscrapers like the one depicted in Spiderman, stroll through a stunning florid garden, turn a corner, and find yourself atop the snowy peak of a mountain. I could travel back in time, visit ancient cities that lay buried or underwater, or in the blink of an eye, watch a day turn into a night or a night into a day. Kisses could transform into flowers, and rainbows into immense forests. Everything was possible in a world where the future didn't exist.

A youngster swaggers on the sidewalk with half of his head shaved and the other half with long braids. He carries a backpack and wears snakes and Christian symbols tattooed on his arms and face. The hieroglyph might convey a friendly message. I figure he must be a guy who survives on marijuana and Caribbean music. I approach him to test my deduction abilities on this planet and ask whether he likes to smoke joints. He sketches a menacing glare and growls,

"Get the hell out of my face!"

I dislike his answer but heed his threat, keep away, and flash at him two of my fingers raised in a "V" shape as a sign of peace. I don't understand his reaction. Curiosity is the basis of knowledge. A society that restricts questions will curtail its growth.

I continue my visit downtown. Dressed in a gray suit, a young man ambles by, his eyes focused on a smartphone, his fingers frenetically tapping a small screen. The Chicago Bank marks 86 degrees F, but an obese lady bears a brown fox stole with the animal's face hanging down. Its eyes look at me as if wondering what in the heck I am doing here. A youthful woman in a blue suit and tennis shoes regards a shopwindow with the mannequin of a fashion model in a blue suit and tennis shoes. These displays seem to serve as stations where everyone obeys the message of how one must dress in this society. Should you deviate from this norm, your silhouette would stand out on this throughway like the carcass of a giant whale in the middle of Vatican Square. When in Rome, one must do what Romans do. I am dressed like everyone else. Daniel's clothes conform to all the fashion rules of upscale stores. The street walls and lampposts feature billboards that bombard the pedestrians with cues addressing all aspects of life on earth: what to eat, when to sleep, where to shop, how to purchase an item, which movies to watch.

At the corner of Michigan Ave and Ontario St, a young black man in a navy-blue shirt and jeans plays the saxophone. The musician has an inverted black hat before him, and his body twists and turns as he blows into the instrument. The melody of "When the Saints Come Marching in" enlivens the area and infuses me with hope for humanity. Some people take surreptitious looks at him, display brief smiles, and slow down their paces as they stroll by the artist and then forge on to their destinations. I stop in front of him. He stares at me and bends over the mouthpiece as his silver-ringed, thick fingers press on the keys. His dark eyes look like two sparkling onyx stones above his puffed cheeks. I stretch my arms out, jostle some room, and dance. I parade like a soldier, turn around, throw my hands up, and tap the sidewalk with my heels the same way Fred Astaire hit the floor in *Swing Time*. Passersby voice loud complaints about my performance, something to do with the song not being appropriate for my dance. Even the musician glares at me and issues me a warning,

"Stop making fun of me, you, weirdo!"

I don't reply. But why should these people resent my enjoyment? I am not interfering with anyone's activities or impinging on their rights. In the Other Dimension, I sang and danced folk songs, jazz, pop music, tango, country, opera, even flamenco. Solo or in a duet with a friend or a monkey, I performed at renowned festivals and receptions for kings, queens, and presidents. These activities lifted my spirit. Daniel always wished to have my ability to carry a tune and dance like a pro, my capacity to smile and laugh with unrestrained joy, love for people, and optimism. To Daniel, fun activities were a waste of time, and games and dancing bored him. He begrudged any hours of idleness and seldom exhibited any sense of humor.

I stay on Michigan Avenue, follow the human herd, and find myself before an enormous black building, the John Hancock. My memory storage also keeps images of this skyscraper. But it does not record the enormity of the structure, the iron belts that crisscross the façade from side to side, and the almost imperceptible oscillation that rocks it. I don't understand why pedestrians don't fear this giant because I feel like Superman, ready to embrace it and stop the swinging. Did something happen with the exchange procedure that made me more sensitive than the rest of mankind? In the Other Dimension, I enjoyed superpowers. Once, I was alone aboard a zeppelin coursing through the sky above a wide street, feeling like a superhero in control of everyone. A gentleman in a sports coat stood next to a lamppost, looked at his watch, and dropped to the ground. He lay unconscious as if thunderstruck. Everyone who gazed at his watch suffered the same fate. I don't wield this superpower anymore, nor do I desire it because I want to be an ordinary citizen on earth.

Up the street and across from me stands the tiny Water Tower flanked and overtopped by massive high-rises. It looks like a medieval toy castle with a tall tower in the middle. This icon survived the conflagration that destroyed Chicago in 1871. Some horse-drawn carriages wait for customers. One with a gorgeous white horse and a coachman in black attire takes two newlyweds for a ride amid the honking of nearby cars. An elderly gentleman in a dark suit walks by me and grumbles between his teeth,

"Too much fuss and a lot of money about nothing. They all get divorced in a few years."

I disregard his words because he must represent those citizens on earth who choose to lead disappointing lives. There are angry and hostile people who begrudge others' goodwill and joy. Diversity sets its rule on this planet. I see the newlyweds' cheerful faces, the groom kissing his bride, the happiness in their sparkling eyes, and the noisy mayhem of well-wishers. The entire atmosphere uplifts my spirit like the basket under a hot-air balloon. Love floats around, an emotion that reminds me of my homeland, "a world of wonders where lovers dwell in bliss." Perhaps, the extraordinary reflection of the Other Dimension on this couple would be worth every penny they have spent, even if their marriage were short-lasting. Earthly life is so brief that one should regret departing it without such an experience.

A few yards forward, I reach the shore of Lake Michigan, where I admire the sandy coastline crowded with beachgoers. A broad promenade with cyclists and saunterers lies next to it. They enjoy the spectacle of lights reverberating on immense blue water and the soothing murmur of waves as seagulls pirouette and caw overhead. The expansive and majestic Lake Shore Drive meanders along the cityscape, framing the littoral like an elegant white ribbon a gift box.

I cross Michigan Avenue again, reach Oak Street, and walk a few steps. A blond guy with long disheveled hair and a black coat accosts me. He opens his garment and flashes several tails of watches. I think he collects them, so I hand him my Seiko, but he refuses it and says,

"No, man, Japanese, that's garbage, keep it, buy a Citizen, the best, just twenty bucks."

I hand him the 50-dollar bill, and he gives me a watch and twenty dollars back. I extend my hand and wait for my ten dollars, but the peddler claims not to have any change. As soon as I call the deal off, a big bundle of bills materializes in his hand. He curses the returned amount and swaggers toward another potential customer, flicking a finger at me. I don't engage in a fight because prudence prevails.

The peddler's behavior exemplifies the greed that plagues society. It accounts for the Great Recession that humans still endure. A few bankers have become filthy rich, while scores of people have lost their homes, jobs, and health insurance coverage. Similar behavior has been part of the creation of this country—Rockefeller, Vanderbilt, Carnegie, Morgan. Thankfully, their cruel capitalism ended up in a competition for philanthropism. Their charity contributions and endowment to the arts and science made a long-lasting impression on American society. Do not expect anything from the bankers responsible for this recession. They are probably sailing through the Caribbean Sea like pirates. Will people ever learn to care for their fellow man?

Some degree of this misconduct afflicted Daniel. He dedicated all his time to accumulating wealth, justifying his behavior because his consuming medical practice provided a good life for his family. But it was never enough as Marlene put it in no uncertain terms,

"You never dedicated enough of your time to your children and tried to compensate for your deficiency by spoiling them."

This vice has never blemished my personality. In the Other Dimension, a salesman delivered a new copy machine to my office and asked me, "How much is the kickback?" I ignored the question and refused any money.

I soon hit N. Wells Street, an area unknown to Daniel because he never visited it. Dusk sets in. People hang out in little restaurants and outdoor cafés, some chat with a smile on their faces, and others stroll into these establishments. The Second City piques my curiosity. Adorned with foliage ornaments and four stern faces, an arcade of three arches rests at the entrance. Three steps lead to the venue that claims to be the best club for improvisation and comedy in Chicago.

I wonder whether my sense of humor in the Other Dimension has survived the filter of my birth. There, I ridiculed inappropriate people. I called Pope Benedict Mr. Popeye, and the popedom a bag of potato chips. I crack jokes to lessen tension in stressful situations, such as the time I was at the battlefront. The enemy sent an emissary to hand me a letter. I asked him to let his general know he must hold fire until I found a copy machine to duplicate it.

I enter the club, order a soft drink, and stand in the back, letting my eyes adapt to the semidark surroundings. Two blondes converse at a table over an almost empty bottle of wine. Their skirts are so short that

26

I see their blue and pink panties matching their dresses. A few rowdies sit at a nearby table full of cocktail glasses. Several couples scatter throughout the auditorium, engaging in animated conversations.

An atmosphere of camaraderie and merriment prevails in the venue. I did not perceive lust or lechery. This insight reassures me. By the way, my newborn human's sixth sense helps me. It does not fully compensate for the loss of my ability to read others' thoughts, but any extra perception is welcome. Homo sapiens has enjoyed this knack since its birth 300,000 years ago. Unfortunately, by adolescence, it disappears in most people. Careful observation and listening prevent its decline. One must open the eyes wide, prick up the ears, and shut the mouth. I wonder whether I can still regrow an amputated fingertip as children do until the age of eleven. I hope I don't need to find out.

The owner of the venue—someone with a leonine face, golden-framed glasses, and a white suit—walks to the stage and interrupts my thoughts. He requests a volunteer. A tall guy in a blond wig and sunglasses rushes toward me, grabs my arm, and lifts it. The lion looks at me, screws his eyes like a myopic person, and beckons me forth.

When I get on the stage, everyone applauds with such eagerness that it makes me doubt whether I should end my performance right now. The crowd displays such happiness with my presence that, from this moment on, the level of excitement can only decline. Everyone stops clapping, and the silence grows intense. I find myself on the platform like a lazy crocodile in the middle of a highway and express my impression,

"I must be nervous since my stomach just uttered a roaring growl of hello to you all."

Everyone laughs. I search behind me to examine my garments. I cannot understand the reason for their reaction. I ask if, by any chance, a paper doll hung on my back. Guffaws break out amid my perplexity. I conclude,

"Please, put your hands together for the owner of this club who has served you alcoholic drinks laced with laughing gas."

Several couples kiss with enthusiasm, whistle, and clamor their approval. The blondes bend in stitches. The boisterous guys mingle with the women and take advantage of the darkness and intense lassitude that mirth brings on. They roll on the floor and grab each other, men taking off their jackets and shirts and women their dresses. Clothes fly off toward me like a cloud of jetsam. Soon everyone strips down to their underwear and encourages me to follow suit. I don't oblige. Barefoot, the impromptu burlesque performers skip on one leg and remove the last pieces of garments as I make off. The leonine owner grabs me before I hit the street. He demands I pay for the soda and then offers me a contract. His threat includes a fine for my lack of compliance with the rules of Naked Tuesdays for nudist clubs' members. I decline.

As it turns out, instead of my sense of humor, I have tested my self-confidence. When I lived in the Other Dimension, this quality received quite a bit of commendation from Daniel. I remember how he praised my reaction when a woman in her fifties opened a door and found me standing up with my pants down in front of a toilet seat. The lady looked at me and saw my private part hanging like a dead parakeet. Her eyes widened in awe. I didn't flinch, wiped myself off, and walked away, whistling a song.

Over the years, shyness plagued my donor. He made an unsuccessful, conscious effort to control it. But compliments embarrassed him, confrontations unnerved him, and asserting himself made him toss and turn all night long. Daniel once said about me,

"I am jealous of the man in my dream, jealous of the audacious freedom and elation he enjoyed when he laughed in unrestrained guffaws. I've never had this kind of pleasure in my life."

Daniel grew speechless and blushed in front of lovely, beautiful women. For example, Daniel and Marlene met for the first time when they were walking their dogs in a park. The animals engaged in fellatio, cunnilingus, and even worse sexual aberrations before their very eyes. Daniel was so embarrassed that his face became red like a beet, but Marlene just stood there, looking afar and smiling as if nothing were going on.

Four

THE WOMAN TRAIL

*D*aniel's praise at the time of my departure from the Other Dimension stemmed from his admiration of my virtues. But he had a harsh opinion of my sexuality. According to him, I was an unfaithful debauchee. In dreamland, I made love to many women, and nothing stopped my lusty binges—the presence of husbands, brave bulls, or ferocious wolves. I bore no prejudice against anyone. I went to bed with his wife, single and married woman friends, and even female patients. Daniel spoke of my legendary ability to unbutton dresses, unlock chastity belts, undo zippers, or strip lacy silk panties off. He admitted to my good taste since I always picked ladies of great refinement and delicacy. His criticism emphasized my wild instincts that disregarded principles issued by institutions that men had created such as marriage or religion. Daniel didn't realize my sexual behavior was standard in the dream world.

My virtues survived the exchange procedure, but none of my above-described skills in dealing with women crossed the filter. I have recovered a significant part of the good looks I enjoyed in the Other Dimension. My power of seduction might have returned, but I still have a long way to go. Lack of knowledge about women and sex on earth strikes me as one of my severe deficiencies. I wonder whether I will help Daniel improve his legacy of his interactions with them. My disappointing performance with Lorna makes me cautious about the steps I must follow. I lack personal imprints in my brain that could act as a reference. Every event evokes a déjà vu impression devoid of emotional charge. In some simple acts, images reflect the associated feeling. Daniel's smiles show that caresses elicited more pleasure from him than kisses. The issue, however, gets confusing when it comes to orgasms because my memory stores reflect images and noises but lack the passionate tracks of climaxes.

To start my training, I make web inquiries about the psyche of the opposite sex. The matter has undergone extensive research with inconclusive results. The main consensus lies in women's intricacy. Scientists document a myriad of tactics for promoting sexual encounters and attracting long-term romantic partners. The exhaustive list of situations includes one-night stands, serial mating, friends with benefits, brief and long affairs, multiple partners, mate swapping, and various combinations. New ways shock the audience on porno channels every day. There are no rules about sex practices of couples or even a proven approach that will always yield positive results. I must gather my own experience.

I start with Daniel's next-door neighbor at apartment 1123, an attractive and single thirty-and-odd-year-old Italian American by the name of Antonietta Lombardi. Her brown eyes conjure up a warm flush in my body that I equate with sexual excitation. I meet her as she tries to enter her condo. I offer to open the door for her, but she throws a nasty look at me as though I were about to rob her. Daniel never indulged her with any act of kindness, let alone intimate pleasure. The whiteness of her skin and her praline scent appeal to my senses. I waste no time to ask,

"Would you like to go to bed with me?"

She lashes her purse against my head and keeps hitting me, her shouts resonating in the staircase,

"Pervert!"

I cover my scalp with my hands and run to safety. I don't know what kind of objects she holds inside her bag. I would have blacked out if I hadn't dashed into my apartment. Some residents come out of their hideouts. Through the peephole, I see how my aggressive spurner rushes into her abode with a smile on her face and a wave of her arm. She must be aware that witnesses distort everything that happens and may blame her for the incident. A day later, Antonietta knocks on my door. She heard I had come out of the hospital a few days ago and expresses her happiness that I have survived such a terrible ordeal. She apologizes for her tantrum and wants to go to bed with me. No sooner do her feet cross the entrance to my condo than her robe drops to the floor and reveals a naked, curvaceous figure, much more voluptuous than I expected. Antonietta praises me as an exciting lover and makes a wish,

"If only my boyfriend knew how."

It is hard for me to judge my performance, but she seems to fake enthusiasm. I check the diagrams Daniel left imprinted on the memory bank, but he was a dull sex partner. I play along with Antonietta and tell her that she may bring her boyfriend next time to observe and learn. She again calls me a pervert, but this time she wraps the word with a coy tone and follows it with a sweet and dire warning,

"He'll kill you if he ever finds out."

I am surprised to learn that people take this mechanical and repetitive act seriously. It is a brilliant invention of evolution for procreation but not so much for recreation. After her probably faux climax, Antonietta becomes talkative and discusses Daniel's divorce. Lovely Marlene seldom conversed at any length, always greeted her, and offered neighborly help if needed. It was me—meaning Daniel—who was a conceited jerk, exuded aloofness, and ignored her presence when we met on the elevator or in the hall.

Now my attention concentrates on the intercourse that has just taken place. In the middle of the commotion, I wonder whether I ever climaxed. There weren't any kisses. The omission somehow stimulated her but might have hurt me. So many sensations, so much attention to details. I blame my deficiency on naiveté. I know the anatomy and physiology involved because Daniel's medical knowledge comes in handy. He kept a collection of old instruments in a cabinet next to his desk. I pick a metal speculum and ask Antonietta if I may dilate her vagina and look inside to confirm my orgasm. A mischievous stare flashes in her eyes as if I were offering her kinky sex. A minute later, she screams, jumps up, tosses on her gown, and scurries to the front door of my apartment. I apologize for my clumsiness and promise to call her later to see how she feels. Antonietta slams the door and threatens me,

"If you ever knock on my door, I'll shoot you."

I must move on with my project. Most of my dreams show Daniel's feats in the Other Dimension—riding whales, making love to Julie atop a rainbow, flying over huge snowy mountains. His face displays the same elation I enjoyed. But I am grateful he sometimes vouchsafes me the protagonist's role. In one dream, I live on Saturn whose ring was damaged by a meteorite, so cars cannot arrive at their destination. A field of asparagus pops up on a sidewalk. Weird and illogical scenes abound. Tonight's scenes surprise me:

I watch a svelte woman in a flesh-colored swimming suit sprawl upon a red rug. Her long legs reach the middle of the room. I stand naked in front of her. Her finger points toward the area where I should insert my erect organ, which stands up like a flagpole. She removes the lower part of her bikini and reveals a smooth and hairless anatomy without the pubic cleft. Her butt then flashes before my eyes with impudence, but the crevice of her vagina is nowhere to be seen. My lusty companion rushes out of the room as Antonietta did, crushing the door and jarring the frame.

Daniel comes in and sits on the couch. I wonder why he chooses a dream that draws attention to my deficient sexual performance.

"You know all about your oversexed behavior," he says. "This is another example."

I correct Daniel. My carnal fiasco triggered a dream that shows my inexperience and insecurity with intimacy on earth. Besides, in the Other Dimension, such judgments don't exist. All acts are innocent and clean for everyone to enjoy, not intended to offend or denigrate anyone. He protests,

"At least you should heed my mother's advice. Check my memory files."

I don't know why he brings this issue up. His erotic debacle represents one of the enormous challenges in my quest to correct the wrongdoings in his life. Granted, he was not promiscuous, but neither am I because I am merely acquiring experience. Daniel refers to some Lorna's teachings that began early in his late childhood with a dire warning—women get pregnant. The word sounded so ominous that the child equated the obstetric state with a menacing tumor. Later, in his adolescence, she issued a second directive:

"Use your organ of procreation, my son, with care... with the right person. Be yourself and stay away from flirtatious women."

These words made a severe impact on young Daniel. He avoided women and never got to know them well. First, he regarded them as strange and mysterious beings exerting attraction and posing a risk—the derailment of his medical career. After this hazard had disappeared, he sought their company and wondered how he could distinguish the right person from the rest. Most men couldn't, let alone Daniel. Whenever he found someone attracted to him, he didn't reciprocate her feeling. Humans don't rule over their hearts and fall subject to terrible infatuations. Some psychologists believe suitors try to return to the safety and love in their childhood. I don't have this kind of problem because I skipped this period of development. My thoughts get interrupted by Daniel's question,

"Why did you have sex with my neighbor Antonietta?"

I tell him of her gorgeousness, admit the episode didn't go well, and hold no grudges against her. But she dislikes him and considers him an arrogant jerk.

"Are you crazy, Sonie? How long do you think it will take for my mother to know about this? And Marlene? Everyone in your neighborhood? Nowadays, with social media, you never know which weirdo in Russia or Pakistan witnesses your performance."

I have disregarded that aspect of the relationship. Why are humans so complicated? In the Other Dimension, no one gave a hoot about what I did, nor did I care about other people's behavior. I advised Daniel to mind his own business. He must allow me to do my work and issue guidance only when I request it.

A few days later, I take my dirty clothes to a nearby coin laundry and regard a young and shapely blonde with blue eyes. I notice how she pours tiny pink panties, large-cupped red bras, and other intimate garments with flimsy lacing into a machine. She has good taste. I invite her to engage in sex with me, and she replies,

"Yeah... but first I must go to the movies with you."

Wow! Perhaps, Shirley—that is her name—wants to watch porn to get into the mood. I read women don't get as excited with images as men do, but she could be different. I look at repetitious erotic photos, videos, and movies on the web. A muscular plumber unclogs a sink and the anatomy of a lady customer. A woman in a horse trainer's outfit lashes the heck out of her lover. A sadist strangles his partner to near unconsciousness to enhance her orgasm. Intercourse abounds among gays, lesbians, bisexuals, heterosexuals, transsexuals, transvestites, transgender, or pansexual couples. It may sometimes turn into bacchanals of three or more players, sexual roulettes, and orgies. The countless positions surpass those of the ancient *Kama Sutra*. Some require more training than Olympic gymnastics. Seldom does regular copulation gather any attention since humans seem to have outgrown the standard intercourse. These pictures bore me to death.

An unexpected occurrence takes place when I venture into these saucy websites. As soon as the images appear on the screen, my GPS points me to a multitude of nearby sex partners. The offers include location and time as if I had asked for a lunch caterer. One can envision the future of this society—a multitude of self-satisfied people who rely on the internet for all their needs. One will request a sexual favor from a willing neighbor as easy as a taxi or a trinket on Amazon. The courtesy might include an enjoyable dinner or even an exciting vacation trip. The family unit could become obsolete since tubes can conceive petitioned children for various human communes. The apotheosis culminates with sex dolls and robots in human form and texture that perform intercourse and simulate orgasms. No need to entice or communicate with another human. No marriage. No divorce. The final triumph of the individual over society.

Shirley takes out and folds up her clean clothes. I ask her what kind of movies she prefers. She shrugs and answers,

"Any movie."

We walk into a theater showing *My Fair Lady*. In the middle of the session, Miss Doolittle makes a mistake at Aston Racetrack and speaks with roughness, revealing her deficient and humble upbringing. Shirley stands up and exclaims,

"I am leaving. I can't stand anyone who makes fun of women."

I point out it is just a movie, and she replies with her eyes filled with pride:

"A movie must depict real life, and this one doesn't. A woman would never fall for that kind of trick."

She upbraids me for inviting her to a movie demeaning her,

"You should have covered my eyes and got me out of the theater so that I didn't have to endure such a terrible spectacle."

A week has passed since her outburst, and Shirley hasn't returned to the laundromat. One never knows what women think. I wish I had kept the ability to read minds.

The experience baffles me. I have a cup of coffee at the Golden Coin, my neighborhood café. Perhaps, I might fit in here and find the right sexual mate. I grab a cup of decaf, sit in a corner, and scout out the area. A pretty and petite brunette sits at the next table, her dark eyes focused on a small laptop, her left hand wielding a paper cup. Her porcelain-like hand passes over her scalp and settles her hair. She seems to be an ideal target. I am about to approach her when a young man in blue jeans and a black jacket stands in front of her. I sit again, regretting my delay that has allowed this intruder to take the initiative. A conversation ensues between the newcomer and the woman,

"Rebecca?"

"You are more beautiful than your profile picture."

"You must be Anthony."

He sits across from her, and the pair praises the "Online Happy Date Website." His crossed left leg jerks back and forth, and her right hand fusses with a paper napkin. She goes ahead and rushes into an interrogatory,

"What do you for a living?"

"I work in a bank."

"What is your title?"

"Loan officer."

"Where do you live?"

"Lincoln Park."

"What kind of car do you drive?"

"Why do you need to know? You'll see it when I pick you up."

"Wait a minute. You are asking for a girlfriend, right? That is what you applied for, isn't it?"

"Yes."

"That is a serious matter. If it were only a one-night stand, there would be no need for questioning. You like me, I like you. That's it. But that isn't our case."

Their noiseless interaction gains a low tone. He gets pale and she red. His foot taps the floor over and over, her hand squeezes the cup hard, and the plastic cover flies off. Her inquisitive eyes frown, and his teeth bite his lower lip. He stands up. His chair staggers back and screeches on the tile floor, her face winces with discomfiture. I can understand the brunette's point since financial strains undermine any relationship. Women are more practical than men, but plenty of gentlemen marry wealth. The famous male's jackpot screw and female's gold-digging. No money, no honey. A price for everything, even a long-term relationship. I watch the brunette and try to catch her eye. Her spurned suitor's steps recede and fade away beyond the threshold of the coffee lounge. I put on a smile, turn to her, and say,

"I overheard your conversation. I'd like to make you forget the whole affair."

"You've no business snooping!"

"I'd just like to have sex with you."

"Oh, beat it! You are not my type!"

Her dismissal makes me think that my improved look and figure might not be handsome enough for the current singles market. Maybe the failures Daniel had with women were inevitable, and I must accept the cruel reality to overcome his handicap. Judging our own appearance can prove difficult. People contemplate their younger version in the mirror and disregard most signs of aging or deterioration. I need an unbiased opinion. Children and drunks always tell the truth. I see an eight-or-nine-year-old boy riding a scooter in a white T-shirt and a red baseball cap. He jumps, negotiates curbs, spins like a pro, and then stares at my raised halting palm. I ask him,

"How do you think I look? Am I a good-looking guy?"

"Mom! A pervert"

"What are you doing to my son? You, pervert! Get out of here, or I'll call the police!"

A bleached blonde with thick black eyebrows and large hips pops her eyes out of their orbits. She holds a big rock in her right hand, hurls it toward me from a few yards, and misses me by the skin of my teeth. An uproar breaks out, a bunch of young mothers joins my attacker, and some wield their children's baseball bats. They blurt out filthy language and call me many names. People are aggressive on earth. No one gives me a chance to issue a word of explanation, and I take to my heels, grateful no one hides a gun in a purse. It would have ended my life on earth.

A few days and several shots of whiskey later, I get a definite answer from Jim—an old patron at the Celtic Tavern on Ashland and Lawrence. He proclaims,

"You must have just hung up your cassock. But you don't look like a priest. I guess you never met your grandma. She'd have told you that you're a good-looking fellow."

I have learned you must smile and ignore a remark if you want to avoid making a comment. I cannot understand my situation, and neither can Jim who already bears five drinks under his belt.

"Let me take you someplace where you can study the art of love-making," he adds with a smile. "Over there, I had my son 'dig into' the subject for the first time, no pun intended, a long time ago."

We walk into an establishment whose name, Sports Babes, flashes with red lights. The lounge lies in semidarkness and brims with giant TV screens showing basketball, football, soccer, and baseball. Men and women sit on stools at the counter over tall glasses of beer. Men wear short sleeves exposing tattoos, and women an abundance of makeup and skimpy attire. Flowery cologne impregnates the area. Jim gets me acquainted with my teachers, Natasha, Marilyn, Dawn, Cameron, Rose, and Monica. I start with Natasha, who charges me the modest fee of 50 dollars for my first lesson.

During the following days, I have several sexual sessions with my other mentors that enlighten me. I must wear a condom because venereal diseases are raging—HIV, gonorrhea, syphilis, and others. I know they engage in prostitution to make a living. Society holds this profession to a low standard. Sex workers feel the need to explain to others how they ended up in such a business. Natasha ran away when she was sixteen because of physical abuse at home. She secured herself a boyfriend who followed suit after her parents, coming home drunk and hitting her every night. Two abortions and two almost fatal beatings forced her to flee and join the trade. Decent-paying jobs were hard to find when one lacked a high school diploma. Dawn and Marilyn recount similar stories. Cameron and Monica claim to be lawyers who abandoned the profession for a more lucrative and less boring activity. Rose praises her sphere of action as her vocation, basking in fornication with a voracious appetite.

The saying that once you do it with one, you do it with all proves to be wrong. Certain peculiarities call my attention. Dawn likes to text her friends from her bedroom to keep them abreast of the lusty event. Rose rides me, spurs me with her ankles, and urges me to continue the motions until exhaustion. Marilyn croons a Zumba hum in my ear to enhance my performance. Cameron keeps her cool, looks at her nails in profound silence, and smokes cigarettes in the brief breaks. I learn quite a few tricks. Monica teaches me how to kiss with passionate delicacy and assures me the technique will open many doors. I confess my previous disappointments, and she blames my parents for my lack of knowledge, surprising me with the following advice,

"Never ask women out of the blue if they would like to sleep with you. You seduce them, flatter them, hand them flowers. Women like to be loved or pretend they are loved."

Five

PROBLEMS AHEAD

A few days ago, my neighbor Allen Roach—the unknowing beneficiary of Daniel's will—let me know he bumped into Daniel's mother, who had just knocked on my door and gotten no answer. Lorna glared at him and warned him against treating her son with so much courtesy, accusing him of toadyish behavior. Taken aback by her sharp tongue, the old man blamed the incident on the possessiveness and illogical jealousy of a mother that could misinterpret any act of kindness. His words make me reconsider whether I should meet Lorna today at our weekly breakfast at Starbucks, but I go ahead with my plan.

Would you believe this place? There are coffee beans from every corner of the world with astonishing prices per package that depend on the size of the golden logo. So far, I have tried Arabica, Ethiopian, Colombian, and Mexican, and they all taste the same. It is just coffee. What is the big deal? Exotic huge coffee-plantation posters cover the walls, which shouldn't provide the establishment with the reason to hit customers with outrageous checks. You shed $3.25 plus tax for a small café latte misnamed "tall," or for an extra dollar, you get a gigantic "*venti*" that swells your tummy and keeps you on the toilet for the foreseeable future. My comprehension doesn't capture the logic behind the esoteric designation until I realize the words small, medium, and large don't sound fancy and expensive. The prices exceed the daily salary of a worker in wide expanses of this planet. Not an ordinary coffee shop, Starbucks caters to a young intellectual clientele who sit next to one another as on the Starship Enterprise. Everyone minds their own laptops, talks to no one, keeps their eyes fixed on the screens, and their ears plugged to phones. They dwell in their thoughts and travel into cloud cuckoo land.

Lorna sits next to me at a table outside and praises the quality of the espresso coffee. She feels loving and kisses me on the forehead. The occasion marks the first time the woman who hatched my body inside hers touches me. Her warm lips infuse a pleasing peacefulness. It must be the closest sensation to what a real son would perceive. Our conversation begins with her usual recommendation for cheap ecologic chicken on Tuesdays at Fresh Market, fresh salmon at Costco, pasta and Spanish olive oil at Trader Joe's. She praises my good looks, weight, wholesome expression in my eyes, and "stunning recovery from death." Her conversation then darts toward Marlene and the beautiful family that Daniel built with her. Lorna thanks God for removing from his brain "the obsessive love for Julie, the dreamed ghost," which he "endured" before his technical death. She again encourages me to make up with her son's ex-wife. Without warning, her artillery of criticisms erupts against me,

"What were you thinking when you went to bed with Antonietta, your neighbor?"

Lorna relentlessly wags her tongue,

"You almost killed her with a vaginal fork... I mean forceps."

"A vaginal speculum," I correct her.

I ask her not to meddle into my private affairs because I am old enough to take care of myself. But she doesn't heed my advice,

"And your saluting soldier wasn't happy enough that you had to stick it into the vagina of every prostitute at the Sports Babe Bar. Do you want your private part to fall to the ground and break into little pieces?"

I had enough of the family for today. Lorna thinks she can snoop on me or do whatever she pleases as if my life were her property. I will tell her off. But what does she gain by doing what she does? Do I observe anger on her face, or is she fighting back tears? Family affairs go over my head. I cannot understand her concerns for me until I notice a change in her complexion. Her face lights up with a warm pink color that irradiates closeness and comfort. Her eyes acquire a deeper blue, opening like a window for me to peek inside. This woman that criticizes me so much wields a powerful force, one that will defend me against anyone who dares to hurt me. If she could, she would cuddle me in her arms and hold me like a mother kangaroo her baby in her pouch.

Yet, I still perceive the same loneliness I noticed when I was born two months ago. Long hours of solitude, eating, sleeping, or pondering alone. No one with whom to share good or bad news or touch at night to reassure yourself you will wake up alive. No foolish squabbles followed by sweet reconciliations or incentive to cook for yourself. A major ill of human society threatens me—isolation. Quite a few people resent aloofness and live alone in their cages, craving for a kiss, a hug, human contact, a smile, a word of kindness. They feel forgotten and neglected in the middle of crowds and families. Some resort to sex that can be secured at any bar; others to drinking, drugs, or even suicide. Daniel was an example. He stayed away from everyone, depression striking him and leading him to an attempt against his own life.

I stand up, kiss Lorna's hand, and bid goodbye as she looks at me as a peasant would a flying saucer. Again, the sensation of warm peacefulness overcomes me. Lorna's voice turns soft and nostalgic,

"I'll see you next week, Daniel, my son."

The meeting with Lorna makes me lose my concentration. A screw slips out of my hand when I remove it from the micro-oven to change a bulb. The little piece of metal drops makes no sound and vanishes into thin air before it hits the kitchen countertop. I search everywhere for an hour, pass my hand over the wooden and marble surface, inspect every tile on the floor, run my finger into every crevice, and even rummage inside my shoes. To no avail. After an hour, I conclude some weird phenomenon swallowed it into the bottom of this planet. To-night, the unexplainable loss triggers a rare prophetic dream that features me as the protagonist:

I am in the apartment of a lady fortuneteller. I ask her for my keys because I want to go home. She hands me several, but none resembles mine. Before I head back, she whispers a warning,

"You'll face problems ahead."

I then swim in the pool of a cruise ship. The water lurches from side to side and spills over the rim down to the sea.

I hope this nasty prank might be what the soothsayer foretold. But I am afraid the evaporation of the screw, the disappearance of my key, and the omen of "problems ahead" have to do with Marlene, my donor's ex. A few days later, I get back from my daily walk and find a letter from her that reads,

"Daniel, I know you have received the final divorce decree. Please, don't dodge me and my alimony payments. I have been trying to get hold of you, but no one has seen your face at your office since you left the hospital. You cannot hide from everyone forever. Contact me as soon as possible, or the next letter that you get will be from an attorney."

The mixture of concern and threat rattles me a bit. I have avoided Marlene. I phone back but pick the times I know she isn't home so that I can leave messages apologizing for missing her calls. Today, Allen informs me that Marlene has visited my apartment building several times and tried to open my door with the former key. She also came across Antonietta and both women engaged in a lively discussion in the hall next to the elevator. God knows what my first sexual partner told Daniel's ex. Allen heard only the word "screw." I don't know if she referred to our intimate episode or a missing piece in my head.

My exchange procedure left up to me to get more understanding of humanity. As my sexual experience taught me, I need to achieve knowledge of civility to relate to others. My memory contains extensive files about proper deportment in various circumstances: on the road, family affairs, social events, and so on. Screaming "screw you" from a car or giving the other driver the finger doesn't have the same connotation as if you did it in a bar. Here you are more likely to get killed for an obscene gesture. Daniel kept clear notions of these norms of decorum his parents and teachers had taught him. But I cannot always extrapolate his knowledge to my case.

The problem occurs with conflicting instructions. One sometimes should be straight and direct, but on other occasions, one must be diplomatic. For example, when people greet you with "How are you?" do they want to know how you are? What would happen if you answer the truth and tell them, "I feel terrible?" Or you are invited somewhere, and the host asks you, "how is the food?" Should you say it stinks or follow rules of civility and nod an approval? All these circumstances require a process of learning how to harness my inborn qualities of honesty and straight-to-the-point attitude. It is difficult to accept the need to beat around the bush. When I watch a man in a suit and a stern-looking woman with a black attaché, both attracted to each other, discuss professional issues, I wonder why she doesn't tell him the truth,

"I have a crush on you. When you are near me, I get turned on."

Or why he doesn't unveil his reaction to her presence near him,

"I have a hard-on."

Why shouldn't they rush to a motel and fuse in a passionate embrace?

The hypocrisy of this world and its need for rituals and avoidance tactics put me out. Yet, if everyone knew what others think, the world would be chaotic, more than it already is. The day everyone gains telepathic abilities, humans will disappear from the face of the earth because of their inability to tolerate the absence of intimate and private thoughts. Only a perfect society—like that of the Other Dimension—can withstand such a level of acquaintance with the facts. This crude view calls to mind the words of Daniel acknowledging his screwup in his marriage:

"We always make mistakes in our marriages that could have been avoided to save the relationship."

Daniel tried to resolve his marital situation but ended up divorcing

Marlene several months ago. He fell out of love with her, whatever that sentence means. In human lexicon, it refers to the romantic feeling artists and poets have sung and praised more than any other subject. This obsession makes me conclude that people don't have the faintest idea of what love is. The commodity must be rare and valuable for everyone to crave it. The dictionary defines it as strong or constant affection for a person. I know little about the terrestrial counterpart of this emotion. If it resembles what I have experienced with Lorna—being abused, harassed, talked down to as part of her rights of motherhood—I am in for a frustrating ordeal.

I must avoid a similar adverse result when I meet Marlene the first time. This event requires careful preparation. I should access my inherited brain stores and review their relationship. Humans have a selective memory and remember what they want the way it suits them best. This defense mechanism reduces their sense of responsibility for their actions. The recorded scenes and conversations lack objectivity and convey only Daniel's point of view.

Marriage doesn't exist in the Other Dimension, so I read on this matter. Humans invented this artificial yoke to tie a pair of individuals through good and bad times. Matrimony of convenience or love. Mind or heart. Cash or lust. The first kind bound the partners in much stronger unions than the second. Society touted the exclusive arrangement of a man for a woman and a woman for a man as the ideal method to preserve the human species. But the official contractual arrangement didn't eliminate the parties' roving eyes and subsequent conflicts. Husbands and wives often entered forbidden extramarital relationships and wove emotional links to others. Individuals could fall in love with two or more people at the same time, but society enacted civil laws and religious commandments to chastise transgressors. Those regulations have changed. Couples of the same sex can now tie the knot in six states—California, Connecticut, Iowa, Massachusetts, New Hampshire, and Vermont— and the number of single parents' children continues to grow year after year. Procreation no longer fits into the definition of matrimony because society has evolved into a more inclusive institution. Nowadays, everyone can decide how to pair with others, regardless of the reason for their intimate liaison—personal growth, children, belonging to a family, convenient setting for sex, tax-relief strategy.

As far as I can gather from memory stores, Daniel and Marlene's union belongs to the marriage of love. He met her as she was walking her dog. He saw a pair of slender legs and a curvaceous figure that held a head with blue eyes, waving blond hair, and a sensual mouth that issued words with an alluring French accent. These qualities prompted his saluting soldier to stand at attention. She probably sensed the military vibration in his eyes and the hormonal pheromones that bathed the air. Daniel wanted her and Marlene wanted him. She disregarded the half-serious bantering of her mother,

"Couldn't you have picked someone else with more charisma than this guy? He is a cold fish."

Likewise, Daniel turned a blind eye to Marlene's shortcomings and concluded,

"Nothing in her character would rock my world."

Like magicians, humans pull out psychological tricks from their sleeves and justify their bonds to their beloveds. Quite a few people base them on their misunderstanding that others need their vital protection to cruise through life. Some proclaim their intent to correct their future spouse's defective personality or even physical handicap. Others misperceive their partners' loneliness and longing for their company when it might be the other way around. Daniel wanted to guide and mold Marlene to his specifications. He subconsciously smoothed out the rough edges of her personality such as distrust for others and an urge for security and stability. He misinterpreted her need as a sign of adaptability to his goals. She must have followed a similar mental process to ignore his hubris, terseness, and humorlessness.

The sexual quagmire of romantic love plunged them to the altar in 1983. Time passed and reality bounced to the surface. Daniel had married a rumba shaker after all, and Marlene a cold fish. She had turned into an obtuse complainer, but he liked her loyalty and devotion to their family. Daniel became a selfish and conceited jerk, but Marlene admired his drive for success and the comforts that his hard work provided.

They were lucky. Their conflict could have exploded out of control. Other couples often woke up and found themselves like two strangers afloat on a piece of wood on the high seas. The Brandons compromised. Yet, the rapid passage of years continued their transformation. Daniel changed, Marlene changed, life changed. Adapt or die. The rule applies to evolution in the universe or marriage. There is no perfect marriage, and you know no one until you face problems together. Marlene complained of Daniel's reticence, obsession with work, and lack of warmth and feelings for her—not even a single "I-love-you." He balked at her lack of affection and even forgot the last time she had hugged him. Her strict religiousness worsened their problem. On one occasion, when Daniel informed her of a patient's frivolous suit, she condemned him,

"You must have done something wrong to get sued. Just leave it in God's hands. If you haven't hurt anyone, you'll be fine."

Marlene blamed him for their marital discord,

"You think marriage is like an accordion that you just keep stretching out more and more and all you get is music. But it isn't. Marriage is an elastic band you can stretch only so much, and then it breaks and hits you in the face."

My birth granted my donor a unique opportunity to redress his wrongdoings with Marlene. As a new Daniel, my brain lacks scars of disappointment, misunderstanding, quibbling, and ingratitude. Neither are there episodes of blaming each other, unmet expectations, heartbreak, and distrust. Nor hidden wounds of infidelity that wife and husband might have accumulated over the years. Prejudices and biases don't exist in my makeup. I will regard Marlene with a clean mind and a warm heart without the distortion that passaging time inflicts on every spouse. She lacks these advantages and will look upon me as Daniel. His shortcomings and her memories of regret, pain, and deception will bristle before her. In dreamland, I was fond of Marlene and even made love to her a few times. Here on earth, reality changes everything. I wonder whether the flames of passion will engulf me. If the human perception of this feeling develops through childhood and adolescence, I might not recognize it, let alone experience it. But if it catches me and burns me, will she reciprocate?

A few days later, I wait for Marlene at The Parisian, an outdoor café on Rush Street, and watch her svelte figure turn the corner of North Avenue. She wears a lovely red dress. Her blond hair hangs over her shoulders and swings in unison with her rounded hips. She remains attractive at her 55 years of age and wields a charming smile that brightens the splendor of her blue eyes. Marlene must have liked my bouquet of white roses and the simple note of apology attached to a hefty check. Her affable appearance makes me wonder why Daniel couldn't get along with the mother of his children.

I stand up, welcome her, and kiss her on the cheek. Her gardenia fragrance enwraps me. She sits across from me and avoids smiling as if aware of the accentuating effect on her incipient crow's feet and laugh lines. Her face retains her original youth that her wavy long blond hair and long slender legs enhance. An array of virtues frames her relaxed anatomy like a rainbow the sky on the horizon. Her look expresses goodness, and her pinkish open palms generosity. With Marlene, you get what you see, a clean upright person without a single evil vibe in her body. She scans me and says,

"You look better than the last time I saw you. You were dead."

"Don't exaggerate. I was very sick."

"Sick? The nurse covered your face with a sheet. No heartbeat. The monitor showed a straight line."

"Nurses get nervous and make mistakes."

The waiter brings her a cup of cappuccino, a double espresso for me, and a few chocolate cookies compliments of the house. I savor the aromatic elixir. I test whether I feel anything unusual for this woman with whom Daniel married in his early adulthood. One would think I should sense some link with her since I bear the genes of her former bedmate. Scientists believe the chemistry between two people is the most substantial reason for a romantic attraction. No flame catches me. In front of me sits a self-sufficient woman with whom anyone can fall in love because of her external and internal qualities. The waiter walks away from our table with an empty tray on his palm, his fading steps cuing Marlene to interrupt my thinking,

"Michael, I mean, Dr. Rosen, doesn't know how you came back from your state. "

"Oh, you are involved with him, aren't you? You have a penchant for neurologists."

"You never liked him."

"You should stay away from Michael Rosen. His presence gives me a bad feeling."

"Daniel, you don't know him well. Please, don't get upset. You get too formal."

"Why should I get upset? You are a divorcee."

"Yes, I am. And you left me for a ghost!"

My lack of reaction to her angry words bewilders her since she expects a lambasting repartee. I don't reply. I wish I could explain to her that Julie is not a ghost, but someone who lives in the Other Dimension. Terrestrials cannot understand. Marlene changes the conversation to Daniel's children,

"The welfare of our children must be an area of communication that should always unite us."

I stare at her perplexed. I thought grownups had control over their lives. Daniel's adult children live out of town. Their dependency on their parents surprises me because I haven't heard from them. They didn't visit their father at the hospital but had registered him as a friend on their Facebook profiles. Daniel could have accessed their pictures and reviewed their adventurous travels. I concluded that, at their ages, the relationship became so distant that no one interfered with one another. That behavior follows the rule of the animal kingdom. As soon as the cubs secure their food and shelter on their own, they abandon the litter to fend for themselves. I don't understand why it should be any different with the highest primate. Marlene breaks my pondering,

"The cat ate your tongue. You never took care of them."

The cat ate my tongue? She has eased the sentence out, her face immutable. I am now the one who appears bewildered by this unexpected onslaught. Ex-wives keep the long dagger for the end. Daniel heard these words before, but I didn't expect this backstabbing. Until then, our quiet chat has made me forget whom I am impersonating. Her face doesn't even change, not even a grimace of disapproval, just a plain cold "I-get-under-your-skin-whenever-I-want." I must look like a pedestrian who, after being hit with an egg on the head, gapes around as the yellow and white drip down his stunned face. Marlene and Daniel's offspring receive monthly checks from their father's account. I don't understand the reason because they are no longer children. She continues her attack,

"You and your absorbing career! Your family means nothing to you."

I keep my mouth shut. I don't know what to tell her. Daniel keeps putting me in a wrong spot. He was such a selfish man. I riffle through his memory files. I don't see him playing with his children or attending their soccer games and parent-teacher conferences. He never read them tales at bedtime or helped them with their homework. Nor did he take them to their pediatricians or walk them to the neighbors' homes on Halloween. The responsibility for these activities fell upon Marlene. Daniel deemed other tasks more critical. He sometimes escorted them to Mass on Sundays and lunched with them afterward. What else did the children expect? He should have been more involved with his family. A father represents the mirror where son and daughters look at themselves. My silence irritates Marlene, who expresses her displeasure,

"Send them more money. There is such a thing as inflation. You, stingy ghostbuster!"

Anger turns her cheeks red; her blue eyes acquire a green tint, and her lips open like a sunflower. I watch her hands fly in front of her with her palms turned up and then drop as in a benediction. She frowns and regards the cups on the table as if wanting to grab one and drown her feelings in aromatic coffee. Her chair retreats, screeches on the floor, and wails a discordant high note. Her curvaceous figure towers over me, her rounded hips staring at me. The vision blocks my ears and restrains them from hearing her ranting condemnations. The epiphany of love then rises before me like a hot air balloon. So, this is love, a new universe that embraces and blinds the lover and transforms the loved one. Words issue from my mouth without a second thought,

"Marry me, Marlene. Let us not waste time. Life on earth is short."

Marlene glares at me, halts for a moment, and searches my face for sarcasm. Her head shifts side to side as though looking around for witnesses that could provide a clue about the offensive or gracious nature of my words. She bolts out of the establishment without shaking my hand or smacking a goodbye kiss on my cheek.

Tonight, a dream scurries through my brain:

I am in a public restroom with no partitions or cubicles. The ample and open room contains an empty stage hemmed by grades like those of an amphitheater. Toilet bowls line up in rows. To relieve my gut, I sit on one in the highest tier and rest my back against the wall. Marlene sits across from me on the opposite side of the room. Her underwear circles her feet, and her eyes gape straight ahead. Before her, a gentleman perches on another loo with his back so close to her legs it almost touches them. He looks over his shoulder and asks her,

"May I tell you a poem?"

The place hasn't the best atmosphere for poetry, but Marlene nods her assent, and the man recites,

"Small verses and stanzas occupy the same space regardless of how large one writes the words."

The guy must be a brilliant poet, but Marlene is unimpressed. She leaves the stand, and after a while, he follows suit. As soon as they vacate the room, Daniel pops up on his ex-wife's lavatory and asks,

"Did Marlene remind you to shut the toilet lid when you finish?"

I shake my head.

"She ordered me around all the time—wash the dishes, take out the garbage, put the coffee cup away."

I tell him he must have been used to fastidiousness since his mother has exhibited the same trait all her life. We all suffer from some weirdness or craziness. He should have sought common ground with his wife and avoided the divorce. Marlene is a good-looking, attractive woman who put up with him and showed concern for him until his last breath at the ICU.

"Being too nice won't get you too far in your new world. After Marlene had berated you, you still asked her to marry you. She thought you were laughing at her."

I disagree with him. She didn't repudiate my offer. I have been on earth long enough to know so. Her expression showed no dismissal of the idea, and a moment of doubt raised my hopes she might even accept my proposal.

"Accept your proposal? She could have strangled you. Besides, after her insulting behavior, it is not appropriate to send her a thank-you note and a bouquet, let alone a gift card with dinner "for her and her friend Michael" at La Française, the best restaurant in the Chicago area."

I remind him he abandoned a despondent woman in this world. I will do all I can to help her regain her happiness either with me or someone else if that is what it takes. He smiles,

"No one can make anyone else happy. Marlene can achieve it only by herself."

I rebuke his argument. His opinion might be correct under usual circumstances. But there are quite a few party spoilers who spread gloom to those around and obscure their experience of joy. The conversation ends with my final remark,

"You had your chance when you were here on this planet, and you blew it. So, mind your own business!"

I drift my attention to the dream. The words of the poet address people's use of thoughtless sentences. Some wiggle their human tongues like snakes and spit venom—slander, false testimony, lies. Everyone must question what everyone else says. With Marlene, she should heed the advice and disregard platitudes, pleasantries, and ill-intended remarks from those around her, notably Michael Rosen. The dream also reveals that self-criticism and self-deprecation haven't affected me. Otherwise, I would have fouled or wetted myself in the public restroom. My mind defended itself with toilet scenes to exorcize the demons of vices, injustice, and prejudice that try to tempt me. Like any other human, I am not immune to them since the war between good and evil embattles us people all throughout our entire lives.

The next day, my mind runs amok. Uncontrolled thoughts grab me like epileptic seizures. I can deal with nothing but Marlene. Her nacreous skin shapes her voluptuous figure, her hips sway with each step. The color of her eyes dabs in blue my whereabouts, her mouth blossoms into cushions aflame, gigantic waves of desire overtake my body. My face flushes, heart races, and breathing halts. I taste her lips and savor every spot of her body. Perspiration crops up on my forehead as my palms and fingertips burn with the illusion of touching her. I wonder whether I can exist without this woman. Whether I can go through life without inhaling her breath, absorbing her perfume, drinking from her mouth, making love to her. My hands and lips search for her. I see her everywhere. Where are you? Come here, my love. I plunge into the cold water of Lake Michigan to block my irresistible passion, but it only causes me to shiver. It takes 48 hours for my ardent desire to melt and engulf me in languorous relief.

I conclude that the episode of fiery sexual arousal reveals receptors in my donor's brain addicted to Marlene. When a man loves a woman, the embers of that fire continue in his mind for as long as he lives. In neurophysiological terms, the feeling behaves like an addictive substance. People might fall out of love, but weeks, months, or even years later, they remain susceptible to rekindle this emotion when exposed to the previous lover. No doubt the withdrawal attack got the best of me.

After a while, my thoughts clear out and pondering begins. I committed an error. I promoted the friendship of Marlene and Dr. Michael Rosen. I behaved like a human being for the first time, for to err is human. I should have studied the issue before sending the gift card. In Daniel's view, the doctor bears a terrible reputation as an egotistic individual and a womanizer. He seduced quite a few nurses at the hospital and flirted with countless women. This vice, however, doesn't disqualify him. This behavior remains standard in the Other Dimension as I can attest.

One could surmise that a woman of Marlene's age and education would wield a practical approach at selecting her new male friends. Logic should prevail over emotion. But after a divorce, ex-espouses grow vulnerable. I hate to admit Daniel might be right. The next day, Marlene leaves a message on my recorder that confirms his assessment. Her voice rushes like a jet of steam from an angry boiler,

"Stop your harassment and don't meddle in my life. I won't put up with it!"

I didn't count on the element of perception: here on earth, once people decide you are a jackass, you are always a jackass.

$\mathcal{Six}$

AT THE OFFICE

$\mathcal{I}$t is October 10, 2009. As I do every morning, I pick up a copy of the Chicago Tribune that lies in front of my door. I usually skip all the other sections and read the comics since, aside from advertisements and sports, the rest bristles with the same bad news every day. But today, on the first page, a large banner stares at me: President Obama has been awarded the Nobel Peace Prize. What a lucky guy! He has been only nine months in office. But he looks like an excellent human being, an exception among so many corrupt politicians. But then what do humans expect? Don't they vote with their pocketbooks, look after themselves first, and consider their country a far distant second? Why would their politicians be any different?

The political species of homo sapiens sapiens exhibits an enormous growth of ego, power hunger, greed, and hypocrisy associated with undeveloped brain memory areas for promises. Like an endemic disease, corruption plagues its members. In the past thirty years, three governors of Illinois went to jail. Governor Blagojevich was also impeached and removed from office last January. He awaits a trial.

It is a miracle that this type of government on earth survives. It has overcome lies, acts of treason, wars, famines, disgrace, assassinations of presidents, marital disloyalties, and even caches of semen. I guess some people wanted to preserve this specimen of humans for future generations. Evolution has mainly grouped these individuals into two subspecies: Republicans and Democrats. They fight and vie for power between them, but in the end, their behavior differs very little. Even experts face great difficulties separating them since mutations are frequent, and until this day, a definite criterion remains elusive. A large chunk of them— about 50 percent in the US Congress—undergo training in law schools. Here, they are taught the art of nitpicking and making a big mountain out of a molehill. Yet, people still wonder why their governmental institutions remain paralyzed.

In the Other Dimension, politicians were closer to their constituents. One could ride on a train with President Bush and kiss him goodbye. Nothing could lie hidden in that world. Everyone knew about the apartment where President Clinton housed all his women and the conveyor belt that he used to supply plenty of milk to them. Relationships between friends and adversaries thrive. Even political rivals such as Obama and Mitt Romney might share the same car on their way to an orgy on Mardi Gras Day in New Orleans.

It has been almost three months since my birth, and Daniel's overhead insurance will end October 15, 2009. In the afternoon, I visit his office to prepare the takeover of his practice. Inside, silence reigns unless the muffled noise of street traffic interrupts it. This place caused such a drag on my donor that stress seems to emanate from every corner. It enslaved Daniel and forced him to toil endless hours to support a prodigious overhead. The pressure on him grew day after day.

His office lies next to the main entrance. The room boasts windows that span from floor to ceiling and open out to the main thoroughfare. It contains a huge mahogany desk, an expensive executive chair, upholstered guest chairs, and a small palm tree that rises from a large pot in a corner. On a shelf in the cabinet behind the desk lie a few charts with the records of the most disreputable patients. Daniel regarded them like tamers the wildest beasts. The infamous Roman Connell, the man who became unhappy with his prosthetic testicle and sued him. Friendly and innocent-looking Reinaldo Torralbo, who even invited Daniel to dinner. The miscreant faked his pain to get opiates and sell them to supplement his income. Attorney Madeline Roscoe, a middle-aged mother and wife, also wrestled a few narcotics from Daniel. She bamboozled him into believing her abusive ex-husband's threat on her life and fabricated a trip to Guyana to escape from him.

Daniel held the opinion that the epidemic of the use of these medications in the US had to do with the loss of the American dream. That people misinterpreted their right to happiness listed in the US Constitution. They thought joy was a government entitlement and substituted their disappointment with drugs. Most ended up sinking into much deeper problems that endangered their lives.

Daniel basked in humane considerations and helped quite a few patients. But, since his malpractice suit, he dreaded the risks involved in his quotidian duties. Every forbidding-looking individual in his waiting room roused his apprehension of impending disaster. He freaked out and feared the stranger was about to hand him a subpoena from another plaintiff. His terror grew more intense with passing time, gaining an almost paranoid overtone. No tangible reason existed because he was meticulous and knowledgeable and cared for his patients.

Daniel never displayed photos of his children and Marlene in his office. He believed the images could distract patients and incite them to ask questions about his family. Photos of the relatives in their offices don't make those physicians devoted fathers or mothers. Hypocrisy abounds on earth. I open the right upper drawer and find two pictures facing down, retrieve them, and turn them around. The first shows fourteen-year-old Steve in a white baseball uniform. His blond hair spills out of the backward cap as he wields a bat ready to strike a ball. His smile lights up his blue eyes that are vivid replicas of his mother's. At this young age, he exhibited a balanced personality with a keen sense of duty toward his family and an ability to prioritize what was important in his life. His handsomeness made him a candidate for the first page of any women's magazine, but he never used his looks to seduce anyone.

He embraced fun and girls with gusto, but they took a backseat to his responsibilities at home and school.

Daniel never developed a close relationship with his son. When Steve was six years old, he drew a picture of his family. Among trees and flowers and under a sky with a radiant sun and scattered white clouds, the boy drew his mother and two sisters but not his father. Daniel was always absent, working, on call 24 hours a day, seven days a week, dealing with patients and hospitals, taking care of business, securing a financial safety net for his wife and children. But what about their emotional safety net? He never attended parent-teacher conferences, soccer games, playground games in the park, snowball battles, throwing of pillows and cushions. Daniel went to Mass with his family. But the child probably associated his presence with that of the parish priest, someone with a role in the liturgy. At the birthday parties, Daniel witnessed the guests like a stranger. He had never met his son's friends or their parents. His obliviousness included the clown and magician Marlene had always hired for the yearly occasions. Her duties involved hanging ornaments on Christmas trees, assembling Nativity sets, or getting children's gifts. Daniel never sat at a table to play a game of cards or parcheesi with his family. Marlene alone shared those joyous times with her little ones. It was she who turned into Santa Claus and the Tooth Fairy.

On Sundays, Daniel was expected to fulfill his paternal responsibilities if the children's misbehavior didn't comply with their mother's entreaties. The father represented discipline and authority, but he lacked the patience needed for this role. On one occasion, the child cried his eyes out for a toy car larger than the one he had received as a gift. The father crushed it under his foot. Another day, Steve borrowed a BB gun and fired at a neighbor's cat from his room window. He missed or just tried to scare the animal, but the plaintive meows alerted Marlene of an impending massacre. Daniel turned livid when he learned of his son's deviltry. He screamed at Steve and grounded him for a week. His loud admonition would have been fine if he had earlier taken the time to praise his son's accomplishments at school. Daniel never complimented him for the good deeds such as shoveling snow or cleaning an elderly couple's backyard. The dad kept waiting for the right moment to start a relationship with his boy, but time passed, and the moment never arrived. Steve graduated from junior high, four years later from high school, and then left for college in Appleton, Wisconsin, at Lawrence University. He is about to get his Bachelor of Arts' degree, and the feeling of near estrangement still looms between father and son.

In the same picture, next to Steve, stands Emmanuelle, blond and beautiful, in her cheerleader's attire with her short blue skirt and sleeveless top, white boots, and pompoms. Her fetching smile and enthusiasm jump out of the photograph. She was the closest child to Daniel because the little girl struck up a relationship with her aloof dad. Since a very early age, she crawled to his knees, stood, and sat in his lap. Her vivid happiness felt contagious to a father whose character bristled with sourness. Perhaps, his trait had developed because of the persistent stress, overwhelming responsibilities, or inherited personality. To hug him, the child waited wide awake until he got home late in the evening because she disliked experiencing his affection while half-sleep. Dad lavished her with the newest members of the Barbie doll collection.

Precocious Emmanuelle could walk at eight months of age, and two months later, control her sphincters. She was studious, vivacious, and charming. Daniel often apologized to her for missing her games, parent-teacher conferences, and other important occasions. He listened to her accounts of these meetings and enjoyed her descriptions and anecdotes. When Emmanuelle grew up, she liked casual dresses that didn't conform to contemporary fashion—leather vests, long floral skirts with matching headbands, jeans of various colors, miniskirts with knee-high boots. She bought them at flea markets or second-hand stores. Her passion for justice and fairness catapulted her to the class leader's position on campus at the University of Illinois at Urbana. Her unwavering commitment to legal causes included animal rights, saving the planet, gay and lesbian issues, children's welfare, and freedom for Tibet. Emmanuelle graduated with a degree in accounting two years ago. To her dad's surprise, she changed her casual attire for a blue suit and landed an

internship at Lawrence, Martino, and Fitzgerald LLC as a staff account-
ant of the famous New York firm.

Ana joins her younger siblings in the photograph. Her green eyes
gaze straight ahead at the camera as her bow-shaped red lips stretch in
a charming smile. Her dark hair reaches the angle of her jaw. The color
matches that of her jeans and contrasts with her porcelain-like complexion and the whiteness of her pullover and tennis shoes. Her striking
face and fashionable outfit with the blue logo of New Trier High School
render her the air of a movie star. As a child, Ana was a loner and lived
in a world of dollhouses and dolls. She chatted to them, dressed them,
fed them, created games and scenes. Later in life, her domain occupied
the hollow area under a loft bed, which housed a computer on a desk,
a wooden chair, and a bookshelf full of science fiction novels. At school,
she overgrew her introverted behavior, enhanced her outstanding intellect, and excelled in creating paintings and collages that teemed with
details.

Ana's aloofness with Daniel turned him away and resulted in a distant relationship that neither father nor daughter could bridge. Rosetta,
her playful white toy poodle, kept her company and understood her
best. Her dad had bought her the dog. It occurred on a rare day when
Daniel walked the children to the school bus because Marlene lay sick
in bed with the flu. Ana lagged the rushing cortege of parents and little
ones. She stopped and gaped at a shopwindow where a puppy sat inside
a cage. The animal rose to its feet, stuck its tongue out, and stared at
the girl, whining and wagging its tail. Her father hollered at her to move
on. But she remained still and mesmerized for a while until he tapped
her shoulder and urged her on. The next day, Ana turned nine, and
Daniel surprised her with the female poodle that had captivated her
heart. Since then, she had taken care of her pet, fed her, walked her,
and cleaned up after her.

Rosetta slept with Ana until she left for the Institute of Technology
in Melbourne, Florida, where she exchanged the dog for a dolphin and
studied marine biology. A picture in Daniel's condo attests to her bliss.
A smiley Ana wears a blue bikini that enhances her statuesque figure as

she rides the mammal in a splendorous and sunny pool framed by palm trees. She completed her studies and now works at Loggerhead Marine-life Center, the injured turtle rehabilitation facility in Juno Beach, Florida.

The second photograph shows a young Marlene. She poses in a white-and-blue scarf, a white bonnet, and a blue coat, the background graced with snowy trees. The blue of her eyes rivals that of a cloudless winter sky, and her mouth sketches a smile that stresses her fleshy lips. I feel an irresistible desire to kiss them. It amazes me the replication in my heart of Daniel's initial love for Marlene. He once remarked that "she wasn't a stunning beauty but had sufficient sex appeal to arouse him without making him crazy." I beg to differ. She has always exhibited a striking beauty. The passage of years distorted his recall. He had enjoyed quite a few ardent fits of intense love making with Marlene, licking and savoring her entire anatomy like vanilla ice-cream.

In the Other Dimension, my protection of Marlene extended to diverse facets of her life. On one occasion, a young gunman threatened her, so I snatched the pistol out of his hand. Another time, I learned of her pregnancy on a public bus where all the passengers had known of her expectant state before me. Someone else might have fathered her baby, but the suspected infidelity stirred no jealousy. In the real world, I supported her marriage to Daniel, but after a while, I backed his decision to get a divorce because the spouses no longer cared for each other. They didn't look happy together for quite a few years. People shouldn't waste so much time in their brief lives.

I place both pictures on what will be my new desk and head down a long hall to the front counter and a large area with internal partitions. Each one contains a turned-off computer terminal. In the darkness, furniture gains an eerie appearance. It makes me feel as if I were on a spacecraft. I switch the lights on, and the place comes alive—waiting room, reception, conference room, and examining rooms. Large paintings with gilded frames hang on the walls—weird rectilinear figures, men covered in bandages, an acupuncture map with needles poked into every imaginable site of the human anatomy—toes, lips, fingers, anal area. Numerous file cabinets stand next to the walls crammed with patient records. Touching them evokes the contained emotional upheaval that contributed to my donor's misery. I wish I could winnow the few that promoted his happiness from the vast number of those that saddened him and kept him awake at night.

I wonder how Daniel could survive in this dungeon. He spent most of his adult life here. All the lugubrious decorations will go to the Salvation Army. I will replace them with joyful pictures of people singing and dancing, having fun, and laughing. Patients have enough problems in their lives and need to feel at ease when they step into a health care facility.

I shift my attention and focus on the empty chairs of the employees that still bear the sense of oblivion of their occupants. Most contemplated the false appearance of an imagined reality. In their view, Daniel was a successful, wealthy doctor in an impeccable suit who basked in an enviable position in the family and society. They didn't realize that he envied their happy chatter, light responsibilities, and shelter from the type of harassment he endured. His subalterns needed not shake off the fear of every unexpected aggressive letter from a law office, a governmental agency, or an insurance company. These fateful missives ended up on his desk for him to deal with.

Daniel resented the excessive intrusion into his practice of the authorities, insurance companies, and medical societies. If he made a mistake, the state could fine him more money than he had earned in his entire career. A percentage of the sum would end up padding the pocket of the whistleblower. Agencies monitored him. They could yank his license away in a matter of days. Anyone could issue a complaint and trigger an investigation: an ill-advised patient, a rogue insurance company, a greedy lawyer, a jealous colleague. Daniel often asked himself whether his sacrifice was worth it. He ended up resenting the practice of medicine that had swallowed up him and his life. If I had to pick an item that symbolized Daniel in this building, it would be the two stuffed pheasants that hang on the wall of the waiting room ready to fly away.

His mood brought on terrible nightmares that featured him in precarious conditions. Naked from his waist down with a shirt that didn't stretch enough to cover his genitals. Attacked by wild beasts, thugs, and criminals. Inside an uncontrollable vehicle that lurches and swerves along a road like a wooden log down a furious river. He didn't recognize the reason for these debilitating night scenes and blamed them on me.

I feel sorry for Daniel, but this expensive cubbyhole was the unforeseen future he had built for himself. He considered it a trampoline to an ambitious career, the budding cell that would grow into multi-specialty offices. But life steered individuals, set its limits on them—time, money, opportunities, adversities, intellectual constraints—and ended up imposing a compromise. Daniel enjoyed the trip to reach its elusive goal because as Roman Emperor Marcus Aurelius wrote 2000 years ago,

"The life of a man is what his thoughts make of him."

Seven

BACK TO WORK

From my apartment in downtown, I head to my main office on West Touhy Avenue in Chicago. Jammed with cars, the Kennedy Expressway crawls. People drive alone, their faces set in indifferent or angry expressions as if in oblivion. No wonder there are so many brawls on the roads. Everyone follows their lane except a few intrepid racers who weave in and out. Advertisement companies hold drivers hostage in their sealed tin cans. Incessant messages bear upon them radio acoustic cues while huge billboards alongside the road display visual reminders of what they should buy. Like stunned dogs or cats, the captives go through a constant bombardment of conditioned reflexes that encourage them to crave useless items. Unnecessary home appliances, bars with topless waitresses and outrageous charges, casinos where patrons get ripped off. Drivers conduct their business from the vehicles and hold in their hands a precious smartphone. Their busy fingers stuck to the screen, and their eyes fixed on the gadget instead of the road. Smart doesn't seem the proper adjective for these devices, let alone for the owners. People no longer remember a single phone number and relinquish their brain functions to these contrivances. I wonder what they would do if they ever lost their phone. Without their GPS, most would wander through the streets and end up in a junkyard instead of their homes.

I have omitted the tattooed, black-leather-jacketed daredevils who ride on their bikes skirting obstacles. They pass car after car unmindful of any rules of the road. A few sane terrestrials spend their time in confinement having fun. Loud music wafts out of their vehicles as their hands and facial expressions engage in wild motions reminiscent of primeval dances. The traffic comes to an almost complete halt. Accident watchers gape at the scene of a fender-bender of two vehicles as their occupants exchange notes and angry words.

Driving in the Other Dimension offers advantages. A road may provide the drivers a helping hand if they face an unexpected block such as the steep face of a mountain. The slope may spin like a Ferris wheel and usher their cars onto the continuation of the road on the other side. During the ascent, the occupants can admire the tallest peak of the range covered with clouds. Rough conditions occur. Your car might impact and ricochet from side to side like a pinball as your body swings back and forth, striking the dashboard and front seat. But you can expect a miraculous hand to grab the steering wheel, straighten your car, and slow it down to safety. You never know how a fender-bender accident may unfold. Neighboring cars could whirl around, ram against yours, and demolish it into a slab of steel and plastic as though a roller had ironed it out. But regardless of the severity of the accident, you will end up standing nearby, alive and well.

I arrive at the office. The receptionist, Linda, and the nurse, Rhonda, wait for me at the door with reserved anticipation. I smile at them, but this gesture only worsens their skeptical looks. They even seem surprised when I ask them how they are and kiss them on their cheeks. Linda sets her hand over the area of my smooch, incredulous of what just happened. Last time she saw Daniel, he passed by her with his eyes staring straight ahead, ignoring her or unaware of her goodnight greeting. In the five years she had worked in this office, the doctor had never been rude but showed no deference, let alone affection. Rhonda passes her hand over her white shirt and black pants and presses down her brush-up hairstyle. She pulls at her small tie, glares at me, and issues a warning,

"Don't you get fresh with me! Your divorce or your illness doesn't give you the right to treat women as sex objects."

I have a few memory files about Rhonda. Daniel must have paid little attention to the woman, treating her like a piece of equipment that assisted him in the care of patients. This approach suited her. His behavior bore no traces of homophobia or misogyny. Linda replaced Ursula, a transsexual who had been his right hand in the practice until their rapport broke down because of the doctor's gloomy moods.

Sexual orientation remains shrouded in mystery. When I was born, my male organ caught my attention. I knew of its existence and have often used it in the Other Dimension. There, I could boast one as big as I thought fit for the occasion. I was a teaser and made fun of Daniel's human banana since it looked more like a small ladyfinger. He measured it in different circumstances—anxiety, coldness, warm weather, after showering or swimming. He even peeked at his college mates in the locker rooms to compare his with theirs. None of his female bedmates ever complained, but their lack of criticism didn't liberate him of the obsession. He considered no lengthening method since he concluded his male member was of average length. Whether or not he stretched the truth, I must make the best use of his appendix. I have not inherited Daniel's preoccupation. The exchange filter got rid of it. Besides, none of the women I have been with made any remark, except Natasha, who reassured me,

"Yours has got girth."

I regard her comment as a compliment, but some people might consider it a deformity. Who knows? I haven't dwelt much on this part of the anatomy. Humans dressed babies with vaginas in pink and those with penises in blue, arbitrarily assigning these colors to sexual orientation. I wonder whether their chromatic choice must have helped pair up males and females because the number of births soared. What would have happened if people had relied only on their instincts for their coupling?

This eye-catching fertile period is now over. Overpopulation poses a significant problem and leads sexuality into unplotted territories. A colorless evolution guides sexual orientation. What exposure or inherited trait influences a child to choose its gender in the new system? I have no experience with this issue since I skipped childhood. Heterosexuality, homosexuality, and bisexuality have become acceptable. But are they equally conducive to the pursuit of happiness? Humans must make them so. Yet not everyone conforms to this admissible triad. Some people behave like unruly asteroids that set their own paths, the spectrum of sex preferences expanding with no limit in sight.

My very first patient interrupts my thoughts—eighty-five-year-old Franziska Martin. In an elegant navy-blue dress, the tall and slender elderly woman shuffles in. Her silver hair stretches back into a bun and reveals a square forehead of flawless complexion, conferring her an air of distinction. Her pale blue eyes regard me with a kind expression.

"Dr. Brandon, I am so happy to see you after so long," she says smiling.

Franziska became a patient of Daniel's twelve years ago. She suffers from arthritis that narrows the spinal canal and causes weakness of her legs. The condition interferes with her daily chores. The old spinster has lived in the same apartment since her childhood. Her parents and a sister died there, but she stayed. Daniel listened to her complaints and issued a treatment plan that afforded her relief. Franziska worked as a diviner. She appreciated his neurological attention and offered the doctor free fortunetelling several times. Daniel always nodded his head and took a rain check because he never crossed the doctor-patient boundary. Their relationship had to remain professional with no taint of friendship, which could cloud his reasoning and undermine his authority.

I examine her and prescribe medications and home physical therapy. Franziska is overjoyed because I accept her invitation. With a grin from ear to ear, she explains that she retired but still does an occasional session of divination for her friends. I have heard the word "friend" quite a few times, but now it applies to me, I must look it up: a person with whom one has a bond of mutual affection. This definition makes me happy. For the first time, someone with no blood connection loves me. I am grateful to Daniel because he built the basis of this relationship I have just ushered onto a higher level. Franziska relaxes and even tells jokes, issuing me a warning before narrating the last one,

"It is an old joke, Doc. I heard it when I was a youngster."

She relates how two friends, a brunette and a blonde, had separate dates with two young men the same evening. The next day, the women compared notes. The blonde said,

"My guy was like an octopus. He had his hands all over me."

"Mine even reached for my boobs."

"Wow! Weren't you afraid?" the blonde asked with her eyes almost popping out of their orbits.

"Oh, no. I had the money in one of my shoes."

In an instant, my brain reviews the concepts of young men and women since I haven't lived through that human stage. I also try to grasp incongruent facts in the plot that works as the trigger of a ludicrous situation responsible for the quip. But, to no avail. I don't understand nor do I smile. Franziska bears a disappointed look. When I tell her that I cannot get the joke because I was born a few months ago, she erupts in whole-hearted guffaws and says,

"My goodness, you are hilarious. Who would have ever known? You are always so serious."

The truth is always healthy, particularly when your interlocutor believes it is a witticism. Most of the time, terrestrials lack experience and fret about distinguishing a real fact from a false one. This planet endures an era of half-truths, alternative truths, and fake news. The web accepts anything anyone posts as preposterous as it might be. Confusion rules nations. It is quite understandable that people erupt in laughter of incredulity or react with callous indifference whenever a proven fact knocks on their door. They don't recognize it. In the Other Dimension, the truth remains the truth regardless of how bizarre it might sound. But on earth, this concept is as unpredictable as a sleight of hand.

A sleight of hand is what I expect Franziska to do when I arrive at her apartment a few days later. She lives in a five-story building in Skokie, a northern suburb of Chicago. An older woman exits the place on a walker, and grateful for my help, she lets me in. A large elevator opens on the second floor, and I can hear a hubbub of parakeets' songs coming from an apartment. After I have rung the bell twice, Franziska takes a while to answer. She wears a long pink gown with printed red tulips and a fake white carnation on the left side of her hair. A big smile crosses her face as she welcomes me,

"Come in, please. Don't mind my birds. They get noisy with visitors."

A parakeet perches on an old mahogany grandfather clock with gilded hands that lies against the main wall of the living room. Another stands on an antique Singer sewing machine. In the left corner next to a window hangs a large cage shaped like a barn that looks out into a sunny boulevard with oak trees. A green-and-yellow parakeet flies from the blue curtains toward the coffee table where we sit at and alights on Franziska's left shoulder.

"Oh, Johnny, behave, would you? A doctor is visiting us." She gazes at me. "I named my parakeets after my ex-boyfriends."

She introduces them: Billy, the blue-and-white bird on the clock. Tony boasts blue feathers with little black dots and rests on the sewing machine, bobbing his head and chirping. A white parakeet by the name of Joe hides somewhere. As soon as Franziska digs into a wicker basket with cookies, the bird pops out, lands on her shoulder, and utters a faint "hello."

"I teach them simple words. They are smart and learn them quickly. Good night, good morning, good afternoon."

She flags down Johnny and he jumps to her hand. At a two-whistle cue and a proffered piece of carrot, the bird talks,

"Good evening, Doc."

"I trained him to greet you. These birds have more brain than the guys I named them after. I got nowhere with them." She takes a deep sigh and adds in a resigned tone, "Better alone than in bad company."

My host holds onto the arm of the chair, wrestles upward, and lumbers toward an attached kitchenette that a granite counter separates from the room where we lounge. I stand up to help her, but she flaps her hand down. She fetches a teapot.

"You like tea, don't you? Your last name Brandon shows your English ancestry. I was born into a German family. But you and I have gotten along fine. Immigrants from Europe forgot our differences as soon as we arrived in America. Cream?"

Franziska opens a wooden chest with a blue velvet cover and pulls out a deck of Tarot cards. A magenta satin bag embroidered with yellow stars holds them wrapped in red silk. As a girl, she ushered in clients for a gypsy neighbor who worked as a diviner. The childless lady took it upon herself to teach her little assistant the secrets of the ancient practice. Franziska reviews the meaning of the twenty-two major and fifty-six minor arcana, suite, court, and prim cards, and the different spreads—one card, two or three cards, Ladle, Celtic Cross, Horoscope, and so on. I ask about the goal of Tarot, and she replies,

"It reveals a client's significant personal life events and character and answers the questions about the future that hide in his mind."

Franziska uses different decks—French, German, Italian, Portuguese, Rider-Waite, Hermetic—depending on her feelings that day. The selected one should evoke unique energy and vibration in her fingers. Some fortunetellers sleep with the cards under their pillows to infuse into them their karma. Some utilize quartz crystals to wipe the residual vibes off used decks before conducting another session. Others smoke them with sage or cedar wood. Franziska found no need to do so because we are all brothers and sisters. I ask whether she reads spreads to foresee her fate.

"No, I am too old. My future is my present."

She selects the Rider-Waite and asks me to sit next to her in silence. According to her, she has known me long enough to gather powerful insight. Her slender fingers with red-painted nails shuffle a deck and grip it tight for a while. Her body remains immobile as she shuts her eyes for about thirty seconds. Franziska instructs me to cut the pile with my left hand. She then picks cards and places them in front of us. The first features the Hierophant with two identical towers, monks, and crossed keys, all held apart by a high priest. The second depicts an identical Hierophant. She frowns, grimaces, stares at me, and says,

"This error has never happened. A card from another deck was misplaced inside this one. But then, it may be the way it should be. In Tarot, coincidences are never accidental."

The third card shows "The Lovers," a naked couple in a valley with a supreme being overhead. Her fingers then ease out of the pile "The Three of Swords," a large red heart impaled by three daggers. Finally, the "Queen of Wand" flashes in front of us, sitting on a throne with two carved lions and a black cat at her feet. It occupies the fifth and last position in the spread. Franziska fidgets, her chair creaks, her left thumb rubs her chin, and her finger-pads impart soft taps on the table as if summoning thoughts with a Morse code.

"Doc, excuse my delay. Yours is not a common situation. We have here two identical twins, or two lives separated by time, a former life and a present one. If I didn't know you, I would also consider schizophrenia or a multiple personality problem."

Her declaration of the existence of another life sounds intriguing and raises my fears that she might find the truth. I express my surprise about her knowledge of psychiatric conditions.

"A professional diviner must read about the human mind, Dr. Brandon. I took a course in Psychology. I've never believed in reincarnation, but maybe now I should consider its existence. I must be true to the intimations I capture in a Tarot session."

I think the Lovers card means Daniel and Julie, who are living their bliss in the Other Dimension. The blatant red heart with the three daggers must speak for Marlene since Daniel hurt her. Like the queen, now his ex-wife stands alone with a wand in her hand ready to hit anyone who dares to come close to her. I ask Franziska,

"Where am I?"

She doesn't answer and instructs me to draw out a card. "The Hanged Man" card bursts forth before my eyes. I see a victim suspended upside down from a tree, his right leg tied to a branch, his left leg crossed behind his right knee, his head surrounded by a yellow radiant halo. It reminds me of the death of Peter, the apostle and first pope. My face turns as pale as a snail's wake. Franziska looks me straight in the eye and proclaims,

"You've got your answer."

At home, the image of "The Hanged Man" haunts me throughout the entire evening. I cannot shake it off. Further evaluation of what I beheld reveals the victim on the card doesn't seem in distress and appears as though meditating and looking at the world from a different perspective. Like a circus performer, he had tethered his foot to a trapeze and let his body be suspended in the air. Blood accumulates in the head because of the might of gravity, and an extra load of oxygen bathes the brain. The maneuver helps reasoning.

Perhaps this position should be the way I should regard everything around me. Huffing and puffing, I stand on my head. Everything gains a different outward aspect. The ceiling turns into the floor and the floor into the ceiling. A chandelier becomes a fancy artistic coffee table made of sparkling glass. TV news adopts a less foreboding look. Upside down, politicians sprinkle off their longing for power and corruption like salt and pepper shakers their savory ingredients. Floods sweep the sky instead of leveling the earth along with its poorest and weakest creatures. Wars no longer kindle city infernos but rather illuminate towns with fireworks. There are no borders in this inverted universe, only clouds that coalesce in the distance. Concepts of nation, state, and country vanish. They no longer attest to people's lack of confidence in their fellow man, the selfishness of humankind, and the tendency to isolate oneself from the rest. Instead, innate rules of brotherhood and goodwill reign on this upside-down planet.

In the Other Dimension, those divisions didn't exist either. You could swim from Ireland to Morocco, jump from Cancun to Machu Picchu in a jiffy, stop in Havana and meet Raul Castro on your way to Rome. Or you might take a brief respite in Tijuana and watch a black cat prowl on a fence on the Mexican border. President Obama could ride a train to Washington with you and plant a goodbye kiss on your cheek. A passenger might leave a plane in the middle of the Atlantic Ocean, return to Chicago to retrieve his forgotten sunglasses, and hurry back into the aircraft, so that he would arrive in Madrid on time. Anything was possible, no limits. Tonight, my frustration with the real earthly world spills into a dream:

I see a huge bookshelf filled with books in a large home office. Beams of sunlight illuminate the naked figure of Marlene. Her splendorous pinkish flesh shapes smooth curves and hills like those of a Greek goddess. Her complexion stresses the beauty of her red lips, sparkling blue eyes, and golden hair. She lies motionless on the bottom shelf and gazes at me with an expectant, wondering expression. I stand naked in the middle of the room, and my private part hangs flaccid. I urge it to rise because Marlene wants to make love. To arouse my obstinate piece of anatomy, I scratch her belly and kiss her lips, but nothing happens. An alarm clock in the room goes off, and I exclaim,

"What the heck!"

As soon as I have expressed my disappointment, I watch Daniel sit on a chair next to a window. His white suit makes him look angelic except for a smug smile on his face and his words,

"Tit for tat. In the Other Dimension, you made fun of me and thought you were immune to penile woes."

His cynical grin doesn't change, and he continues his teasing,

"'The Hanged Man' didn't mean a different view of the world. It warned you of your dead parakeet. You are not ready for Marlene. I wonder whether you'll ever be."

Payback time has arrived. I confess I pestered him in excess because of his penile neurosis. I don't give a hoot about the size of Mr. Peanut. My telescopic organ shows deference and shrinks into oblivion at rest. When I walk or run, I don't have to grab it with the edge of my underwear, shift its position through the pocket, or stifle it in layers of clothing as bullfighters do. It obeys me and grows in arousal. I protest Daniel's intrusion into my life and his disregard for my efforts to redress his mistakes. But he disappears before I utter my first sentence

Eight

THE AFRICAN MASK

I walk into my office. From the mahogany wardrobe in the back of the room, I pluck a doctor's gray lab coat with the name "Dr. Daniel Brandon" embroidered on the front pocket. Behind the garment, atop a small shelf, a wooden object catches my eye: an African tribal mask, a gift to Daniel from a patient who owned a museum of exotic art. The dark brown mask bears an oval shape with openings for the eyes and the mouth that render the object a truculent aspect. It feels rough to the touch and reeks of a rancid odor but fits well on my face.

My appearance seems most appropriate for today's task because, on Tuesdays, Daniel spent the day performing electromyograms (EMGs). The dreadful procedure involved repeated poking of long needles into various muscles of the scheduled victims. He could not anesthetize the area because it spoiled the results. Patients swore the Spanish Inquisition invented and perfected this torture in their cruelest jails. A few scientific pioneers developed this test, among them Étienne Jules Marey who worked in Paris and named it in 1890. Since then, it has evaluated the integrity of nerves that supply muscles.

74

Daniel bore no sadism in his personality and disliked performing EMGs. He came up with thermography as a painless way of gaining the same information. The photographic technique mapped out the temperature on the skin of the subject. It was based on the anatomical fact that a single nerve contained cutaneous and muscular branches that innervated a long strip of skin and one or more neighboring muscles at the same time. The damaged nerve caused a hypothermic area on the skin, which this technique detected. From the finding, the physician figured out which muscular branch was affected. Thermography proved to be accurate. But unscrupulous practitioners abused it and discredited it, prompting health insurances to deny payments. Daniel had no other choice but to use the well-reimbursed EMG.

As I walk down the hall, I regard the deceitful appearance of the EMG machines. They look like harmless robots with a long arm that extends forward like the boom of a crane. I sit next to it and open a package that contains a sterile needle. I attach it on an electric wire, lift the sleeve of my shirt, and poke the needle into my biceps. A sharp, burning feeling bores into my flesh. No blood comes out, but deep pain squeezes a tear out of my eye. I cannot subject my patients to multiple insertions like this one in ten to twenty muscles.

Daniel performed a moderate number of EMGs, which helped him cover a costly overhead and a pricy malpractice insurance policy that had escalated to an obscene amount. I have dropped the coverage and gone bare. From now on, the thermography apparatus will replace the monstrous EMG androids regardless of whether I receive any payment. Lorna heard about the changes I had made. I received several calls and her voice showed irritation. I erased them to eliminate aggravation. I already inherited enough in this world.

A few unwelcome certified letters lie on my desk in the office. I have yet to open them. I don't wish to do it in the evening because it might disturb my sleep, nor in the morning because it might spoil my day. Daniel had to put up with so much harassment. To his defense, I must admit he was compassionate with his patients amid a dark environment. It rushed him down the chaotic stream that the practice guidelines of medical societies had set for practitioners.

I write a letter to Daniel's patients:

"I would like to apologize for the suffering you endured during the numerous needle insertions in your muscles. Another test could have reached the same diagnosis, but medical societies and health insurance companies didn't consider it reliable and disallowed it. I will no longer perform electromyograms, nor will I bill you for the alternative method. All dark clouds have a silver lining. In the past several months, payments for these services have resulted in an extra-cash bonanza I want to share with you..."

Four days later, I have a long queue of people lining up from the front desk of my medical building to the hamburger place across the street. They collect their checks and make appointments. The stroke of fairness turns into a feat of genius and catapults my practice into an auspicious beginning.

The following week, I perform injections into the knee, hip, and spinal canal. Many pain specialists perform them in surgical centers where sticking one needle turns into a costly operation. A few interested parties brought to bear stringent requirements to get rid of the cheap office procedures of their competitors, among them Daniel. Money ruled on, and these guys mastered the technique of disguising the wolf. To line their own pockets, they set out to inveigle insurance companies and medical societies into imposing their arbitrary and expensive requirements on all practitioners for these simple treatments. Daniel never yielded to these pressures and continued offering them in his medical building at a much lower fee.

In the Other Dimension, injections require a less rigorous approach. You can stick a needle into the chest without removing the shirt. You might even plant a giant syringe full of Lidocaine into anyone who dares to walk by you. Procedures contain a dire warning: these methods may be harmful to the physician. The needle may take on a life of its own and force the medication into the doctor instead of its intended target. Or one assistant could go berserk and poke the practitioner and everyone around. A patient could turn into a ferocious animal, grab a needle, and make the surgeon run for his life.

Today, I am surprised to read on my list the name of Marlene Brandon. I knew Daniel injected her carpal tunnel with cortisone every six months. I expected her to cancel her appointment. But she didn't. Anxiety might have increased muscle tension, compressing the nerve in her right wrist and worsening the painful numbness in her fingers. It must keep her awake at night. She wears a green dress that reveals her shapely knees and legs. When I enter the exam room, her eyes shift toward me and glow with a nonchalant expression. I welcome her, and she comments,

"You are not wearing your Burberry."

She notices my perplexity and clarifies her remark,

"Your aftershave is different."

I tell her that I cannot tolerate the smell of that *eau de toilette.* Baby cologne seems more suitable for my age. She laughs and says,

"I told you many times... too strong for you."

The truth hidden as a witticism drew human mirth again. This trick might be the key to earthly humor. I spare Marlene my daily battles with shaving. The vengeance of blades against my skin, the roughness of an electric shaver on my sensitive complexion. My unavoidable looks in the mirror as I hope to find the right pose to enhance my attractiveness. A hopeless endeavor. I hate this part of human life. In the Other Dimension, you don't worry about growing bald, trimming your beard, or barbering your whiskers. You enjoy a clean-shaven face and cropped hair. Marlene's expression interrupts my thoughts because it acquires a stern appearance,

"Daniel, please don't misinterpret my visit. You are a jerk, but you are the best neurologist in town. I wouldn't trust anyone else to stick a needle in my wrist."

I thank her for her kind words and tuck my hands into a pair of sterile gloves.

"Before I let you do anything, you must promise me to behave like a professional. You won't send me flowers, invite me out, and so on."

I shrug my shoulders, express my love for her, and explain my intention to try my best. In her case, my heart runs away with me. She springs to her feet, but I rest my hand on her shoulder. I agree to her request and make a conscious effort not to stare at her. Like phosphorescent lights, the blue in her eyes spreads a celestial hue throughout the room and mixes with the pinkish splendor of her cheeks. I focus on the procedure. I insert the needle, the plunger goes down, and the white solution eases into her tissues. Marlene winces a little and says,

"It doesn't hurt." She then stares at me with a wondering expression and adds, "There is something bizarre."

I ask her what she means.

"I don't know."

Marlene doesn't elaborate but studies me like an impromptu physician who attempts to diagnose a new patient. That evening, thoughts about her visit unsettle me. I fear she might have discovered my identity. Women enjoy intuition, a powerful internal perception that can detect a secret long before it becomes evident. They have been catching men for as long as humankind exists. Tonight, nightmares besiege me with barely any pause between them:

I perform another carpal tunnel injection in Marlene. Her wrist swells up as if I had emptied a large syringe loaded with cortisone into the wrong location. She does not complain or grimace in pain and makes me wonder why her eyes are locked on mine. I try to inject her again, but she withdraws her hand in fear and causes the needle to jump out of my fingers and stab my left arm. In the next dream, I insert an EMG needle in the leg of a young black woman. She springs up on her feet and kicks the needle that flies like an arrow and sinks into my right elbow. There is no blood nor pain. The next scenes find me at a building in a town made of iron with grim and dangerous passages. A threatening-looking man in a dark suit watches me from a large window three stories above the floor. He accuses me of killing a patient, grabs a syringe with a colossal needle, and rushes down an elevator to get me. I run through long halls where rats as big as dogs sit in cages. The rats escape. I scream out at the top of my lungs, boot two of them, a black and a white, and in the process, kick the sheets off my bed. The night ends with a bite on the tip of my tongue.

In the morning, I slur some words for a while because the injury has left bloody spots and teeth marks on my flesh. It amazes me this mishap didn't occur earlier because of the faulty design of the human mouth. I wonder how a large muscle such as the tongue survives two rows of sharp blades every day. One expects that such an arrangement would result in a tragedy. But this harm usually happens only in epileptic people during grand mal seizures since, normally, a reflex mechanism retracts the tongue to its hideout and prevents its severance or a major laceration.

My mind, however, remains sound, and I must again focus on my task in hand and learn how to achieve my goal. For months, Daniel derived strength to pursue the love of Julie from a collection of items he put together and stowed away in a box under the bed. I bumped into his cache a few weeks ago but have yet to open it. Daniel decried the fingerprints of someone else on it as if the alien hands could desecrate it. My prints are the same as his. I need human clues about how I can conquer Marlene's heart.

I open the box and regard his treasure. Atop the pile, I find the composite picture of Julie. Daniel drew this portrait from a dream and captured the enthralled impatience of someone who had long awaited her beloved. Peaceful happiness graces her expression. I observe the coiffure that allowed Daniel to date the image back to the middle eighteen hundreds. He sought an explanation for the presence of this woman in his dream and found an answer on the next item I come across—a rolled olden photograph of Julie McIntyre, his ancestral aunt. His mother kept it in the bottom of a chest. The dry touch of raspy cardboard, stale and opaque odor, and yellowish gray discoloration speak of the passage of time and her ephemeral existence on earth. She held her lips anchored in a self-conscious expression as if questioning the meaning of life. This appearance contrasts with the ethereal smile I observed on her in the Other Dimension.

At the bottom of the pile lies the picture of her naked portrait that Daniel found at the Museum of Fine Arts in Richmond, Virginia. He sat before this painting for hours, arousing the attention of the guards who thought he might jump on the voluptuous woman and break the canvas. I admire the splendor of her pinkish flesh, rouge on her cheeks, and flirting sensual stare. Unfortunately, her seductive veneer does not convey her true spiritual beauty.

Julie's handwritten love note rests inside a small box wrapped in blue velvet. For two hundred years, it was hidden between the pages of an original golden hard copy of the "Scarlet Letter." Daniel's grandfather had bequeathed the book to him when he was a child. It was Julie's sister who, through a medium, alerted Daniel of the presence of this letter. The discovery proved his tenacity in the pursuit of his love for Julie. I open the container and pick up the note. I expect the ephemeral texture of documents in the Other Dimension that makes them disappear as soon as one reads them. But the ancient parchment maintains its whiteness and squeaking stiffness and still exhales a scent of roses. The poem was addressed to a Daniel. My donor believed the verses were aimed at him despite the centuries that separated the poetess' life on earth from his.

The last picture in his collection served as further proof in Daniel's mind of the existence of his beloved in the Other Dimension. It shows the epithet on the marble stone at Julie's grave,

"I lived my life in dreams, and now Life dreams of me forever."

I am dumbfounded by the crucial message. Some people believe human spirits communicate with the living but provide no proof that the world of the dead interacts with terrestrials. But tonight, an event rocks my belief at 3:00 AM. I come back from the bathroom, lie in bed alone, and hear someone's slow and restful deep breathing next to me. An invisible being seems to be sleeping in profound repose. I hold my breath and focus my concentration. The noise continues, and my whole body turns into gooseflesh. The next three nights, the episode recurs at the same time. Tonight, I have my recorder and some questions ready. At 3:00 AM the noise booms, and I set the machine to register the sound. I stand up. I can hear the respirations with equal intensity in all the corners of my bedroom. Several times, I ask about its identity aloud. No answer. The device keeps registering the phantasmal sound. I open the window, but nothing comes from outside. I walk out of the bedroom door and pace the hall, but the place lies in absolute silence. The entire event lasts ten minutes. I check the machine in the morning and confirm it documented the sound from beyond the grave. The ghost might have felt betrayed because several weeks have passed and it doesn't show up.

Now, I don't doubt the veracity of the famous medium who helped Daniel reach Julie's sister. I learn from my donor's proofs that one must weave the loose ends surrounding a goal to understand it and accomplish it. Daniel's success had to do with his tremendous sacrifice that amounted to a superhuman feat. Mine doesn't lag. I have given up my eternal life to redress his mistakes on earth—his divorce from Marlene being the major one. I wonder whether his ex-wife will ever fathom the love I feel for her.

Nine

COURTSHIP

My planned attempts to conquer Marlene's heart begin on November 13, 2009, the same day NASA's LCROSS mission confirms water in the lunar south pole. It is excellent news.

If humans continue mistreating their planet, they will soon need to colonize any celestial body they can reach. I hope my quest on earth is also successful and don't end up with giant impact craters in my heart like those from the rocket explosions on the moon.

In the evening, I spy on Marlene when she leaves her apartment. She goes to the sports bar "The Goalkeepers." From my parked vehicle, I see a bunch of guys and gals in animated conversation. They sit at the counter over large mugs of beer. Marlene may try to fine-tune her sexuality as I did with several bed partners. Her long abstinence and divorce might have caused her to feel rusty. Perhaps, she wants to prepare herself for her next husband. Marlene doesn't hit on any hunk but sits with a group of female friends and chats. A few days later, she visits the condo of Laura Davidson, a fellow volunteer at Christian Charities. Through a window, I espy six women playing cards, having fun, and telling jokes that make them burst into peals of laughter. On another occasion, she gets into a taxicab and meets with Dr. Michael Rosen at La Petit Maison Restaurant. Their dinner lasts almost two hours. The doctor drives her home and tries to kiss her on the mouth, but she inches her head away and plants a goodnight smooch on his cheek. The cat-and-mouse game is well underway.

I experience qualms because Marlene has no assurance that marrying me will make her happier than tying the knot with Michael Rosen. In the Other Dimension, young women liked me. Some reacted to my presence with weird familiarity such as popping their breasts out of their bras to squeeze their big nipples and spurt milk at me. I seduced them with my reckless romanticism and made passionate love to them one after another like a butterfly that jumps from flower to flower. I had no regrets about my acts. The notion of faithfulness to a sexual partner didn't exist.

Here on earth, winning a woman's heart requires more efforts. The suitor should be ready to relinquish everything for her, even surrender her to someone else better than himself. I am supposed to be perfect. But I was born with the same potential vices as Daniel. The human downgrade renders me an opportunity to correct defects that might have oozed through the filter of the exchange procedure. I recognize them, arrest their development, and strengthen their antidote virtues. My concern includes integrity and fairness to judge Michael Rosen. How will I know Michael Rosen's intentions? Yet, if his goal were sincere and laudable, I wouldn't feel uneasiness. Tonight, a dream surfs through my brain:

In a light gray shirt and pants, Marlene holds me on a leash like a dog. I lick her heel and her toes as we rest on the ground, kissing each other on the mouth with avidness. We then saunter joined in a lingering peck without missing a single step, her blond hair swaying in the wind. We enter an apartment where Lorna waits for us. Marlene goes to the kitchen to prepare roast turkey, and I stay with my donor's mother in the living room. She whispers,

"I like this woman. You must get rid of someone."

I ask the targeted person's identity and the way that elimination should occur. No answer. My mind loads my brain with images and noises. I wonder whether I am awake. I lie on my left side to rest my growling stomach because I ate my first lobster last evening. My heart pumps, my thoughts sound loud, music plays, rap music, hip hop music, country music, neighbors chat, engines grumble. I am asleep, awake, or in between. The lack of an answer to my questions in the dream pops into awareness on and off. The alarm clock tracks passing hours. Naked and alone, I then find myself seated on the floor of a hospital waiting room. I go through a long corridor. I end up at a yard with lush grass and flowery bushes next to an athletic-sized swimming pool. I strip off my clothes and find myself before a vast crystal syringe-like building with a very small access door. A long line of people waits outside to go in. Someone explains the object of the enormous artifact.

"This machine eliminates people or shapes them up."

I watch a man walk into the bottom chamber, sit, and lean over. A heavy piston then glides down and squeezes him.

I wake up and realize the weirdness and impracticality of the contraption. I am sure a similar one exists somewhere on earth. Humans are the worst enemies of mankind and have devised many instruments to torture their fellow man.

The dream expresses the need to apply pressure on Dr. Michael Rosen. The physician's lounge at the hospital cafeteria bustles with white jackets and noisy silverware. Heads bow over meat stew with potatoes, grilled chicken breasts with green beans, and roast beef with carrots. Some push their glasses up against their foreheads while others look down at the plates as though reading their futures on their bottom. A bland smell slaps me as soon as I poke my nose into the room. I don't know whether I will ever get used to unsavory terrestrial food. A recital of cacophonies follows—whishing noises from swallowing, suction slurps from straws dipped in soda, chewing, smacking.

At one table, Daniel's fellow members of the unofficial Save-Mankind Lunch Club engage in animated conversation: Dr. Ravel, Dr. Mantras, and Dr. Matthew. Dr. Ravel wields his left index finger like a gavel as his right hand holds an arrested fork with an impaled piece of potato at midair. He bolts the last bite of meat and proclaims a solution to Medicaid woes,

"Get a bunch of patients together and go to Springfield to complain. Politicians expect us to take care of the sick without remuneration and..." he stops cold as soon as he watches me walk into the room, exclaiming, "Daniel, the resurrected!"

The doctors regard me like a weird potato. Not everyone dislikes my donor. His cadre rushes toward me, wiping their fingers to shake my hand and pat my back. The uproar stirs up another table in a corner. Dr. Michael Rosen sits with the gorgeous anesthesiologist Dr. Roberta Pryor and the head nurse on the neurology floor, Louise Landau— a slender blond with a flirtatious smile. He raises his head like a peacock, stands up, and flashes a half-smile that must afford him the best pose in his mirror. His two companions remain tethered to their seats, their eyes fixing on me and bracing for what may develop.

"Daniel, finally you came. Your follow-up visit with me should have been three months ago."

My proffered hand surprises Michael Rosen, but the gesture doesn't change his air of conceit. I explain my visit has nothing to do with my health, which is fine. He doesn't wait for me to mention the subject of my inquiry, and asks,

"Marlene, your ex, right?"

I assent and say I don't want her to suffer as she did at the end of her marriage. I need to make sure of his good intentions. If he has her best interest at heart, he shouldn't be concerned. But my reservations abound since his reputation with ladies precedes him. He tries to interrupt me, but I don't let him get a word in edgewise. I ask whether he ever *googled* his name to refute complaints from unhappy women. He grits his teeth into a sarcastic grimace, scans right and left, sniffs like a night ghost, and boasts,

"Many happy ladies too."

Michael Rosen and Daniel's mutual dislike comes through, but his attitude doesn't dissuade me. I mention his complaint to American Airlines, his insistence on carrying on an oversized suitcase. Ground personnel refused to abide by his demands. An ensuing melee caused him to miss his flight. After a 3-hour delay, he ended up at Milwaukee Airport, catching a Metra train to Chicago. He arrived at his destination eight hours late. The incident reveals his poor judgment. Yet, he wanted monetary compensation for the inconvenience. A big guffaw erupts from his mouth that unveils his perfect and immaculate white teeth. He puffs and hacks because the unexpected criticism seems to suck the air out of his chest. The food odor intensifies and stifles the atmosphere. Everyone remains paralyzed and silent, gawking at us, eyes popping from their orbits. They must wonder where this argument will lead. Michael Rosen stares at his female friends to find comfort, but the spellbound nurse knits her brows, the anesthesiologist scrapes her nails, and their visions search past him.

I walk toward Michael Rosen and whisper a warning—not to mention my visit to Marlene. I add that he committed malpractice when he signed my death certificate. The body he sees in front of him could have been dead, buried alive. I could sue him for all he owns. He adopts a poker face. His eyes gaze at a picture of a little Italian village on the wall as though his mind were shuttling itself to the idyllic place. It doesn't mitigate the stressful situation. His right hand fiddles with the golden pen in his jacket pocket, his head shakes in disbelief, and his chest erupts in a deep sigh. Michael Rosen blames the hospital for his carelessness. He signed the document as required of an attending physician even though he never diagnosed the death. Someone else had made the determination, and he copied it. There were plenty of proofs of my body's demise, flat tracings, no breathing, no pulse. I insist those arguments wouldn't fly in court because they show flagrant neglect.

I fish for another reason. As a member of the Credentials Committee of the medical staff, Daniel had reviewed Dr. Rosen's application in 1996. The office of the Department of Professional Regulation investigated an alleged infringement but issued no public reprimand. A private reproof was not ruled out. The lack of documentation forced the hospital to grant the applicant admitting privileges. I fabricate a poignant remark,

"What about the sealed letter of reprimand for your conduct hidden at the office of the Department of Professional Regulation?"

He turns livid and glares at me. I don't flinch. A grimace of disgust crosses his face as his hand scratches his forehead and smooths down his hair. A murmur of disapproval arouses the place as if someone prodded a beehive. Forks and knives clutter the plates, and before I reach the door, Dr. Michael Rosen counters,

"Daniel, people can change."

Michael Rosen makes his point that everyone is capable of redemption. But can humans change? I am four months old and enjoy the keen perception of infants. Here, the answer is "no". I notice his sleaziness permeating the place and crawling over the walls. It behaves like clouds of cigarette smoke that foul everything and stain furniture and walls with viscous layers of yellowish carcinogenic poison. But tobacco users' rude disregard for the health of their fellow man amounts to a joke in comparison with the evilness I sense in front of me. If Michael Rosen wants to win the heart of Marlene, he will have to contend with me. I have never experienced this human warning system to this degree. I wonder whether it is reliable or just ill-will on my part. Michael Rosen reads my thoughts and balks at me,

"We all make mistakes and conceal skeletons in our closets."

Ten

SKELETONS IN THE CLOSET

The words of Michael Rosen about hidden skeletons prove prophetic. In a shoebox inside the bedroom closet, I chance upon the boy voodoo doll Daniel used against the malpractice lawyer.

He purchased it at a casino from a black lady who claimed to be a mambo, a priestess who performed only white magic. Daniel tried to keep it secret, but the fetish didn't escape the detection of his mother, who approved of it,

"Good for you! Those lawyers deserve a little voodoo. I hope you didn't tell your religious fanatic wife, or she'd cross herself in your presence from now on."

I don't understand how someone knowledgeable like Daniel could rely on pieces of cloth sewn together into a figurine. People on earth assign supernatural powers to statues of saints, goddesses, and even idols. Many pray to them, ask for their protection, and request favors from them. I wonder whether mankind will ever move beyond these false deities. Daniel believed the magical toy worked well once, but its power dissipated. He disregarded the possibility of coincidence. I dislike the doll's sad eyes, bury it back in the box, and dump it into a garbage can. My routine eases the day along until a dream disturbs my sleep:

From a dark street, a Chilean gentleman and I walk downstairs into a basement. My companion has a striking resemblance to the Nobel laureate poet of the same nationality, Pablo Neruda. We reach a corner where a jazz band stands on a stage in front of several rows of chairs that accommodate a small audience. Pablo takes the only empty seat, and I go to the back of the venue. A bunch of broken chairs stands piled in a corner: some have two legs, some three legs, some missing seats. Amid the wreckage lies a boy doll dressed in a running suit. I hold it in my arms and place it on the floor. It then turns into a child and ambles around. A striking svelte young woman in a light-blue dress shakes her long brown hair and looks at me with wondering eyes. She carries in her hand a book with a gilded black cover. I tell her about the transformation of the toy into a real boy. She drops to the ground in stitches, and I join her laughing. The next scene takes place at my apartment. Here, she instructs me to take off my suit and tuck it into the wood-paneled ceiling like a tile. She then proclaims with fanfare,

"The Catholic Church expects you to place it there, or a legal clause will ruin you."

She disappears and I see Daniel, who addresses me,

"You shouldn't have discarded my voodoo doll. It might have gotten you what you need."

His words upset me. I call out the farce of this religious practice that preys on uneducated individuals. In the dream, the doll turned into a boy because I had no use for it. If Marlene falls in love with me, it will happen because she chooses so without evil coercion. She must convince herself I am the best person to walk the path of life with her.

Daniel laughs.

I don't react. I ask him what he did to conquer his ex-wife.

"I did nothing. She was more in love with me than I was with her."

His conceit knows no limit. He thinks one can measure affection like the content of a bottle of perfume. Here I am trying to persuade a woman who seems to have erased her love for him. No embers in the ashes of that fire. I wonder what he did to Marlene to cause that. He shrugs and says,

"You will never learn how to live on earth."

I wake up and digest Daniel's last sentence. He might be right, but if I never get used to life on earth, it won't be because of my lack of effort.

In the Other Dimension, my relationship with religion showed the contradictions of the dream world. Sometimes, I was a priest, officiated at Mass in churches, and founded religious orders. Other times, I mocked the ecclesiastic hierarchy and showed contempt for religions because, as I told a priest, "They all have the same output," whatever that meant. I seldom thought about God. Nor did I pray, invoke Its name, or request favors. The Supreme Being had done Its job by placing us there and granting us eternal life. We had to do ours. We basked in our blessings and let God enjoy Its well-deserved rest. Here on earth, I follow the same rules. It is up to humans to share their divine gifts, help one another, and build a better place.

I dwell on my last dream, where the Catholic Church plays the same dictatorial role in the real world. I have visited Holy Name Cathedral in downtown Chicago. I admire the yellow cream brick of the façade, graceful spire, and expansive plaza over which the building presides. Inside, oval mahogany arches rise in sumptuous patterns and rest upon Corinthian marble columns, all illuminated by stained glass depicting biblical scenes. I don't sense God. In these churches, the faithful—many of whom think they own their creator—read from sacred books that condemn everyone except themselves. It seems as if they had shackled their deity and jailed It for their own use. Within these organizations, there are some well-intentioned individuals who strive to improve Mankind and relieve suffering. I respect them. But one must wonder whether the Supreme Being should interrupt Its repose to indulge them with additional presents.

Here on earth, I feel the Almighty when I watch sunbeams ricochet on green oak leaves as their lacy shadows swing on the ground with the breeze. In the afternoon, when sunlight caresses the crests of lake waves that edge toward beaches of blond sand, and seagulls pirouette over-head. At night, when the moon wheels toward its zenith and silvery rays dress sidewalks like embroidered carpets. Only the Almighty can be-stow such opulence upon these surroundings.

Until her father's death, Marlene had practiced Catholicism only on Sundays. The loss transformed her into a deeply religious devotee who attended parish events several days a week and joined various Catholic charities. I accept her beliefs. Everyone should be free to embrace what-ever religion they see fit. In the dream, the attractive brunette with a Bible in her hand substituted for Marlene. The ceiling represented the structure I needed to support my integrity with—my suit of qualities and virtues— so that I could get Marlene enamored of me. I send her a bou-quet every day. She likes autumnal colors—yellow, orange, brown, pur-ple. I include soft violets, elegant white daisies with yellow heads, delicate yellow buttercups, fragrant pink peonies, slender yellow and orange lilies, and flamboyant yellow and brown coreopsis. I attach notes asking her out to dinner, a movie, or a cup of coffee. She spurns my invitations and writes back,

"Why do you lavish me with flowers and love notes? You had your chance to charm me for many years, and you didn't. You went to bed with Antonietta, who has been our neighbor for ten years. Your behav-ior shows a deranged mind. Visit a shrink."

Frustration takes hold of me because I cannot explain to Marlene the reason for my lusty behavior. After a brief dinner of macaroni and cheese at home, I sit to read comics. I enjoy Batman climbing on the walls to catch evil men. Or Superman, who dons his super costume, rockets into the skies, dives into the clouds, and crosses the planet from pole to pole, his vision penetrating any solid matter. It makes me rem-inisce about my superpowers to control the forces of the occult in the Other Dimension. I remember the day I walked into a dark room where evil nested. I wrote the letters of the alphabet in black on my chest, lifted my hand to the heavens, and exclaimed "amen." I watched how a huge mattress freed itself from the ceiling and lifted off like a helicopter as a bright light illuminated the room. But here on earth, I lack those powers. At night, a nightmare stirs me up:

A sinister nave of concrete houses a long and dark gallery. At the bottom lies a gigantic swimming pool where numerous abused women are jailed underwater. I perceive their sadness and fear. They dress in long drab gowns and roam their confined space like zombies or brainwashed citizens in *The Handmaid's Tale.* A boardwalk extends along the entire length of the building over the aquatic prison. It inches forward like an electrical walkway at an airport. In dark attire, a group of stern-looking corpulent bodyguards stand nearby. One shouts,

"Stay away, let him pass."

I then see how my alive severed head bears a grave expression and marches along the moving path in silence. Only the bleeding neck supports it because the rest of my body is absent.

A scene impacted me the day before and could have triggered this dream. I met my 12th-floor neighbors and their dog in an elevator of my building. He was a cocky and lanky man in his early thirties, and she, a short brunette of twenty-odd years of age. A few times this week, they had engaged in shouting matches, using words that challenge my knowledge of human language. He put on a friendly face when he saw me, but she huddled and hid behind him. I still caught a few glimpses of her face. Her eyelids swollen, her expression sad and flat, her lips pale blue. I remarked to them that, every day, scores of wives and girlfriends died at the hands of criminal men who believed women were their personal property. The scoundrel frowned at me and turned his face away with a grimace of disgust. She stared at me like a butcher at a group of animal-rights fanatics. I informed her there were domestic abuse lines, violence shelters, and restraining orders to stop abusers. He growled,

"Mind your own business!"

I told him it was my business to help victims. The woman remained silent. He then set his German shepherd on me. I stood against the corner of the car, paws against my belly, his bare teeth gripping my jacket. The dog would have torn my head off had the door not opened on the third floor and let elderly Mrs. Berman in.

The women immersed underwater represented abused girlfriends and wives. My frustration selected gloomy images from my memory store and cut my head off. I am happy Marlene was not among the victims because she should never suffer such humiliation and pain. When I am about to wake, I see Daniel and Julie sitting in the chairs next to my bed. He wears a white suit, light-blue shoes, and a tie of the same color, and Julie a green dress and white high-heeled shoes, her green eyes sparkling like emeralds. Holding hands across their chairs, they smile and gaze at each other with affection. Daniel opens the conversation,

"The path to a woman's heart is rough. You witnessed all I went through to win Julie's."

As soon as I move, my twilight state ends and so does my hypnopompic hallucination. The loving couple vanishes. Daniel set an example for me. He devised several ways to breach the distance between this world and the Other Dimension where Julie lived—visual cues, steering dream scenes, visiting a famous medium, endangering his life in experiments to split mind and body. I must follow suit and not give up.

Time passes, and I come across a scheduled local marathon on Sunday, April 25, 2010. The itinerary incorporates the street where Marlene lives. I am sure she will watch it from her balcony since the primary goal of the event consists of raising money for breast cancer. When the day arrives, I don a tee shirt with the sponsor name on the back and a message for Marlene on the front:

"Marry me, Marlene."

I use a trick that worked in the Other Dimension: running backward to seduce the woman you want to take to bed. I practice, master the technique, and achieve the same speed as running forward. Here I am, in the middle of this crowd of joggers who regard me with expectant expressions. Venturing to imitate my skill, another runner nods and stares at me with a nasty gesture, spitting a large piece of gum and pointing with his right thumb down. He must like me and feel a sense of camaraderie. I reach Marlene's building and greet her. She doesn't seem amused, raises her thumb, and points it down with brisk motions.

I sprint, lose my concentration, and bump into my fellow backward runner. We fall to the pavement. I don't understand why he reacts with violence, grabbing my neck and thrashing me around until other joggers stop him. I look back to where Marlene stood a minute ago, but I see only an empty balcony with shut blinds.

The incident doesn't detract me from continuing my pursuit. I review my memory files and find out that Daniel's dad had conquered Lorna's love with nocturnal serenades. Under the spell of the moon and stars, he played his guitar and sang romantic tunes before her window. For weeks, her mother stood behind the curtains and watched him shout his head off. One day, Lorna came out, cut a flower from a pot, and tossed it at him. Neighbors and passersby noticed their display of love but walked by and pretended not to pay attention to them. It was as if their own world had wrapped the pair and made them invisible to everyone.

In the Other Dimension, I sang well and danced even better. I performed tangos at a cabaret where my voice sounded as melodious as Carlos Gardel's. The audience broke into roaring applause. But I have not tried this on earth. The next evening, I sit on a bench in a small plaza in front of Marlene's. I settle my record player next to me, play music, and bellow the romantic songs she enjoyed as a young woman— "Strangers in the Night," "Unchained Melody," "When a Man Loves a Woman." But this artistic quality was one of my innate talents that didn't survive the filter. Some neighbors shut their windows; others shout "Go away! Your singing stinks." Two teenagers throw buckets of water on me. Only an old woman with a hearing aid cheers me. Marlene never acknowledges my presence and sends me an angry note the next day,

"Stop embarrassing me in front of my neighbors. Next time, I'll call the police."

Eleven

TRIP TO A BUSY BEEHIVE

Almost a year has passed since my birth. Humans are an imperfect species. An apocalyptic catastrophe occurred in the Gulf of Mexico one month and a half ago. The explosion of the Deepwater Oil Rig killed eleven workers and opened a hole that still gushes almost 65,000 barrels every day. No one knows how to seal it off. Countless numbers of seabirds, turtles, and fish perish drowned in nasty brown sludge. One-third of the fisheries and beaches in the area are decimated.

But there is hope for humankind. The year began with a terrible earthquake in Haiti that devastated the island and killed 250,000 people. Survivors suffered horrendous calamities. A Doctors-Without-Borders physician described a young woman who had lost her entire family—her husband and four children. She did not remember anything. The poor lady believed she was a movie actress who worked for the government in the refugee camp. She was beautiful and bore an emotionless simper as if nothing had happened. But her eyes always stared straight ahead at emptiness. People have shown love and generosity for the victims. Donations and pledges topped three billion dollars.

I must continue the mission on earth that Daniel assigned me. It is time for me to meet his children. I will start with Steve. I cannot picture the bond between fathers and sons because my inherited memory files contain contradictory data. Some scenes feature Daniel's dad looking at curvaceous blondes in lingerie with enthusiasm. His face then lights up with a warm smile as soon as he shifts attention to his son. I consider the mighty power of sex in humans and evaluate the way the father regards his little one. The overwhelming preference for him speaks for a strong attachment. Daniel lied to his mother to protect his dad, a behavior that showed a strong linkage with him. A few similar images occurred on other occasions, but Daniel got used to the absent father at home and seldom remembered him in his quotidian life. His dad's death didn't make much difference either.

My neighbor Allen Roach believes the relationship of a father and a son resembles that of two kids that meet at school and go through the same courses for several years. The youngsters swear they know each other well because they read the same books, eat the same cafeteria food, and see the same faces every day. Yet, neither of them ever lifts their gaze to look into the other's eyes to understand who he really is. Familiar affection develops in them like osmosis. It spreads side to side into everyone in the household because everyone happens to be there. The other day, Allen was thrilled, and I asked him the reason. He said his son—who lives in a western suburb of Chicago and hadn't seen him in six months— sent him a card for his birthday. I don't understand why the older man felt happy. People who greet you only with a card either have no time to waste talking to you or belong to advertisement companies that want your money.

The case of Daniel and his son might be even worse. As Marlene points out, her ex-husband neglected his parental duties. Years of a poor relationship created faulty conditioned reflexes because humans are nothing more than well-developed monkeys. Have you ever wondered what would happen if whenever you fed a banana to a gorilla, you whopped its head with a hollow plastic hammer? The next time you approach the cage with the tempting fruit, a change of behavior will occur. The animal will ignore you, run away, or grab the banana and smash it against your head. You will never convince the ape the treat won't lead to a bang on the noggin from then on.

I must go where Steve lives because he is a busy bee. Children hold the weird belief that their earthly parents have all the time in the world on their hands. In the evening, Vincent, Antonietta's boyfriend, knocks on my door and asks me if he could use my corkscrew to open a bottle of Chianti. He wants to celebrate her birthday. The Italian hunk swaggers into my kitchen and uncorks the elixir with masterful deftness and offers me a drink. I take a rain check. He slips out of my quarters armed with the bottle and borrowed utensil. A mixture of heavy metal rock and hullabaloo wakes me up at 3:00 A.M. It comes from my neighbor's. Unending songs erase the nocturnal silence. She performs *O Sole Mio* at the top of her lungs like a contestant of America's Got Talent. Earplugs don't block the noise. I put my ear on the door to make sure the brouhaha originates from her apartment. I knock, and Antonietta opens the door ajar. Rock music and heavy moaning boom out, and a stench of alcohol and humanity slaps me. Her hair lies in disarray, and mascara smudges her face like a raccoon's dark mask. She wields a mischievous smile and invites me to join her group of chem sex. I decline.

After this experience, any inveterate whiner would proclaim the death of civility in modern human society, but not me. I grant my neighbor the grace of spending a wild night once a year on her birthday. My request to lower the volume of the music goes unheeded. I fall asleep, and their racket becomes incorporated into oneiric scenes:

I am in a luxurious apartment where a large group of people attend a party. A rumbustious young man smokes in the middle of the crowd. I reprimand him, but he ignores me and kicks me out of the place. I find myself lost in strange streets. I try to call Lorna but forget her phone number, and the screen of my iPhone goes blank. I curse automatic dials that discourage me from memorizing important numbers. I call a taxi. Instead of giving me a ride home, the driver takes me through a long country road flanked by a few homes and open fields and no buildings in sight. He abandons me in a deserted plaza far from my apartment.

The dream scenes showed my apprehension about meeting Steve. The raucous young man who kicked me out of the apartment represented him. My mood selected distressing images of forsakenness in an unknown plaza and the quagmire of lack of communication in the middle of nowhere. I never got home. From now on, I will always punch in my office phone number and those of Lorna and Marlene without using autodial.

The next morning, I am alone in my car on my way to Appleton, Wisconsin. On both sides of the unending road, the early June scenery of green foliage turns vivid at the northern counties. Green maple trees, tall oaks, red barns with silos, and white little shops scatter along the path. The asphalt reveals the drying cracks and graying of the past gelid winter. Afar, cattle and horses graze in peaceful pastures in the countryside. I review my memory files about Steve. As a youngster, he enjoyed baseball and kept to himself most of the time, reading adventure novels or playing with toy cars in his room. A smile lit up his blue eyes that bear a striking resemblance to his mom's. It is no wonder that mother and son fit together like a hand in a glove.

I admire the pristine blue water of the Fox River. Small streets flanked by oak trees lead to the small home that Steve shares with three schoolmates. I park my car next to a large green garbage can and several disposed pieces of furniture—a wooden rocking chair, a stained mattress, a dilapidated coffee table. The discarded accessories are part of an initial selection that didn't meet the roommates' needs. Students often furnish their abodes with items thrown away by previous school year's graduates. A hullaballoo arises from nests of sparrows atop the trees. I thought these birds had disappeared from earth because I didn't see one in the Chicagoland area.

Steve greets me with a jovial grin. He is taller than me and takes after Marlene much more than I expected. A breeze sweeps his locks of blond hair that fall toward both sides and cover the upper part of his ears. I watch him amble with unmotivated steps, brushing away with parsimonious touches a few wayward tufts that hover over his eyes. A petite brunette arrives after him. She has an attractive smile and wears an oversized orange pullover with "University of Wisconsin" printed on the front. He pats my right shoulder and then introduces Marie. She stands on her toes and plants a kiss on my right cheek. Steve's words confuse me,

"This is the famous neurologist Dr. Daniel Brandon, my old man."

I don't know why I am considered an "old man." I guess everything is relative in this earthly life. I am only eleven months old and pay no attention to the signs of aging that worry many people. Middle-aged men and women watch their mirrors panic-stricken, holding their breath for any new wrinkle or change in skin turgidity. These people listen to the clicks of their biological clock like the choo-choo sounds of a train, feeling their bodies smarting from the ravages of time. Quite a few attend Botox parties and turn their faces into pincushions to erase wrinkles with the most poisonous substance known to mankind—botulinum toxin. A single gram can kill a million people. The venom smooths the injected area only for three months and ruins your health and your pocket with the outrageous expense. Steve stares at me as though searching for some clue or feature that will associate my person with him. His scrutiny reaches a conclusion because his face exhibits an involuntary frown, probably of disbelief and resignation. After his girlfriend has excused herself, and I am about to recover from his humbling concept of aging, Steve pitched a question at me with a sarcastic edge sharper than that of a knife,

"What have I done to deserve the honor of your visit?"

I want to explain my sincere intention of building a father-son connection that should have been present a long time ago. His right hand tames the unruly lock of hair on his forehead that threatens his vision again. And before I can articulate a single word, a new smart-alecky remark pierces the stormy cloud around us,

"I am glad you've got nine lives like a cat. If only I inherit that gene from you and nothing else, it will pay for all my years of filial disappointments."

I ignore his witticism and tell him that I am glad that he takes after his mother whom I praise as an extraordinary parent and wife. A smirk crosses his face, and he corrects me adding an "ex." We walk into a nearby tavern and sit at a table over burgers, fries, and a locally brewed beer. I make an exception and eat the poisonous killers for the sake of camaraderie. His mouth adopts a scornful wince as his attack persists,

"When Mom called to tell me about your unconsciousness, I thought that state had been the norm since you'd always been unconscious of anything I did. Anyway, you still didn't tell me why you are here today."

The prediction of last night's dream materializes. His words also remind me of how the human world works. It is hard to live up to anyone's expectations. Children hold their parents at a higher standard than they hold themselves. Bosses expect more from their subalterns than they do from the managers of their companies. Religion preaches morality that numerous priests and pastors skip. Grownup humans feel entitled to food, shelter, and money, and consider the bonanza their birth right. Voluntary contributions turn into duties and sacrifices into ungrateful expectancy. My memory files register disappointing data. Since Steve reached the age of reason, he hasn't strived for a close relationship with his "imperfect father," who toiled to provide his family a high standard of living. Why should the entire fault fall upon Daniel?

My thoughts drift to the Other Dimension and my behavior with my parents. I did anything for them. At a movie theater, I even tore two armchairs from the floor and set them in the middle aisle so that they could comfortably watch the movie.

Here on earth, we deal with a different world. Children call the shots in the household, expect every gift their heart desires, and give nothing in return. They believe their mere existence should provide enough reward to their parents. Parents relinquish their authority and become their offspring's friends as if playing house. No concept of discipline. As youngsters grow, the one-way relationship consolidates. Mom and dad become a drag when they reach their old age, turning into disposable hot potatoes at a nursing home or other facility. Sons and daughters get busy with their lives, exert strictly necessary efforts, and set aside no time to communicate with them, let alone dote on them. In the past, deference entitled the elders to special regards and treatment from their children. But humans stopped this filial practice years ago. The elderly often lives alone, and some face hardships. No air conditioning in summer, no heat in winter, scarce food, no money for both medications and nutrition. Quite a few die forsaken. Over and over, newspapers report the discovery of mummified corpses that have lain in an apartment for weeks, months, or even years, next-door neighbors oblivious to what has happened before their noses.

I shake Steve's conceit. I tell him that I don't care about our relationship at this point; that I came here to ask for his help. The young man stops cold, his eyes wide-open, his face red like a beet, and his lips twisted in a grimace of surprise. His bewildered expression remains motionless for a few seconds until it melts down into one of disbelief,

"My help?"

I explain I want to marry his mom, whom I love with all my heart. I know he has always been the sibling closest to her. He scratches his chin and frowns, staring at me with cynic incredulity. He gazes past me and probably recalls incidents that were due to a conflictive conjugal relationship and his father's insensitivity. In the archives of memories, I can't find any instance when Daniel praised Marlene or even acknowledged her contribution to the happiness in their household in front of their children. Her detailed care of the house chores, guidance with their homework, and daily trips to their soccer games and ballet classes. Her efforts to feed everyone healthy food and her attention to their perfectly laundered garments. I am sure Steve doesn't remember the last time Daniel brought flowers to his wife. Nor was he surprised to find them sleeping in different bedrooms when he came home from college for Christmas two years ago. His mother made up an excuse and blamed their estrangement on the husband's snoring. But the unhappiness of the couple turned the atmosphere of the home and hearth as thick as tallow. Steve and his sisters fretted over the marital discord. He says,

"You just divorced her. You and mom were not happy for a long time. You didn't pay much attention to her."

I counter that divorces arrive from the behavior of husbands and wives, not just one. Here, the husband felt compelled to focus his life on the practice of medicine and financial matters of the family. I hope he believes a broken long marriage deserves a second chance. The young man looks me straight in the eye and frowns. He acknowledges my sincerity and realizes I must have said the same words to his mom, but hardheadedness runs in the family. He laughs. His affability then changes into stern hesitation as a realization dawns on him,

"Your words seem aboveboard... but the way you speak."

I underestimated Steve's intuition, for he must have sensed a sign that threatens to reveal my real identity. It reminds me of my last conversation with Marlene when she perceived bizarre feelings she didn't know or dare to put into words. I reiterate my straightforwardness and my goal of keeping the Brandons together. A stable and close relationship among all family members remains crucial regardless of the ages of everyone. The future cohesiveness of siblings, grandparents, grandchildren, aunts, uncles, nephews, and nieces will suffer an irreversible setback with the permanent separation of mother and father. He lowers his eyes and nods in agreement, completing his remark,

"Your voice sounds different, but it lacks any inflection of remorse about your screwups."

I assure him that I have given up the selfishness of my former way of life. Besides, one can always find excuses to deny a favor to others. I urge him to consider the elation that would follow a charitable act for one's fellow man. Steve ponders and tilts his head as though wanting his eyes to contemplate a straight world without the imbalance of lies and dishonesty. He then shakes his head and states his refusal to become an accomplice to an act that would spoil his mother's life with misery. He says he wants no money from me and hopes his next comment doesn't offend me,

"Your behavior shows defective mental health. Otherwise, how could you bequeath your fortune to a stranger, your old neighbor?"

He has hidden this rationale in the pocket of his mind since the be-ginning of this visit. Like most magicians, people hold the best trick till the last. Marlene must have seen the testament lying on the floor when she walked into Daniel's apartment, or maybe an infuriated Lorna told her. Less likely, Steve might have intended to pay a call to Daniel at the hospital but read the document and returned to Wisconsin. It doesn't matter what path bad news follows because the result doesn't change.

My task escalates onto an even steeper uphill course. Money is the source of great evils capable of breaking any family ties. Here on earth, arguments and deals always come down to money. It determines your social status, the friends you have, the woman you marry, the way the law treats you. You are worth the money you own. Wealth won't buy health, but otherwise it will get you anything else. I grab a card from my wallet, write the name and phone number of Attorney Samuel Gold-stein, and say,

"Call him up."

Money should have nothing to do with visiting a dying parent. Even I, who have skipped childhood on earth, know that. I tell him his selfish behavior doesn't speak for a decent son whose father can be proud of him. Filial love should prevail over monetary issues. Bequeathed wealth should be considered an unexpected and welcome gift and not some payable dues to a greedy recipient that feels entitled to it. Besides, I recall no words of gratefulness to an inadequate father who worked his ass off to afford him a good life. Steve gapes straight ahead, flabber-gasted by the unexpected upbraiding. He lowers his head, looks down, and mumbles,

"Dad, I went to see you at the hospital."

With a resigned look, he relates the experience. He stood at the nurses' station waiting for a resident physician to finish examining Dan-iel. There were no visitors present in the unit. An immobile old lady lay on a bed in a partition next to his dad's, her mouth gaping at the ceiling. The waiting room behind him droned with the whispers of rel-atives of the ill. Steve watched how two nurses, one tall and thin and the other short and Filipino-looking, placed a large white sheet on his father's body. They then edged toward their station and expressed their regrets about the death of Dr. Daniel Brandon, a decent professional, the best neurologist in town, who had worked too hard for his own good. A young resident-on-call rushed past Steve. He wore green surgical attire, a stethoscope hung from his neck, and an identification card with his name dangled from his pocket. A few minutes later, the rookie doctor returned and hurried instructions to a clerk in a conceited tone,

"Dr. Daniel Brandon didn't make it. Please, print his straight-line EKG and PCG before disconnecting the wires."

The clerk asked if he could talk with the son of the just departed colleague. The physician shouted he had to attend another emergency at 4B and boarded an elevator. Steve couldn't find the strength to approach his dad's remains and lift the sheet from his face. He walked down to the chapel and prayed. The son confesses his difficulties expressing love to his father as a child, his illogical idea that kissing him would bring about his dad's death.

My eyes must reflect bewilderment because I had no idea Daniel misjudged Steve. He would have enjoyed exposing the youngster's heart and beholding the treasure hidden in his soul. I misjudged him too. My feet seem to sink under me. For the first time, I experience the agony of regret and the gigantic force of paternal love. I am truly human after all. My face flushes, heart races, throat tightens, and tears flow down my cheeks. Words burst out in an explosion of contrition,

"I am sorry, my son, I misjudged you."

Steve has never heard an apology from his dad before. Daniel blamed someone else for any wrongdoing. The inability to accept mistakes extended to every displeasing minor incident, including the day father and son missed a plane while they sat reading in a waiting room. Daniel had failed to pay attention to the screen where the change of gate had flashed for a while. He blamed Steve because, an hour before departure time, the youngster went to purchase a T-shirt and caused an "unnecessary distraction." Daniel would rather hide, twist, or bend screwed-up errors than admit to them. He would never express regrets. To him, it meant disrespect to himself, a weakness that could incite others to disapprove of him, deride him, or even show contempt for him.

My words have an effusive impact on young Steve. He appears more bewildered than me, tears well up in his eyes, and a veil of tenderness covers his face. He rushes toward me and clasps me against his chest, his head resting on my shoulder and his hair caressing my cheek. I plant a kiss on his forehead. His hug is more valuable than a bunch of meaningless months of lingering on earth. It makes me feel the awesomeness of being a father and the grave responsibility.

Twelve

THE TURTLE'S PATH

aniel and I stand on a massive mountain atop the world, a bustling place with buildings and roads and crowds of people. Conversations and opinions swell around us, and the process of life and its meaning sprout into lively discussions. An open microphone allows everyone, everywhere, to listen to what everyone says. A four-or-five-year-old girl with brown hair wears a school uniform and walks next to me. I become the father of the world and emerge dressed like Samson, naked except for a loincloth. I lift an enormous cylindrical stone like the trunk of a huge tree and throw it down a cliff. Daniel shouts,

"Sonie, be careful. You will destroy the world."

I hear no cries, only a loud crash, and I watch how a new path paved with pink rocks opens before my eyes.

The dream expresses the need for dads to open a path for their children and let them walk through it into the puzzle of life. It is up to their offspring to find their goal. The child must be Ana, the elder daughter of Daniel, for I plan to attend the celebration of her 26th birthday on June 25, 2010. The communication between my donor and his daughter bristles with difficulties because of their reserved personalities. Ana had enjoyed the advantage of owning a pet and channeling her love to another living being. This propitious experience filled her with happiness and supplied her with the strength to endure a father who hung in the background of her existence like an image in a mural by Picasso. She contemplated him from afar and assigned creative meaning to his deeds as one would to each of the images in the abstract painting.

Some memories confirm this view. Daniel watched Marlene, Steve, Ana, and Emmanuelle from the podium at the convocation annual ceremony of the American College of Physicians. They witnessed the event as their faces shone with enthusiasm and affection. In black doctoral attire, Daniel praised his teachers for the unselfish imparting of their knowledge through lectures and books. He also thanked his patients for sharing the signs of sickness with him, which taught him the intricacies of the human body. No words of appreciation were directed to his wife, children, or mother. Was he oblivious to their sacrifice? No, Daniel suffered from an emotional paralysis that impeded his expression of feelings to his loved ones. One could extract a tooth from him easier than a single "I love you." He knew of the deficiency but justified it in his mind because "his affection for them needed no reminder."

A few weeks later, the thump of the plane tires against the asphalt wakes me up from my reverie in West Palm Beach, Florida. At the exit, I meet Ana for the first time, and her beauty takes my breath away. As tall as I, she boasts emerald-green eyes that stand out against her bronzed face and raven-black hair. She kisses me, hugs me, and introduces her boyfriend Richard, whose athletic figure towers over me. He wears long blond hair, short pants with big pockets on the sides, a yellow T-shirt with "Florida" printed in black on the chest, and flimsy flip-flops.

In the back seat of his pickup truck, I learn he and Ana have been living together for the past two months. In the daytime, Richard runs his own school of surfing in Juno Beach and waits tables at a local restaurant in the evening. The conversation goes on and on about the 60-foot waves he rides in competitions all over the world: Hawaii, South

Africa, Australia, Spain. He met Ana when he volunteered at the Loggerhead Marinelife Center during the yearly migration of green sea turtles in May and June. His team checked their eggs for damage from predators every day. A fantastic spectacle unraveled every evening when little hatchings rushed to the seashore to start a new cycle of life. The little ones defied the dangers of birds, fish, and humans. His verbosity continues until I interrupt him,

"I didn't know you were the celebrant at this meeting."

I say it with a smile as a joke, but no one laughs. I use this language device on purpose for the first time in my human existence. But my knowledge of the subtleties of earthly humor still needs honing. My donor had no sense of it, nor have I acquired this concept either. In the Other Dimension, I cracked jokes and did pranks. I defied the laws of physics and sat crammed like spaghetti in a package inside a lamppost in the middle of a shopping center. As soon as a shopper stood nearby and placed a bag or a box on the floor, my hand sneaked out under the rim of the post, snatched it, and pulled it inside my hideout. I laughed myself into stitches when I contemplated the awed faces of the perplexed dupes looking everywhere for the missing merchandise. Ana breaks the silence,

"You open your mouth to embarrass me, don't you?"

She details my donor's flaws. Selfish, I always act like the center of the world's attention. Conceited, I cannot allow anyone to be better than I, even my family members, lest I suffer an attack of relentless jealousy. Insensitive, I just proved my disrespect for her and her boyfriend when I spoke without proper consideration. I ask her if she had anything good to say about her father,

"You contributed your little grain to my conception and have sustained me."

Ana qualifies her response since one expects those essential aspects from a parent. It is my responsibility because she never asked me to bring her into this world. I realize the tense relationship between Daniel and his children. Any little spark triggers a conflagration as though I trod through a minefield. I discuss her introversion and how she has achieved happiness despite her handicap. Like anyone else, I improve at a different pace. One might expect to hear rude words from someone who might have built a reputation for insensitivity. Richard comes to our aid,

"Ok, you two, let's sign a truce for this weekend."

He asks how many turns of his wrist a doctor needs to screw a bulb into a lamp. We don't answer, so he follows up his question,

"Only one because doctors think planet Earth rotates around them!"

He and Ana break into big guffaws, but I still cannot catch jokes. They ignore my perplexity. Richard palavers about a few large snappers he found grounded in tiny puddles of seawater on the beach and threw back into the ocean. He goes on to recount the shark migration and how during those weeks one could walk on top of them in the water near Jupiter Pier. I envision those beasts chewing his feet and laugh. Their askance scowls notify me of my crossing the wrong line, but the arrival at Ana's saves me from further battles with human drollery.

We enter her dark apartment, the lights go on, and the hullaballoo of a crowd ensues in a room full of multicolored balloons, banners, and garlands. Blindfolded Ana wields a baseball bat and swings it before her, right and left, up and down until she hits a burrito piñata that hangs from the ceiling. A significant gap opens in the belly, and a rain of colored condoms falls to the floor amid the guffaws and commotion of partygoers, who grab as many as they can cram into their pockets. Music hammers my ears. Guys and gals flock to the middle of the room, alone and as couples or groups. Limbs and bodies thrash around with wild movements that negate everything I have learned about dancing in the Other Dimension. I cannot rely on Daniel's experience because he never had the faintest idea about leisure activity. Ana approaches me and shouts over the noise,

"You look good. The mustache made you older. You have a new happy look on your face. Divorce agrees with you... and mom too."

Ana remarks Marlene seems to enjoy going out with Dr. Michael Rosen, following her comment with a surprising statement,

"She always liked him since the day he came home for the interview."

It happened in 1996, fourteen years ago when Ana was only twelve years old. The child observed her mom's expression when Marlene opened the door and met the handsome visitor. Young humans enjoy a sixth sense of how adults feel around them. I hearken back to that day in the memory files. A subtle blush dabbed her mother's face, her eyes opened wide and irradiated some greenish light, and her voice gained a sweet intonation. Ana noticed the sudden crush of a woman for a man. Not that Marlene would have acted on those feelings since her religiosity put a brake on her and wouldn't have even allowed her to fantasize about him. But one never knows. Humans often hide a secret personality in the waking world. This concealed part sometimes escapes the control of the mind and manifests to a few select witnesses. Daniel was oblivious to her feelings as most adults would have been. He had been searching for an associate and scheduled an interview of this well-trained neurologist, four years his junior. He carried it on at home because of some construction in his office building.

It was a sunny spring morning when Dr. Rosen knocked on the door. There he was with his tall and muscular figure, a youthful face with a dimpled chin, in an impeccable gray suit, a red tie, and a square handkerchief in the front pocket. His shadow was already inside the house as if he had been impatient to walk in. A gentle pass of his hand over a full head of dark hair betrayed his nervousness. Next to his polished black shoes rested a square white screen that spanned from the ground to his upper chest. Marlene asked him in.

Dr. Rosen admired the white marbled hall and spiral staircase but lost track of his large piece of canvas, which rubbed against the lower frame of the entrance and tripped him. His balance proved to be excellent. He settled his contraption on the floor at the threshold of the living room in front of Daniel, who sat opposite to it on a sofa.

Michael Rosen tacked different pictures on it, illustrating his curriculum vitae—his birthplace in Toledo, Ohio, on May 13, 1959, college degree with honors at Ohio State University in Columbus in 1981, medical diploma at the University of Pennsylvania in 1985, neurology certification at the same institution in 1988, and attending physician at Jefferson Hospital in Philadelphia, 1988-1989. Michael Rosen had practiced in a hospital group in Cleveland for the past six years. But he sought a higher monetary compensation at a world-renowned institution such as the one where Daniel worked. The colleague paced back and forth and pointed with a long metal rod as he spoke with assertiveness in a fastidious English whose Oxford accent seemed pretentious. He blamed it on Philadelphia. After an hour, the young doctor concluded with,

"I will be a rainbow in your practice, a beacon of attraction for wealthy patients."

Daniel wondered where this guy came from because his conceit loomed like a blood-dripping head hanging from a tree. Unaware of his own deficiencies, Daniel didn't recognize the aspirant shared his own vice. The inability of humans to identify their defects lies deep in their psyche. The Bible records it,

"Why do you look at the speck of sawdust in your brother's eye and pay no attention to the plank in your own eye?" (Matthew 7:3-5.)

Often, this obliviousness grows from hypocrisy. Mindful of the defect, individuals ignore it, intending to deceive their fellow man. I must admit Daniel didn't suffer from this vice and labeled it the capital sin of our time in America. Lorna warned him,

"Not everything is fine until someone catches you as a lot of people believe. Be yourself. You don't have to air your dirty linen in public, tout your weaknesses to the world, or pontificate about morals, virtues, and principles you lack. Keep your mouth shut and don't explain your position in those matters."

Daniel looked more into the background of the aspirant and found a new patient had accused Dr. Rosen of ogling her and attempting to seduce her. She complained to the hospital but furnished no proof. It might have even been the other way around since the young divorcee had endured the lack of attention of a male for a while. The attraction of the good-looking young physician might have exceeded her capacity to control her sexual desire. The administration knew that more than one patient had made indecent proposals to the young doctor, and the successful had hushed their lusty feasts.

Clinical personnel provided no evidence either. No one could distinguish the moaning and other suspect sounds originating in the examining rooms from the painful cries resulting from palpation of sore areas. Nor could their sweaty brows, stale odor, and facial flush reveal the enjoyment of intercourse. The acknowledgement of normal lab tests or an apropos joke might cause similar signs. Since then, the cautious doctor asked a nurse to witness his encounters with female patients. Michael Rosen and Daniel Brandon never agreed to the contract terms. Fears arose from Daniel's intuition that he would end up working harder to sustain the new associate without foreseeable benefits. In the past, junior partners had engaged in hobbies and dedicated insufficient time to building the practice.

Rosen opened an office and got privileges at Riverfront Hospital where Daniel had been a consultant for five years. But the relationship of the handsome neurologist with his family didn't end. Marlene and Michael Rosen belonged to the same French group that met twice a month at the local library on Saturday mornings. Ana often accompanied her mother and stayed in a reading area while the session went on. For an hour, the members spoke the aristocratic tongue, sharpening their skills. Marlene and Michael Rosen often interacted in conversations that spilled out of their conference room within Ana's earshot. Michael Rosen sometimes invited mother and daughter to lunch. Marlene excused herself because her husband would soon arrive at home after his weekend duties. Language meetings flourished for a while and then fizzled out as attendance dropped. But they created a bond between the members. It explained why Marlene picked Michael Rosen as her ex-husband's doctor when she happened to find him in a coma.

Daniel knew his wife attended a bimonthly meeting where his colleague took part in the discussions. He lacked any insight about her platonic relationship. A man and a woman can enjoy friendship without sexual connotation in the World of Dreams. But here, people wonder whether this disinterested relationship occurs on earth. Humans suspect sexual collusion whenever a man and woman meet alone even if they discuss work issues. In their myopic view, the phantom of romance would loom in the back of the mind of at least one of the pair. What a sad state of affairs, no pun intended. Daniel shared the same belief. But his conceit allowed him no admittance of any possibility that his wife would prefer someone else over him. He never asked Marlene about her daily activities and took her faithfulness for granted.

The next morning, I present to Ana her birthday gift, a green parrot with a yellow beak. As I introduce her new pet, the bird flutters and whines a loud and angry litany of Spanish expressions,

"¡Me cago en la Iglesia! ¡Curas asquerosos! ¡Hijos de puta!"

They are a barrage of swearwords because my inherited daughter's face turns purple like a beet. I bought the bird from an old Cuban who sat with a fishing rod in hand at Juno Beach Pier. He called Federico— that is the parrot's name— *"loro charlatan,"* which meant it chattered Santeria prayers that his late wife had taught it. He had kept him by his side as a companion during long hours of waiting for grouper and red snapper to bite. I showed curiosity about the animal. He perched in a cage amid flocks of pelicans, Jamaican and Floridian fishermen with chatty girlfriends, and a pungent reek of fish gutting. Ana remarks that I bought him in a heavenly sunny place of white boats, paradisiacal water, athletic surfers, and multicolor bikini beachgoers. But the parrot is a mascot in the army of the Devil. Smiling, Ana plants a peck on my cheek and adds,

"I'll teach him good manners. In two days, he will have uttered more words than you ever talked to me all my life."

I nod my assent.

On my way back to Chicago, my thoughts drift toward the difficulties I face. The relationship of Marlene with Michael Rosen seems stronger than I believed. Most people would feel insecure under these circumstances. But I lack the sense of inadequacy since this human frailty stems from early parental rejection or disappointment. I wonder whether this attitude serves a purpose and spurs people to overcome nasty experiences. Or maybe, it paralyzes them, renders them defense-less, and sinks them into a depression. I don't know whether I have lost a powerful mechanism of compensation or saved myself from a plague that afflicts many humans on earth. If only I could use the powers I enjoyed in the Other Dimension. There, I made a square hole in the pavement, filled it with problems, placed a wooden cover atop, and whistled my worries away. Here on earth, I need to remain confident. But one cannot be sure of anything when one lacks superpowers.

The next morning, I phone Marlene to clear my doubts. She must have just awakened because her voice sounds strained. My question upsets her. She engages in a battery of profanities and insults, screaming at the top of her lungs,

"How do you dare suggest I had an affair with Michael while I was married to you!"

I tell her, I am just asking for my own knowledge, but that infuriates her even more,

"You, son of a bitch!"

Marlene sounds angrier than Federico, the parrot, and hangs up on me. People on earth don't like straight questions and would rather beat around the bush.

Thirteen

A VISITOR IN TOWN

I cannot achieve physical attributes that equal or surpass Michael Rosen's, but at least I should exceed his command of foreign languages. I am becoming trilingual. Daniel endowed me with his fluency in Spanish, and my French improves every day. In this language, quite a few words are written the same way as in Spanish or English, but most have evolved to unrecognizable articulations for unknown reasons. For example, "place" is pronounced "plas" in French and the Spanish *"jardin"*, "shagda." I have difficulties with the "r" vibrating in the back of my throat like a gurgling "g", conjugation of verbs, and reversal of pronouns. French follows guidelines. But this feature didn't carry over into English, whose unruly words wield whimsical enunciations that put kindergarteners and English as a second language students through their paces. Daniel did the work for me and saved me from that torture.

Knowledge of the new language grants me an unexpected bonanza: a deeper understanding of France and new insight into how Marlene's childhood environment influenced her. Daniel thought he knew French society because he had once visited Paris and the Louvre as a young man, feasted on escargot, and read the English translation of *Les Misérables* by Victor Hugo. One doesn't comprehend another ethnic group well until one understands its tongue and bridges the two cultures. Accents, idioms, and grammar usher students into an alien universe. Once they fall head over heels for a foreign tongue, their love for its native speakers experiences exponential growth. French let Michael Rosen comprehend aspects of Marlene that her husband couldn't. My rival commands superiority over me in this area—*mais pas pour longtemps.*

On the morning of July 4th, I wake up with a full agenda. My inherited daughter Emmanuelle attends a convention at McCormick Place in downtown Chicago. She plans to lunch with me at home. I look forward to meeting the child closest to Daniel. A few TV culinary tricks come in handy. I sprinkle a pinch of salt and some beer on thin pieces of chicken breasts and sauté them in a hot pan dabbed with a thin layer of olive oil. I load the salad bowl with leaves of lettuce, a few tomatoes, two avocados, and several slices of onion. Tears flood my eyes when the bell rings. At the threshold stands one of the most beautiful young women I have ever seen, her turquoise eyes sparkling like aquamarine. She rushes to hug me. I feel her long silky blond hair on my cheek and have the impression of walking into a garden of red and yellow hibiscus in bloom. She talks fast,

"I hope you don't mind my pregnancy. I'll make you a happy grandfather in six months."

I smile and place my hand on her belly. The miracle of human procreation arouses bells of joy inside me and brings to light an enormous deficiency of the Other Dimension. Only earth gives birth, the other world is a mere recipient of the fruit that sustains it. Life begins here. What a privilege to walk upon the face of this planet and be part of it. If I ever thought I was shortchanged in my trade, this advantage surpasses all my losses. God seeds this earthly world with life and grants its creatures His biggest gift, the award of co-creation. I am now one of them.

"Aren't you curious who the father is?"

Her question surprises me. Does it matter? The important news overwhelms the minor consideration because she will soon be the mother of a gorgeous baby. Her arms embrace me tight and happy tears mix with onion tears, and we both laugh. She stops, stands before me, contemplates me like Moses descending from Mount Sinai, and says,

"I thought you would give me a hard time like Mom."

I don't understand the reason anyone would object to this glorious event. The unknown identity of the brief contributor and out-of-wedlock nature of the birth are minutiae. Society maintains a rigid attitude about these issues but ratchets ahead with the cloning of humans. The unnatural newborn will replicate the donor's physique. The personality will emerge from the same human template, but it will develop into a unique individual, distinct from the giver of the cell. Events change us. A mother won't regain her lost child, nor society a missed Einstein.

I turn off these thoughts and regard Emmanuelle like the heroine of a Biblical saga. I cannot stop grinning. I offer her to stay with me through her pregnancy and delivery. Free like the wind, Emmanuelle probably planned the baby long before conception. She scrutinizes me for an instant and then rushes down the elevator to grab her belongings. Her lovely smile makes me realize I have reached an essential stage of my life on earth. I have completed the mental assimilation of Daniel's children as my own, a process that began when I confessed to Steve my misjudgment of his behavior.

My elation at hearing the good news of her expectant state surprised Emmanuelle. She was unaware of the late estrangement of her parents and thought her mother had contacted me about the pregnancy. Marlene did not welcome the news. Emmanuelle returns with two large suitcases.

The next morning, I call her mother and offer her to move in with her daughter and me until the delivery. I have accommodated for the future grandmother a bedroom with a private bathroom so that she shares this unique experience with us. I get a jealous fit for an answer. Marlene grumbles that my proposal is nothing more than another devious attempt on my part to bring her back into a marriage I have destroyed. She accuses me of bamboozling her daughter into staying.

I try to get in a word edgewise, but Marlene's ranting continues. She has taken care of Emmanuelle all these years in health and in sickness, in schools and sports games, on birthdays and at pajama parties. She handled the situations when her daughter bullied classmates at St. Mary Elementary, got into fistfights at St. Therese High School, or sneaked boyfriends into her room. Marlene spoke with Sister Antonia and dissuaded her from expelling Emmanuelle from school. My mind uncoiled memory recordings to expose what Daniel knew of his daughter's misbehavior. Nothing. He knew nothing. Marlene overprotected her. Mothers often defended the behavior of adolescent daughters as a private matter within the realm of womanhood. Marlene continues her tirade,

"Now, you want your daughter for yourself alone. You want to be the good father and assign me the role of a bad witch."

She hangs up before I can reply.

At dinner, I voice my concern about the H1N1 swine flu pandemic that rages in the country. It affects young adults and causes severe illness in pregnant women. They lose their babies and even their lives. I will make sure she gets a vaccine as soon as it is available. She welcomes my words but declines any overprotection,

"I am aware of the danger. But I have been avoiding exposure as much as possible."

Emmanuelle then goes on to recount her encounter with Marlene the previous evening. Her mother became outraged in front of Michael Rosen who had dropped by and stayed for dinner. After a while, the hostess calmed down but blamed herself for what she considered a failure of her daughter to exercise responsible parenthood.

Emmanuelle appealed to her own maturity to defend her free decision. Marlene refused to accept the explanation. Her daughter offered no excuse. She had craved a child for herself alone without resorting to anyone's help or advice. Artificial insemination fulfilled her desire. As a single mother, she will rear her worthy child without the interference of a father. Her own dad contributed little or none to her upbringing. Emmanuelle expects my reaction, but the joyful smile doesn't

118

abandon my face. She praises me because I value my feelings toward my first grandchild more than those toward her or my ego, and adds,

"Grandfathers are a special breed."

Marlene disagreed with Emmanuelle's decision and adopted a defensive attitude, feeling singled out as the parent responsible for her daughter's screwup. Michael Rosen had been a mere spectator until he stood up, patted his girlfriend on the back, and suggested,

"Since this pregnancy is artificial, perhaps Emmanuelle will reverse it."

The way the expectant mother looked at the meddlesome witness might have burned holes in his skin. Marlene's failure to react to the hint of abortion turned Emmanuelle livid. Her mother, the upright Catholic, the one who had taken turns to worship at the tabernacle day and night, lady of charity, benefactor of the poor, sat oblivious to the sinful proposal during a long pause. The prejudices of society impacted her. Marlene shook her head in disapproval, and Emmanuelle rebuked the uninvited interlocutor,

"Again, doctor, another woman does not go along with your selfish and inhumane suggestion."

A flush reddened the face of Michael Rosen, who averted his eyes and returned to his seat. But a sulky expression betrayed his resentfulness. Marlene overlooked the words of her daughter and called for a peaceful evening. The male guest adopted a nonchalant attitude, strived to ignore the repartee, and toasted to a long and pleasant friendship. Yet, a scalpel could have dissected the congealed atmosphere in the room.

At our lunch, Emmanuelle talks about Michael Rosen and repeats the same information that her sister Ana provided. She fears the long superficial friendship of her mother with him has developed into a deep attachment. Marlene never listens to her warnings. Two years ago, she recounted to her the story of Michael Rosen's daughter, Geraldine, a college fellow student at Notre Dame University in Indiana. The young woman exhibited the raven-dark hair of her French-Canadian mother and the blue eyes of her father. Emmanuelle had known her by her last name at the enrollment, Mailloux, but she changed it to Rosen-Mailloux in the second year. The classmate explained her father had recognized her as his daughter.

Geraldine's late mother had been a novice at a convent when she was admitted to Jefferson Hospital in Philadelphia. There, she met the father of her child. The pair seemed to have fallen in love and started a brief relationship that dissolved three months after the mother had become pregnant. Michael Rosen asked her to get the money for an abortion from her wealthy family in Canada. But she refused to end the life of their offspring. He moved out, provided no forwarding address, and never inquired about the outcome of his girlfriend's pregnancy.

The death of her mother prompted Geraldine to search for her father. Afraid of scandal and financial responsibility, Michael Rosen rejected her overtures to meet and denied his parenthood. She took him to court and won, vindicating her mother. The judge ruled he had to repay child support with interest to her mother's estate and imposed him a penalty of 100,000 dollars. Geraldine added his last name to hers as an accolade to her mom's victory and never contacted him again.

Emmanuelle continues to relate the incident at Marlene's, picking up where she left off. After dinner, Michael Rosen posed like a peacock, straightened his blue and white tie, and smoothed his dark blue jacket. He then wished the daughter a happy stay, congratulated his girlfriend on her excellent culinary aptitudes, kissed her cheek, and swaggered out of the apartment with an *'au revoir.'* As soon as the door closed behind him, Marlene reprimanded Emmanuelle for her rude attack on a gentleman friend,

"You know better than offend a guest at my house. What kind of respect do you show for your mother? Besides, you don't even know the truth about this Geraldine."

Marlene recounted Michael Rosen's side of the story. He had fallen in love with the Filipino novice and enjoyed a romance. As soon as Miss Mailloux got pregnant, she no longer showed any affection for him or even for this country, desired an abortion, and longed for Quebec, Canada. Michael Rosen opposed ending the life of his first child. The woman remained adamant. He relented, helped her, and furnished her the money for the procedure and the move north. Michael Rosen then left for Cleveland to prepare his new place, and after two weeks, called his ex-girlfriend. She had disconnected her phone. A friend walked to her apartment, but no one lived there, and the last occupant had provided no forwarding address.

Michael Rosen concluded his ex-girlfriend had returned to her home country and heard no more from her until Geraldine contacted him. The initial call flabbergasted the father who couldn't believe his ears. He met her, welcomed her into his life, and offered his love and unconditional financial support. He felt robbed of all her years of growing up without his presence and asked his child's pardon for his inadvertent absence in her life. The girl became hysterical when he requested a DNA test to confirm his paternity. Geraldine considered his petition an offense to the memory of her mother. The case ended up in court. The test came back positive but ripped an unbridgeable breach between father and daughter. Michael Rosen complied with the court ruling, but the episode saddened him. Marlene added,

"The fact that he and your father don't see eye to eye doesn't make Michael Rosen a bad man."

Despite Marlene's statement, the words of Emmanuelle still cause me great concern. Her mother could fall for someone whose evilness surpasses by far the blemish of womanizing. Women and men are often the gullible prey of bad guys and gals. People look at the surface of humans, their physical beauty, elegant dress, fake attitude of uprightness, apparent gaiety. They turn a blind eye to signs of moral turpitude and callousness. These suitors hide their evil under the screen of religion, liberal professions, and institutions of charity. Tonight, a dream surfs through my mind:

A large cave opens before me. It boasts walls that sparkle with encrusted diamonds, rubies, and emeralds. Rainbows emerge from stalactites and stalagmites that encroach on the entrance like teeth in a mouth. On a marble table rest five one-gallon crystal containers. Four sit empty and unlabeled, and one marked with the word "FAIRNESS" stands full to the rim. I lift this bottle and hear Daniel forbid me to carry it with me. He explains the unnamed jars contain the three "L" ingredients of romantic love on earth—LURE, LUST, LUCK—and one "F" for FANTASY.

Daniel explains that LURE entails physical and emotional attraction. LUST means a strong need for physical and passionate love. LUCK involves the spark or cupid's arrow that triggers the imagination of the beholder—an act of kindness, a look, some words, a dream, a perceived interest or need in the other person. FANTASY carves a new makeup for the potential lover, so he or she fits in the expectant niche of the suitor. But the last component might create a beloved whose perceived qualities may have nothing to do with reality. He adds,

"FAIRNESS, the other "F" choice, never made it into the irreversible formula."

There is nothing fair about romantic love. No one deserves this gift from nature. Some even joke and equate this lofty feeling to temporary insanity because it changes behavior and mood to an enormous extent. A perfect woman or man awash with virtues and attractiveness may not capture the other person's heart. The explosive formula causes terrible mistakes, brief love affairs, short marriages, terrible quarrels, fatherless children. In contrast, common sense love adds trust and admiration as requirements for the beloved, but this advanced and logical affection belongs only to a few privileged minds on earth.

As a corollary to the lack of fairness in love, Daniel urges me not to dismiss any approach to win the heart of his ex-wife. It is an all-out war. If I shy away from any scheme, I will lose. I understand his point but will use only reasonable means. Daniel's position as a member of the Credentials Committee grants me access to the release of information that Michael Rosen signed for the hospital. He handed it in at the time of his initial application for appointment to the medical staff. Armed with this document, I contact Dr. Horacio Torres, the head of the same committee at Jefferson Hospital in Philadelphia. A review of documents discloses the applicant's infraction that had to do with a hospitalized young Filipino novice by the name of Sister Monique

Mailloux. The patient suffered severe intractable headache and neck rigidity, receiving a provisional diagnosis of meningitis. The emergency room assigned the case to Dr. Michael Rosen. Patient and doctor started a romance during her hospitalization. The religious woman's radiant beauty and nacreous skin she exposed during a spinal tap might have been too much of a temptation for the junior neurologist. A nurse overheard a bet between Michael Rosen and his colleague, Dr. Frederick Lerner. Michael Rosen would pay for two tickets to a football game of the Philadelphia Eagles and an expensive dinner at the Café de Artistes if he failed to seduce Sister Mailloux. The allegation could never be proven. The day before her discharge, a few nurses witnessed how the neurologist proffered her a bouquet of roses with a note and kissed her on the cheek.

Sister Palermo, the mother superior of the convent, learned of an intimate encounter between patient and doctor in the afternoon of that day, a few hours before her subordinate returned to the convent. It remained unknown whether Sister Mailloux had volunteered this information, or the superior had wrung it out of her. In 1988, Sister Palermo sent a letter of complaint to Leonard Davies at the Department of Registration of the state of Pennsylvania and a copy to Lyndon Manteaux, president of the medical staff at Jefferson Hospital. The main sentence reads,

"Michael Rosen, MD, used his dominant position as an attending physician to engage in a sexual relationship with his patient, Sister Monique Mailloux."

The mother superior specifies that, while the initial seduction occurred at the hospital, their sexual intercourse took place at the doctor's apartment. She concludes,

"Dr. Michael Rosen degrades the medical profession and poses a danger to society."

It seems odd the patient didn't start the complaint. Michael Rosen hired a lawyer to defend himself. By the time the board ended the investigation, the pair were living together. Some members considered their free union as Dr. Rosen's attempt to justify his severe infraction.

Others viewed it as a case of two young people who fell in love at first sight and wanted to join their lives. The committee of the Department of Professional Regulation imposed no disciplinary action on the young doctor. No mention was made whether a confidential letter of admonition was sent to Dr. Rosen.

The papers I had received shed no light on what might have happened to the couple that prompted their separation a few months later. I phone Geraldine Rosen-Mailloux, introduce myself as Emmanuelle's dad, and explain the reason for the confidential call—the impending admission of her father into our family. The following Sunday, I take a Metra train to Milwaukee, Wisconsin, where she lives. She stands up to greet me at a local café. Her wondering smile towers over me as her aquamarine eyes sparkle under an undulating sea of long raven-black hair. Her mom never talked about her father until Geraldine reached the fourth grade and asked questions. Little by little, she culled scraps of information about him. Her father grew up in an orphanage under the care of nuns and put himself through college by working at UPS in the evening. At first, he seemed to love her mother but turned aloof when she got pregnant. He preferred to be around the same cadre of friends and left her mom six months before her delivery. Her mother always denied knowing his whereabouts and discouraged her daughter from searching for her father.

After Monique Mailloux's death on February 3, 2007, Geraldine went through her mom's belongings. In the bottom drawers of the nightstand was a square black box with golden edges. Inside were three closed envelopes addressed to Michael Rosen MD, University Hospitals Cleveland Medical Center. Someone marked them with the written words "Return to Sender" and an arrow toward the address of her mother. The first one contained only a photograph—a baby with big eyes, black hair, and chubby cheeks rested in the mother's arms wrapped in a pink blanket. On the back, Monique wrote,

"Your daughter Geraldine was born at Jefferson Hospital on August 14, 1989, at 1:03 PM."

The second contained another photograph. It features a sleepy

Geraldine in white silk baptismal attire with lace and a white embroidered cap with a rose-like pompon on each ear. On the back, her mother wrote,

"Christening at Our Lady of the Immaculate Conception, October 2, 1989."

The third letter dated May 5, 1997, bore another photograph. Geraldine appeared dressed in a blue ice-skating outfit striking a pose like an Olympic champion, her face radiant with happiness. This time the envelope had a small note with pink edges where Monique jotted a sentence,

"Michael, this picture will be the last one you will receive unless you acknowledge it."

Geraldine believed her father had opened the correspondence and resealed it before remailing it to her mother. But it was difficult to find any evidence of tampering in the envelopes. Geraldine then phoned her father at his office to notify him of her mother's death. She provided her name and always received the same answer,

"Dr. Rosen cannot attend to your call, please leave your number."

He never contacted her. She used a fictitious name and got an appointment as a self-pay new patient. Dr. Michael Rosen greeted her at the door of his office with a handshake and then perched behind a lustrous semicircular mahogany desk. Behind him, the wall teemed with diplomas. His face turned pale green when she identified herself and the reason for her visit. He expressed no condolences, drew a grimace of indifference, and said,

"Didn't you follow your mother's vocation and join a convent?"

"I am studying psychology. I am trying to understand fathers who abandon their pregnant women and their newborn children."

Michael Rosen didn't react. He leaned back on the armchair, crossed his arms on his chest, acknowledged knowing the mother, but cast doubts about his paternity. Geraldine refrained from exposing her anger and resented the implication her mother had been promiscuous. She affirmed that Monique went out with no men and invited no male into her home. Her mother remained faithful to the man with whom she fell in love. He remarked with sarcasm,

"What a pity."

"You, evil son of a bitch."

"You, daughter of a nun, this consultation is over."

"No, it isn't. I'll see you in court."

The story causes me consternation. My newly found paternal love for Daniel's children afforded me a feeling of fulfillment worthy of the trade of my eternal existence. Michael Rosen's childhood in an orphanage doesn't explain his callousness. I cannot warn Marlene. She wouldn't listen or forgive my intrusion. But marrying an evil man would be the worst sequelae of Daniel's misguided behavior on earth because it would destroy her.

I find Michael Rosen at 7:30 AM, getting out of his red Porsche at the hospital parking garage. The twilight of dawn dims the lamps of the solitary place. Plumes of breath rise as he readjusts his dark blue coat and bends over to smooth the folds of his gray pants. I approach him and his neck jerks toward me in surprise. He rests his left arm on his car, leers at me, and says,

"Is this your idea of a good morning greeting?"

I make clear to him that I have talked to his daughter, Geraldine, and found out the secret side of his life. He answers me in an emotionless voice, his finessed Oxford English flushing down the drain. He related to Marlene everything about the issue—the whole truth, nothing but the truth. His poker face shows not even a disturbed grimace. Besides, I should have asked my ex-wife's opinion before this encounter. Marlene wouldn't approve of this behavior from the man who married her, made her miserable, and dumped her. Nor would she expect her ex-husband to interfere with her life, let alone impede the companionship of a friend who helps her through the sadness of her separation. I correct him. Lack of love didn't break up the marriage but a poor relationship. I wouldn't object to any decent man trying to conquer her heart, but she doesn't need a scoundrel. He must end his farce or else.

"Are you threatening me?"

I answer yes, but he must not fear a physical threat and figure out his penalty. He snickers. His expression of indifference turns into a rictus of hatred. His breathing quickens, forehead scowls, eyes spit venom, left elbow presses against the roof of his car, tongue pushes his left cheek, and right hand makes a fist. I stare at him. He tries to push me away, but I keep my pose and ground as his voice thunders,

"I am sick of you, Daniel. Stay away from Marlene and me. A story has at least two versions!"

"Maybe so, but in your case, the two accounts are the sinister and the evil."

I leave him, his face ashen gray with anger, and walk into the lobby by the chapel. Father Ruston stops me and makes a joke,

"Have your horse ready."

I respond I own no horse. He chuckles and elaborates. He said hose, not horse. I look perplexed as he admits having witnessed my quarrel with Dr. Rosen. My apologies for my lack of sense of humor prompt his repartee,

"Yeah, blame it on your coma. Jesus Christ and you and the two resurrections."

He sits at a table and says,

"I don't think you know what happened to the nurse who testified against him at Jefferson Hospital. Be careful."

He explains. The concerned woman overheard Dr. Rosen make a wager with Dr. Lerner. The latter would purchase two football-game tickets and foot an expensive-dinner bill if Dr. Rosen seduced Sister Mailloux. She corroborated her story at an initial inquiry of the Department of Professional Regulation. The nurse also presented an anonymous note that had threatened her,

" *Why did you accept to testify against Dr. Rosen? It was just a joke about a stupid nun. He has done nothing wrong. If you go ahead and do it, I will make sure your husband learns of your ongoing affair with a doctor in the hospital. You know who he is. I have definite proof of your indiscretions. Watch your back, you, gossiper!*"

A handwriting expert didn't identify Dr. Rosen as the author of the missive. The unknown sender didn't know she had gotten a divorce a few days earlier. The Department of Professional Regulation did not impose any disciplinary action on Dr. Rosen but issued a cautionary confidential reproof. It warned the physician that future attempts to blackmail or threaten witnesses would end up in the hands of the law. Any suspected obstruction of the proceedings of their department would cause the loss of his license. For the community's sake, they would take these actions even without definite evidence of wrongdoing. After the addressee had read it, the commissioner sealed the envelope and hid it in a file cabinet away from the public eye. The published official documents never mentioned this private letter. But it leaked out to Bishop Torrent because the committee suspected that Dr. Rosen held a grudge against Catholic institutions. When Dr. Rosen applied for admitting privileges at Riverfront Hospital, Father Ruston also received the information but couldn't divulge it.

"I fear for your safety. I know I can trust your judgment. Please, don't repeat this conversation to anyone."

I now understand Michael Rosen's face when I speculated about a hidden letter back in November 2009. I have no idea how I guessed this info. Perhaps, Daniel suspected it, and I had access to this intelligence. Michael Rosen's violent streak worries me quite a bit. I ask Emmanuelle to hand a note to her mother when they meet today. It reads,

"Marlene, please excuse my audacity in writing this letter. But I fear for your personal safety. The Department of Regulation of the State of Pennsylvania issued a hidden letter of reprimand to Michael Rosen because he tried to intimidate a witness with physical threats. Please, be cautious, heed my advice, and keep this man at arm's length."

Fourteen

EPIPHANY

The next day, I find a threatening message from Marlene on my recorder:

"Stop pestering Michael and me, or we will get a restraining order!"

She spurns my warning. Humans lack control of their hearts because the FANTASY ingredient in the formula of romantic love on earth causes deaf blindness. Lovers cannot accept any argument against their beloved, nor will they catch exhibited defects in plain sight for everyone to see. Marlene's voice sounds angrier than her usual tone of displeasure. People change their nuances and timbre under certain circumstances, depending on their emotional state, but this instance must be an extreme case.

Her irate twang causes a mind-searching effect on me. I wonder if Daniel seduced Marlene and if she even fell in love with him. I hearken back to their initial courtship in my memory files. The first time the couple made love occurred an evening in July 1982, a few months into their relationship. A downpour drenched them and, laughing, they took refuge behind the Foster Beach House on Lake Michigan. Daniel licked the water dripping down from his girlfriend's body, and the flavor lit up his passion. She planted a soft kiss on his lips and waited for him to finish. Marlene was not a virgin. Daniel observed no honey hue of desire in her eyes. Their last intimate encounter happened during a trip to San Francisco, three years before Daniel met Julie in a dream. That evening, he and his wife had dinner on the terrace of a fifteenth-floor suite that overlooked the bay and the Golden Gate. The main entrée was a delicious plate of seafood—shrimp, oysters, scallops, crab legs. It calmed their hunger and ignited his passion. Again, there was no color change in her eyes.

Marlene was a good wife who took care of Daniel, supported him on most issues, and kept a joyful hearth and home. But she never exhibited enough sexual attraction for her husband. Some people never feel this inclination. Men can also be responsible for their wives' frigidity. With Daniel, his conceit rejected any doubts about his charm. There were other signs. On one occasion, he turned into an aisle on his way to the wine-and-beer display in a local supermarket and bumped into Marlene. She was picking up two yellow boxes of Earl Gray tea. He rushed toward her and hugged her, but she remained frozen as if she hadn't recognized him, her arms hanging at her sides. A minute passed before she smiled at him and kissed him on the cheek. Marlene never settled any dispute, she quibbled with Daniel before going to bed and always waited for him to make up with a conciliatory peck.

The couple never discussed their previous love affairs prior to or after their wedding. It was an agreement. Daniel had two former girlfriends. Vicky had green eyes and made him laugh despite his deficient sense of humor, but her assertiveness intimidated him. Choka boasted an athletic figure and engaged in a relationship that ended when she parachuted from a single-engine plane and Daniel freaked out. The husband knew his wife had endured the disappointing relationship of her mom and dad. As a teenager, Marlene caught her mother red-handed with young men in the back of her parents' bakery. She witnessed the disaster of her elders' heartrending divorce. Marlene often said a woman would encounter only one man who could fit into her heart in a lifetime. Love was not a single-sized garment adaptable to anyone. Daniel believed he fulfilled her requirements. He once asked her about her past love affairs, and she replied,

"As we agreed, we started from zero when we met. Nothing in my past will change my feelings for you."

Her evasive answer ignored that the past forged the present. A significant occurrence in the brain alters the perception of our senses, reaction to events, mood, and temperament. It changes life around us. Her words reassured him that Marlene loved him. She must have believed it herself because she fought the divorce and didn't want to split from him. The evidence also points toward her marriage being a beneficial relationship for her. Marlene might not have behaved like a social climber. But she took a comfortable ride, bamboozling her mind into avowing that she had fallen head over heels for Daniel, a promising young doctor. Psychological need can distort people's thinking. At night, these thoughts tire my mind out and drag me into a dream:

In the middle of a large square stood Reputation, a fence where life transactions hang from the upper edge. From this balustrade, one can grab women and men of various ages and races, love, friendship, money, dresses, alcoholic beverages, soft drinks, toys, cigarettes, perfumes. I pick a white girlfriend with a squint in her left eye. She dresses in a tight dress that enhances her plump but well-contoured figure. The young woman has a boyfriend and suffers from the paranoid idea that someone intends to steal him. I select another—a good-looking and svelte Chinese lady. I feel intense desire to urinate. She ushers me into a vast public restroom, immaculate and dry. Several people of both sexes loiter around the place. There are no cubicles, toilets, urinals, or holes. Large yellow Xs lie written on the floor, each separated two yards from the next. My oriental girlfriend walks over, points at one and says,

"Do it here."

What a mess! I then select a tall and thin young brunette as my next bride. She dresses in a blue suit, carries a black briefcase, and requests I wear a loincloth and a feather on my head. I refuse her demands. The dream carries a distinct meaning: everyone bears flaws. It is the catastrophe of the earthly world, an unstoppable course of decay that grows with time, eroding perfection day after day in an endless process. It behaves like a jack hammer lashing against the pavement. In this shattered mess, we must rummage in search of shards of flawlessness that make individuals who they are. Nothing remains perfect. Marlene is not an exception. Can she fall in love with someone like Michael Rosen? I keep visualizing them together, walking hand in hand, kissing, making love. The scenes hurt me, but I cannot block them. My insides run amok. Did she forget she had defined herself as the exclusive woman of one man? Don't I own that person's blood and flesh?

These thoughts still plague my mind as I catch the elevator to my apartment at the end of my workday. I find Emmanuelle enjoying a cup of tea with Geraldine, who came to Chicago on an errand. She volunteers information about her estranged father. A schoolmate read the decision of the court in a newspaper, found her phone, and contacted her. He identified himself only as a graduated member of the (Χω) Chi Omega Fraternity, an organization formed by former alumni of Saint Augustine's Orphanage, where her father had grown up. Tears well up in her eyes, and blood reddens her cheeks as she recounts the story:

Six-year-old Michael Rosen entered the institution in 1965. Sister Martha, his mother, was slim and beautiful. The novice walked around with long strides, her arms swinging with the nimbleness of a pair of wings. She looked like an angel with big blue eyes, long eyelashes, and a ton of energy. Sister Martha then fell in love with her confessor, Father Philip Rousseau. She got pregnant with Brigitte and left the convent, and he the priesthood. They settled in a small town near Toledo, Ohio. He worked as a salesman at Sears, and she stayed home with Brigitte. Michael was born two years later. Their marriage never sailed across smooth water but achieved a certain degree of contentment. He barely made enough money for basic food and a roof over their heads. Their sexual naiveté granted them the only reward to look forward after a long drab day.

Philip's resentment for his truncated religious vocation surfaced on and off. Martha begrudged his moods and scolded him, calling him a weak black beetle whose only brave deed had been to seduce a novice. Philip began to drink heavily, and soporific unhappiness set in at home. He threw himself upon the railroad tracks as a train was approaching. His suicide subjected his family to dire poverty. Martha struggled to manage the meager dollars from Public Aid. She missed Philip, and bereavement made her neglect her house and her children. Michael grew unruly and engaged in frequent temper tantrums and squabbles with his sister. At home, dirty dishes and clothes piled up. Martha sent her children to school dirty until social services threatened to take them from her. She prepped them up and cleaned the house but failed to find a part-time job. Martha decided to start her life anew in her homeland, Quebec, Canada. She kept the apple of her eye, Brigitte, and left Michael under the nuns' care at the orphanage. Martha planned to retrieve him as soon as her situation allowed her to do so but never came back.

Six nuns and two novices kept the orphanage for males under strict control. One large dormitory housed fifteen boys younger than ten and the other, twenty youngsters less than eighteen. Three sisters had motherly instincts and lavished on the children as much loving care as possible. But the degree was inadequate because of the dismal disproportion of the number of orphans for each caregiver and institutional rules. Physical endearments such as kisses or hugs were forbidden to discourage an "inappropriate mother-son attachment." Corporal punishment abounded. Some children endured the stings of wooden rulers on their palms or forceful pulling of their hair. Some bore their ears tweaked as their punishers dragged them to a corner of a classroom. Others suffered a reenactment of the crucifixion for several hours. The penalty consisted of kneeling in front of their classmates, outstretching both arms, and supporting a book on each palm. The anonymous caller described how Michael Rosen ended up in a closet for 24 hours with a limited supply of bread and water because of an "obscene" joke. Sister Theresa had overheard him say to a sick classmate,

"You look paler than a nun's breast."

When the caretakers transferred Michael Rosen to the youngsters' dormitory, his height and look made him a target of abuse. Frequently, a nun ushered him to her cell, stripped off his clothes, and caressed his genitals. When he got older, another sister in her fifties often spent nights with him "at sacral vigils" of sexual orgy. The nun engaged in endless tongue kisses, vaginal and anal penetrations, fellatio, and cunnilingus until the youngster lay exhausted. She labeled the crime an act of sacrifice for God and warned the victim not to disclose it under threat of severe punishment. The penalty consisted of banishment to foster homes on a farm where he would be subjected to constant labor and utter perversion. Michael never found out whether this bucolic hell existed. Other children fared even worse than him since their teachers handed them to their confessor, Father Louis Gomes, an insatiable pedophile.

The whole affair reached the press, which published it in The Toledo's Daily on October 10, 1978, with a banner headline,

"Hellish Saint Augustine's Orphanage, Bordello of Sexual Abuse."

Religious authorities questioned the existence of these crimes and cast a shroud of secrecy and impunity over them, forcing the newspaper to retract the accusations. The rogue nuns and novices were moved to other convents. A new crew arrived to oversee the institution whose name was changed to the Christian Children Group Home. The story brought pangs of guilt upon Geraldine who checked with her friends before contacting her father again. She now wonders whether he needs psychological help and maybe another chance to establish a father-daughter relationship.

The information doesn't awaken my forgiveness for others or my sincere readiness to help even my enemy. I can only think of Michael Rosen's terrible act of deceit and egoism, the abandonment of Geraldine's mother and denial of his fatherhood. Nothing justifies his abominable behavior. I wonder about my compassion and unconditional generosity that Daniel used to praise in my makeup because he lacked them. Like any other human on earth, I have been caught on the unstoppable wheel of decay that erodes the perfection of mankind since its inception. This process accounts for the deterioration of my personality as jealousy creeps under my skin like scab mites. The relationship of Marlene with Michael Rosen drives it. Obsession grabs me. Her images appear everywhere. Marlene's figure jumps out of her picture on my nightstand, rides on the clouds overhead, rests on the sands of Lake Michigan beaches, and pops out of roses and tulips like mists of perfume.

I am behaving like Daniel when he searched for his beloved in statues and atop Indian totems. My fixation on his ex seems to play the same role as his fixation on Julie. This state contributed to his downfall. I wonder whether my love for Marlene will follow the same course. The lights of dawn used to bring a smile to my face every day. Now I wake up despondent. Defects besiege me—insensitivity, mercilessness, jealousy, lack of happiness. An overwhelming force churns my metamorphosis into another Daniel.

The epiphany surprises me. Are life circumstances exerting a transformation on me and molding my character? Or does the inexorable command of genes dictate the rules? If the latter is the case, I will turn into another Daniel, a distraught individual who might even consider suicide. I hope the former is true, and humans may mold their inherited genetic template the same way an artist can chisel a piece of marble. At night, my fatigued mind rests and lets a dream flow:

A young woman hands me a plant of tea—*camellia sinensis*—as a gift. It is long and guarded on the sides by two long and narrow wooden stakes. I live on a large white ranch, so my guest and I look around for a place to cultivate it. The back yard lies covered with shadows of tall dry trees and shrubs. We consider it unsuitable and walk to the front of the house. A considerable prairie opens before us and displays a few trees and plenty of green vegetation. I reason the brittle tea twig will grow best exposed to sunlight. On a knoll runs a stream with a little waterfall that provides continuous irrigation to a field of white daisies. I pick the elevation where this variety can grow and gain a strong flavor. I bend, dig a hole into the dark soil, and stick the root inside. As soon as I finish my task, the young woman no longer stands next to me.

Instead, I find Daniel, whose mustache arches like a feline's as he groans,

"Was I so bad that you fear to turn into me? You won't be able to survive on earth without imperfections. Jesus and Aristotle were killed. Buddha had to lower his expectations. And so did Confucius who endured a long exile before returning home to die. Abraham Lincoln lied to abolish slavery."

"Those events happened centuries ago"

"Man hasn't changed."

Fifteen

TIME OUT

The tea-plant dream prompts changes in my environment. The oneiric scenes point out a way to forestall my transformation into Daniel, an event that would overturn my purpose on earth.

Sharing a large portion of my donor's milieu created the ideal culture for the bugs of his imperfections to grow in my mind. Daniel was not bad on earth, but negative influences around him promoted his flaws and deficiencies. They also derailed a significant portion of the virtues and innate abilities that an unobstructed development of his personality would have brought about. Society trains people for a cruel world and bolsters their blindness to the goodness around them. External factors change the expression of human genes and modify people's physical and spiritual traits.

In preparation for my grandchild's birth—at least, that was my excuse—I have refurbished, repainted, and redecorated the entire apartment at Marina Towers. The place commands such a magnificent view that I didn't move. I took the pictures of Daniel off the walls and furniture and put photographs of Marlene and the children. My donor's clothes, shoes, and belongings lie on shelves or dangle from hangers at the Salvation Army thrift stores. I left no traces of him and purchased a new wardrobe at Macy's.

Now, as I drive, I watch the rearview mirror and observe how the silhouette of the massive Riverfront Hospital fuses with other high-rises in downtown Chicago. I turn onto Michigan Avenue, and it finally disappears. Daniel spent so many years there that this piece of real estate must bear quite a few of his joys and disappointments. But those emotions belong to him not me. I like my new hospital, John H. Stroger, near the Eisenhower Expressway. It boasts spacious and clean lobbies with large glass windows. This advanced medical center has replaced an old building with a lush façade of ionic marble columns that now lies empty. I don't miss my previous surroundings and exited them without inflicting damage on anyone. Riverfront Hospital bought my practice, so Daniel's employees still enjoy their jobs to make a living and support their families. I placed the proceeds from the sale in a trust for my future grandchildren.

The new institution allows me to observe a somber side of America. The place is located near a poor neighborhood. Blacks and Latinos brighten up their bodies and faces with tattoos. What a cool way to cover human nakedness. I haven't figured out the message of these patterns. Nor can I translate the graffiti symbols posted on the walls of dilapidated buildings. I cannot understand these people. They speak their own dialect,

"Hey, you, *muh-fuh*, what you' doing? Get the hell out o' here!"

Their language doesn't sound friendly. But I like their murals. They turn the area into a museum where young artists express their feelings about human weirdness. This degree of poverty should be eradicated in the US. Here, it mainly affects Afro-Americans. Sadness, despair, and desolation permeate everyone. Drugs abound. People struggle to survive amid gangs that behave like wild beasts. Rapes, robberies, and murders rage. It is no wonder residents forgot how to smile and laugh. This poverty is not the one Christians mention in the Gospel. If the purgatory existed, this neighborhood would be what the priests had in mind.

Many of our forefathers died to free black people from slavery. Why are they now abandoned? Is it the color of their skin? If it is, it makes no sense. A white orchid isn't more beautiful than a black orchid. Nor is a seagull's white feather nicer than a raven's lustrous black feather. It all must boil down to family values and education—many don't even speak well. Why are parents and schools failing? Where are the irresponsible fathers of so many single mothers' children? What are their organizations and local churches doing to correct the problems? American Society never completed its job.

At work, my new job reinforces the change in my environment. I spend most of the day walking from room to room, treating severe cases of stroke, head injuries, meningitis, encephalitis, seizures. Long lines await me at the outpatient clinic where rare diseases and unknown conditions challenge my diagnostic acumen. No other institution in the world can match the extent and rarity of its pathology.

Numerous daily gunshot wounds overburden our emergency room. The proliferation of guns has become a deadly danger for ordinary citizens in the US. Their availability has been blamed on the Second Amendment to the Constitution. But the outrageous number of firearms in our society has more to do with the Wild West and cowboy romance than with anything else. Arms sales grow every year, and manufacturers, protected by legislation from lawsuits, reap obscene profits. Corrupt politicians render them untouchable. Even schoolchildren are now targets of gun violence and mass shootings.

John H. Stroger Hospital faces a gigantic task. It provides care to an enormous population of indigents, undocumented immigrants, and the uninsured working poor. The old hospital opened in the 1800s, and since then, the public had lauded its work all over the country. Annual statistics are staggering: 464 beds; 24,000 admissions; 150,000 emergency visits; and 500,000 outpatient visits.

In my new hospital, most patients are uninsured. This adverse reality affects a large portion of our population in the US. Fortunately, Congress has just passed Obamacare. It provides coverage to twenty-six million uninsured individuals. It also removes the unfair preexisting condition clause that has denied coverage to sixty million people, among them the sicker members of our communities. It still leaves out twenty million unprotected people who belong to the working poor. My new facility caters to them.

My dealings with old ladies and little children restore my compassion and unconditional generosity. Images of Marlene flash in front of me on my occasional breaks and arouse my longing. I exchange them for scenes of patients fighting for their lives, relatives in tears for their loved ones, and children holding on to their sick mothers in the lobbies. Jealousy sometimes surfaces. I envision Marlene preparing food for Michael Rosen, spoon-feeding him French onion soup, and kissing him with his mouth full. The scenes last for a few seconds until I tear them from my thoughts and dice them into pieces as with an electric knife.

In the evening, tiredness makes me fall asleep in front of the TV. I wake up on the sofa with the screen off and a blanket on. Emmanuelle tucked me in with it. Her eight-month belly has grown large, gorgeously pink, and lustrous like vanilla ice-cream. She spreads avocado oil over it to avoid permanent stretch marks. Tonight, she and I sit next to each other, reading. Half of the time, I stare at her and wait for my grandson's kicks, which lift the drum-like surface of her baby bump and bring giggles of rapture to the mother. I go to bed, and a dream inundates my mind:

I see a massive hospital with enormous facilities that bristle with patients and nurses. Dressed in a white gown, I am on the top floor and decide to go down long vertical stairs. The steps are made of narrow metallic planks attached to the façade like a giant bookshelf or a firefighter's ladder with no ropes. Confident and relaxed, I stand straight, face emptiness, and one by one, descend three steps. Fear then paralyzes me. I regret choosing this path instead of the elevator and risking a fall into the abysmal void. The way back to the top of the building looms frightening. Panic throws my balance off. My feet float in the air as I clutch a metallic step tight, and my nose and mouth press against the wall. My right hand releases its hold, reaches out, grabs my foot, pulls it down against the stairs, and stabilizes me. I creep back to the top like a lizard, one hand first, the opposite foot second, followed by mirror movements of the other two limbs. After a few never-ending minutes, I have made it.

The scary dream seems to portend an end to the deterioration of my personality and the subsequent recovery of my virtues. The gain should happen after serious efforts and dangerous vicissitudes. The oneiric scenes ended before I walked into the elevator and rushed down to the lobby. So, they never specified whether I would reach my final goal since I could have remained stranded on the top floor.

A few weeks later, I settle on the sofa until Emmanuelle's shouts stir me up,

"My boy is coming!"

The clock displays 8:00 PM, November 19, 2010, a beautiful day to welcome my first grandchild, Thomas Brandon. Emmanuelle's water breaks, and I hurry her into my new red Honda. I place a towel on the front-passenger seat and help her sit, her belly rubbing against the door. She puffs off and on, and the stress of giving birth begins. I ask Emmanuelle if she wants me in the delivery room. She declines. Emmanuelle has been so independent that she did not even let me or her mother accompany her to the obstetrician and childbirth classes.

I call Marlene from the hospital. An hour later, she and Michael Rosen walk into the waiting room hand in hand. I kiss her on the cheek and shake the hand of her companion. They settle across from me, and their presence distresses me, but I do my best to endure it. I haven't seen or talked to them for five months. He arches his eyes, takes sidelong looks at me, puts his arm around her waist, and squeezes her body against his as if afraid she will fly away. The cloud of malevolence around him persists, creeping over him like dark clouds on the Himalayas. A nearby dispenser of hand sanitizer lets me squeeze some foam out and wash the hand that touched his. I remain silent and hear them whisper words I cannot make out.

A nurse allows Marlene and me to walk into Emmanuelle's room and spend a few minutes encouraging her. We come back to the waiting area, and my nerves get the best of me. I must focus on something else before I go crazy. My mind settles on the issue before me: Marlene and her boyfriend. She looks content, but her facial expression is not that of a woman in love. Everyone on earth has the right to make mistakes, including Marlene. I wish I had accomplished my mission of repairing the damage Daniel caused her. But I have continued to pursue my quest:

A private detective, William O'Connor, handles the investigation of Michael Rosen's background. I found him in the Chicago Tribune. He introduced himself as someone who boasted "logical and carefully crafted conclusions." The words discretion and confidentiality appeared in bold font, essential requirements to avoid Marlene's temper tantrums. Dark and narrow spiral stairs with a moldy odor led to his office and prompted complaints about the unsanitary access. He answered with a grunt,

"What in the heck do you expect to find in an old hound's den?"

He uttered these words, knitting his bushy salt and pepper eyebrows and shaking his head. His bumpy nose reddened, and a few locks of whitish hair flickered on his convertible-roof-like baldness. He sat on a large dark-leather reclining chair before a faux fireplace with a marble mantel and hearth. I perched on a dark wooden armchair with scuffed yellow upholstery and faced him. The red office walls featured gilded framed pictures of Sherlock Holmes with the original pipe and hat. Each depicted the famous snoop in various scenes, looking through a magnifying glass, examining the penmanship on a letter, watching the full moon reflect on the water. I relayed the info I had gathered in the case. He looked straight ahead as though paying no attention and scribbled occasional remarks on a clipboard. He accurately summarized my report and remarked,

"Listen to some of your sentences, 'the divorce took place a year and three months ago,' 'I hope the intensity of my love will conquer Marlene,' 'I don't want to allow Michael Rosen to deceive the woman I love more than anyone else on earth.'"

I balked at his comments because I didn't understand what he meant and assured him of their accuracy and relevance.

"Did you hear yourself talking? I have heard hundreds of ex-husbands and ex-wives relate their issues. You filed for divorce and want to remarry the same woman a few months later, don't you? Are you insane? You never used the words "again" or "our" and utilized phrases like "on earth" rather than "in this world." Who are you? Where in the heck are you from? Where were you raised?"

I replied he should stop his esoteric divagations and tackle the problem I had contracted him for. People remarried all the time. I blamed my speech on the multiple nationalities of the patients I saw every day at my workplace. He made a grimace of disbelief, nodded his head, and grabbed the one-thousand-dollar retainer check.

A few weeks later, I attended a briefing. Mr. O'Connor confirmed that former inmates of St. Augustine Orphanage had founded a fraternity at Ohio State University in 1977 and named it Chi Omega (X ω). The X of the symbol stood for "love of Christ" and ω "for eternity." It presently had thirty-five students who had either graduated from Christian Children Group Home or had been raised in adoptive households. The investigator interviewed a few children at the retitled institution under the guise of a reporter doing a freelance study on orphanages. Louis Ryan, the president of the ninth graders, recounted an oral legend of the members of Chi Omega that had passed down from one class to the next for the past two decades.

Mr. O'Connor summarized the info. The fraternity symbols had borne a different translation from the very beginning. The X meant "screw," and ω depicted the pendulous breasts of a nun, the signs composing the sentence "screw the sisters." At that point, the brotherhood recruited graduates of the orphanage with highest levels of intelligence and valor. The number ranged between twelve and fifteen. Students endorsed the alliance to their cause, swore absolute secrecy, and underwent a strict initiation ceremony.

The exploit consisted of pasting obscene comics of nuns and monks on the main door of a convent and setting fire to a large cross in front of it. The blaze scared the wits out of the sisters who frantically yelled in fear. The candidate wore a white mask and a black pinecone hat and rode away from the scene on a dark horse, giving the slip to the police through nearby alleys. His success was rewarded with a sexual orgy with prostitutes in religious habits. The fete took place amid rich mosaics, sacred images, and gold and silver decorations at Rosary Cathedral, the monumental gothic church that boasted the same architectural style as its counterpart in Toledo, Spain. The brothers, mayor, and bishop joined a crowd of civil and religious authorities at an event that lasted until the wee hours of the morning. Everyone wore elegant black tuxedos and top hats and hid their faces behind masks. Hookers flaunted their stark-naked bodies crowned with sisters' white cornettes.

There were some traces of truth in this legend. Reviewing newspapers brought to light a nocturnal cross burning in front of St. Augustine Orphanage on October 29, 1977. Pornographic cartoons surfaced pinned to the main doors of the convent, featuring nuns in lesbian acts and in group sex with priests and monks. The perpetrator escaped through narrow alleys on a mountain bike, and the police made no arrests. The FBI investigated the incident and concluded it might have been an initiation prank by a college student. Up to the orgies at Rosary Cathedral, Mr. O'Connor discovered an instance of sacrilege committed by fake Buddhist monks with Bishop Torrent and Governor Limerick in attendance. The police had raided the place in the evening and shut the lavish ecumenical party as soon as religious authorities had realized the cruel prank. The Court disregarded the case because organizers had obtained the permits required and the diocese had approved the celebration.

Mr. O'Connor traced the current whereabouts and activities of the five founding members of the fraternity—Michael Rosen, Louis Vaudeville, Anthony Lenoir, Vincent Gustine, and Frederick Lerner. Louis, Anthony, and Vincent had married, moved away, and lived with their families of several children in Florida, California, and Oregon. The two bachelors, Frederick Lerner and Michael Rosen remained in the Midwest, Dr. Rosen in Chicago, and Dr. Lerner in Cleveland. The investigator met Dr. Lerner at an outside café and learned a few more details. Michael Rosen had spearheaded the creation of Chi Omega

Fraternity and recruited the other four co-founders. Organizational activities didn't differ from those of the rest of the groups at the university. Members engaged in philanthropic efforts for scholarships and charities, played sports, threw parties, and arranged chess competitions. As far as Dr. Lerner knew, no one committed any hateful prank against the nuns. He added,

"That's preposterous. We loved the sisters."

Dr. Lerner expressed his gratitude to teachers and caretakers for their motherly care and indefatigable efforts at the orphanage. The fraternity founding group petered out when members scattered around the US and lost contact with one another. He hadn't seen Dr. Michael Rosen since he moved from Cleveland. He admitted to a bet with him in the case of Monique Mailloux, regretted the silly incident, and meant no harm to the sister. Since then, his life evolved into religious endeavors. He became a member of Opus Dei, a Catholic organization that stressed the holiness and sanctifying value of daily work. Dr. Lerner lived at a residence for single members who had taken a vow of chastity and stood ready to embrace ordination to the priesthood if needed. The detective concluded the whole feud with the nuns and novices was Michael Rosen's personal vendetta.

His conclusion reassured me that I did not confront an evil sect with an infamous purpose. I informed Mr. O'Connor that at Riverfront Hospital, the staff knew that Dr. Michael Rosen had engaged in a few long-lasting relationships with several alluring and elegant women. They bore no connection with the medical establishment. He flaunted them at some annual galas of the medical staff. Daniel neither met them, nor did he learn their names or occupations. Michael Rosen holds high positions in the Alliance Française de Chicago and the Groupe Francophone de Chicago. He meets a lot of people and has access to a lot of information in the French community. I asked the detective to find out about them, and he agreed after I handed him a five-thousand-dollar check.

Butterflies in my stomach wake me up from my induced reverie. I wonder whether Daniel was as nervous as I am when his children were born. I survey my memory stores and find out my donor spared himself the stress of sitting in a waiting room before the happy news. He didn't witness the deliveries of his children since this practice only began a few years ago. A brief halt in his demanding job let him welcome the new-borns on their days of birth, but stolidness dampened the joy on his face. As for me, tears well up to the rim of my eyelids as the arrival of my first grandchild approaches.

Emmanuelle has refused any type of anesthesia and will rely on ex-ercises to decrease her pain. I envision the normal process of delivery. Muscle spasms and pressure build inside an overstretched uterus. The child pushes down the bony walls as amniotic fluid buffers the process that threatens to drown the baby. There is not enough room for the mother's bladder and gut, let alone for the offspring's head. The pelvic floor tenses like an arch, and the woman's heart rushes. Hot flashes and paleness alternate on her face. Waves of pain interrupt her breathing, and a shrill cry announces the first inhalation of air that breaks through into her newborn baby's lungs. The mother's pain disappears, forgot-ten. Humans undergo passage through the birth canal with worse symp-toms than those associated with death. Lucky for them, they will bear no memory of the event.

Minutes and hours pass, and my impatience worsens. I can no longer trick my mind into concentrating on something else. Magazines and TV aggravate my anxiety. I pace the hall back and forth, return to my seat, and then go back to loitering around the corridors. Marlene keeps her eyes closed and rests her head on the shoulder of Michael Rosen who stares ahead. At 6:00 AM, a nurse comes in and ushers Marlene and me into the room of the new mother. Dimmed lights re-veal the gorgeous scene of her first encounter with the baby. Emmanu-elle has her head bent toward little Thomas who lies in her bare arms wrapped in a blue blanket. The ravages of delivery disfigure her face with bluish spots, parched lips, a reddish nose, and circles around her sunken orbits. But her eyes sparkle with excitement and gaze at the mir-acle before her with immense tenderness.

Clouds have just turned pink and purple over Lake Michigan and peek into the window as if to render homage to the new human. Marlene kisses her daughter and Thomas' hairy head. Tears stained with mascara run down her cheeks. I dab her tears and mine before they reach our necks, and Marlene stares and scowls at me with a wondering expression. I feel joy for the birth of my first grandchild and pity for myself because my mind hearkens back to the cold marbled intensive care room where I was born alone. Humans learn to rein in their emotions in their childhood. In the case of Daniel, Lorna went too far and repeated over and over "A man never cries." But a man should cry when he should, laugh when he should, sing and dance when he should. Displaying emotions don't make humans weak. Marlene smiles at me, holds my hand, and whispers,

"I want our daughter to feel close to her parents. I read that somehow our grandson will also experience this attachment through his mother's hands. But my feelings for Michael haven't changed. Do you understand?"

I nod my assent. The warmth of Marlene's hand sends shivers down my back. My daughter lets me hold the baby. The materialization of human creation lies in my arms with his eyes open, his straight gaze absorbing the earthly world. The fragrance of innocence wafts around and floods the surroundings. I cover him with the blanket because he seems so defenseless, but he pushes it off. These grounds are his worldly domain where he orders everyone around and masters everything that walks on the face of the planet. Marlene watches my face of excitement, huddles next to me, and says,

"Thank you for our grandchild's college fund."

I never told anyone about the new account, not even Emmanuelle. But nothing escapes the eagle eyes of the lawyer of my donor's ex.

Sixteen

SECRETS BEHIND DOORS

mmanuelle waits for me to have dinner. She remarks that Geraldine, the daughter of the groom, has received no correspondence from the hosts. Marlene commented that the young woman had harassed and blackmailed Michael Rosen with "psychological threats." But her version is erroneous. The daughter visited the father, offered him her love and friendship, and expressed her willingness to attend sessions of family therapy with him. The treatment would have addressed the gap of years of separation and coaxed father and daughter to come to terms with settled legal issues. But he stared at her and balked,

"I want you to return my money and stay the hell out of my life."

I tell Emmanuelle to disregard her mother's position on the issue. At this point in the relationship with her boyfriend, nothing will convince her of the truth. When a woman sets her mind on a suitor, she turns a deaf ear to entreaties and arguments. Marlene lies closer than ever to marrying someone with no heart. People often get caught in a spiral of mistakes and lack the vision to stop it. The absurd process starts like a game and ends like doom because most people don't even notice when the blunder occurs. I have warned her many times and can no longer advise her. Tonight, a dream disturbs my sleep:

I tread on a long movable bridge. A submerged canoe plods along in the water channel under me. It wields robotic arms that grope around and try to grab me. I run away to escape from them, and at that precise moment, the bridge opens, and an imposing metallic wall looms before me. Fear seizes me. I cannot cross to the other side. I retreat and watch a blue bus halt and pick up passengers. I rush and ask the driver to take me to 2020 Acacia Plaza. He declines because the vehicle follows a different route. Somehow, I get to my destination—a building with a brownstone façade of arcades like those of elegant Spanish squares. The main arch bares an inscription in French that reads,

"Les mots ne peuvent pas être écrits en anglais car le bâtiment est trop petit pour abriter la traduction."

That is, the words cannot be written in English because the building is too small to house the translation. I figure out the bridge means my relationship with Marlene; the threatening robotic arms, my difficulties; the stone building, her strong-headed mind; the bus, my hope to reach her; the French words, my convincing arguments; and the lack of translation, her deaf ears.

I suppress my passionate desires for Marlene with hectic work and caring for my grandson. I have accepted her preference for Michael Rosen. But my human nature surfaces when I least expect it. I am not the full master of my thoughts, and this dream reminds me of what brews deep inside my heart. The letter of invitation has behaved like a cathartic. It stirred up my love for Marlene in the forgotten areas of my brain and steered it to the fore of consciousness. I cannot afford this weakness and must keep my feelings dormant.

A few days before the engagement dinner, I research the attire for the event and come up with a royal blue suit. Marlene praised this suit when Daniel wore a similar one at Paradise Casino in the Bahamas ten years ago. She remarked "he was dressed to kill." I hope she reacts the same way to mine. I complement the blue garment with a white shirt, a red tie, and a red pocket square, selecting the three colors of the French flag to honor the bride's heritage. Emmanuelle approves of my attire. But Lorna frowns and stares at me as a gorilla would a basket of rotten bananas. She wears a dark green dress adorned with sequins and patterns of black damask, a green hat with two black feathers, and black riding boots as if going to a hunting party.

Emmanuelle has taken good care of herself and recovered the svelte figure she enjoyed before her pregnancy. Her turquoise gown enhances the blue of her sparkling eyes and the fiery blond of her hair. We catch a cab to the John Hancock, and a few minutes later, the elevator to the 95th floor. The cage takes off like a plane lifting and floods my ears with hollow pressure. The nearness of Lorna in such a close space stresses my discomfiture with my donor's mother. If I were not a self-restrained person, I would scream. She makes me feel claustrophobic and instigates conflicting feelings. I dislike her aloofness and selfishness but treasure her straightforwardness and bluntness, which we share.

The elevator opens into a semi-lighted hall where a hostess in a dark dress receives us with a charming smile. It takes a little while for my eyes to adjust to the penumbra. She ushers us to an expansive salon with a large table set for a formal dinner. Groups of guests stand next to the floor-to-ceiling windows, admiring never-ending long paralleled lines of illuminated city streets that abut downtown. Everyone enjoys the spectacular view of Lake Shore Drive under a starry sky. The road snakes along the beaches up to the dome of the Baha'i Temple far north in the cityscape. Near the corner of the north and east windows, Marlene and Michael Rosen chat with their guests— Father John Roche, her parish priest; Laura Davidson, her best friend; Roberta Pryor, MD; Louise Landau, RN; and Frederick Lerner, MD.

I jostle my way in to greet the future husband and wife. I shake Michael Rosen's hand, put on an honest smile, and thank him for inviting me to their engagement. His hand conveys doubts about my sincerity. I clench his fist tight and say,

"I apologize for all the grief I caused you and Marlene."

He forces out a smile. I have practiced this meeting for so long that the desensitization succeeds. I bear no bad feeling toward him. I figure if I did, Marlene would sense it and resent it. She has a life before her and must make her own right or wrong choice because her future lies in her hands, not mine or anyone else's. I kiss her on both cheeks. Her lips pucker and two tiny parallel folds rush down to the space between her eyebrows. The splendor of her eyes seems to flood the room with azure. I excuse myself and leave to greet other relatives. I see Steve and Ana with their significant others, petite Marie and beach boy Richard, in an animated conversation. Before I get to them, Father John Roche waylays me and asks whether he could have a few words,

"Marlene wants to marry Michael Rosen at our parish church."

Now I understand the reason for Marlene's invitation, but his words still surprise me since Catholics don't accept divorce. I express this doubt, and he ignores me. The priest talks about the conditions for a real marriage of both spouses— freedom to wed, uncoerced exchange of consents, intention of marrying for life, promise of faithfulness, openness to raising children, desire to be fair to each other, and acceptance before witnesses and religious authorities. If the union falls short of at least one, there will be grounds for annulment. The lengthy procedure requires two tribunals of the Archdiocese of Chicago. He adds,

"The resolution might take ten months to two years. It depends on you, Daniel. I hope you find in your heart the strength and generosity to help Marlene. You want her to be happy, don't you?"

I let him talk. The Church will appoint a defender of the bond of the first marriage. The petitioner will require the testimony of two witnesses acquainted with the situation of the spouses at home. Finding people aware of frictions between husband and wife has proved difficult. The children cannot take part in the proceedings. Father Roche volunteers to participate as an attester because he has known the family for many years. The serious illness of Marlene's mother makes her an unsuitable candidate. I suggest her mother-in-law as the second one,

"Your mother?"

I tell him Lorna adores Marlene and would do anything to help her ex-daughter-in-law have another chance at happiness. I will convince

Lorna. I omit that she prefers I marry Marlene and views my failure to persuade Daniel's ex-wife as a painful disappointment. The children will object to the annulment. They will dislike being born out-of-wedlock even though the Church will later dispense them of this technicality. Besides, from their point of view, the matrimony fulfilled all the requirements for a real marriage. Father Roche welcomes my remarks, augurs a reasonable and prompt resolution, and adds,

"God will reward you,"

His words stink of hypocrisy, but earth teems with this garbage. People accept false axioms, embrace half-truths, bend their beliefs, and repeat spurious claims over and over until they convince themselves of their correctness. I watch Father Roche whisper words in Marlene's ears, and she gapes at me in awe. Steve approaches me and puts his hand on my shoulder to console me, but I reassure him of my solid emotional state and best wishes for his mother. He shrugs and lifts his eyelids in impotence. Marie strolls toward us, stands on her toes, and kisses me. Her story resembles Marlene's. The young woman was born in Paris and moved to this country when she was two. History repeats itself once and again as if fate were imprinted in the genes of our family. I hum the French song "Petite Marie" and articulate the first line,

"*Petite Marie, je parle de toi...*"

Her wide smile displays dainty teeth as Steve hugs her and proclaims her his little French sweetheart. She kisses her boyfriend on the mouth and lets her lips linger, no qualms, no inhibition. Ana and Richard admire the grandeur of Lake Michigan and the luminosity of Navy Pier with the incessant Ferris wheel before changing their attention to me. No sooner do I plant a peck on Ana's cheeks than the lights of the salon flicker to announce dinner. The names of the twenty-five guests rest on the table. I find my seat next to Laura Davidson, who shakes her long brown hair and stirs her neck like a butterfly breaking out of its cocoon and stretching its wings. She must be ten years younger than Marlene, and the soft tapping of her fingertips on the tablecloth reveals boundless energy. The excitement in her voice and her eyes expresses happiness for her friend's good fortune. Laura has never married. We engage in conversation enlivened by glasses of muscatel wine. She asks me what I think about her. I grab a napkin and write,

"Let me worship what your eyes see and your hands touch."

The unexpected reply shocks Laura, who blushes and shakes her long hair. But she doesn't capture the meaning of the sentence and throws me a questioning stare. My smile reassures her of the poetic compliment. She has no clue I have turned her eyes and her hands into surrogate instruments of my love for Marlene. My two gift boxes for the future spouses, hers wrapped in pink and his in red, pass from Laura to three other guests at the table and end in front of the couple. I hear protestations that I should have given the presents at the end of the dinner or at the wedding, but I disregard the comments. I tap my glass a few times, stand up, and address the future bride and groom, toasting to their happiness and adding,

"*D'un arc-en-ciel, les ailes battantes le regardent se précipiter vers une flamme qui frémit comme si elle était agitée par le vent.*"

I translate the riddle into English "From a rainbow, flapping wings watch it rush towards a flame that quivers as if agitated by the wind." The sounds of the original language fit Marlene's heritage and the nature of her romance with Michael. The answers to the brainteaser lie in the two boxes facing the future bride and groom. I ask them to open them. Marlene hesitates for a second, and then peels off the box that reveals the blue velvet cover of a tiny container. A gilded clasp unlatches and discloses an 18-k white gold necklace with a heart-shaped ruby pendant that emits an intense red glow on her hand. She slips it down her head under the guests' spellbound gaze. Michael opens his gift, two white gold cufflinks with Cupid ready to aim an arrow.

Attendees enjoy a fabulous dinner with appetizers of caviar, shrimp cocktail, and endive salad followed by entrees of duck *a la orange* or filet mignon. Bordeaux wine enhances the flavors of the food. Before the dessert pastries and engagement cake arrive at our table, a musical group sits in a corner and the piano plays the notes of "Strangers in the Night." A young vocalist imitates Frank Sinatra. Marlene and Michael Rosen start an awkward dance, their feet tangling as embarrassed expressions emerge on their faces. People applaud their performance. Laura takes me to the floor and clings to me tight under an elegant chandelier. I don't flinch, let her sway and spin like a ballroom pro, and catch sight of Marlene looking askance at us. Several couples join us and block her view. The song ends before two waiters place a large dark chocolate cake with two big "Ms" on the table. We return to our seats. Laura talks about the future wedding of her friend, her life as a single woman, her parents in Alabama. She stops, looks at me, and remarks,

"You are a nice man. I don't understand why Marlene divorced you."

I correct her. Marlene didn't ask for the divorce. Laura expects me to elaborate, but I change the subject. She insists on talking about it, addresses the pending annulment, the grounds for it, and my inevitable disappointment after so many years of sharing my life with her friend and the children. I explain my position,

"The important issue is Marlene's happiness. I will cooperate with the Church to support the annulment."

Marlene must have arranged our seats next to each other with a clear purpose. I will let the Church find the excuse and abide by the decision. I cannot speak for the children, but she assures me their mother has their support. Pieces of cake silence the table, and after a few smacking noises and praises of the chef, guests abandon their seats, scatter through the salon, and show off their talents on the dance floor. Laura ambles away to confer with Marlene. I remember what my patient Victor Rossini taught me,

"If you go to an event and take a fancy for a woman, don't approach her in the salon or the bar. You will compete with quite a few suitors for her favor. Go to the bathrooms and wait for her outside. You will soon have her undivided attention."

I heighten the advice an extra notch and put an out-of-order sign on the door of the ladies' room. A few women express disappointment and head for the toilets on another floor. I soon see Marlene and Laura coming. I remove the sign, sneak inside, and hide in a toilet stall. Their conversation continues. I can hear them over the noises of basin water, flushing toilets, and blowing driers.

"You don't mind if I go out with him, do you? He is so handsome and romantic."

"Romantic? He was never romantic even at the beginning of our relationship."

"I showed you the poetry he wrote on the napkin. "

"He never wrote a poem in all the years he spent with me."

"It sounds beautiful, but I still don't understand the meaning. Do you?"

"I don't know."

"And the French riddle... is so romantic, and the gifts so lovely and thoughtful. Did you train him? Did you teach him French?"

"No. Daniel showed no interest in my first language."

"Do you think he is hitting on me?"

"No, Laura, he is not the type."

"I wish he were. Maybe, a new girlfriend is inspiring him."

"He has no girlfriend. He had sex with one of his neighbors and a few whores two and a half years ago. I haven't heard of any other affair."

"He has such a gorgeous mole above his right upper lip."

"What mole?"

"Are you sure you paid attention to your husband when you were married? In Chinese astrology, such a beauty spot shows wealth and a reserved personality."

"You and your oriental interpretations! Yes, Daniel has always been a loner."

"I think he still loves you. You don't mind if I go out with him, do you? I keep fantasizing about his big muscles pressing against me."

"Oh, stop it! Be careful what you wish! Men go to bed with you and forget everything they promise."

"He is..."

The bathroom door creaks shut, and their conversation continues out of earshot. I slip out of my hiding place and slink into the men's restroom before someone detains me and accuses me of perversion.

Seventeen

CARDBOARD UNDERWEAR

Scientists have concluded that man is born polygamous but buckles down to monogamy. A month after the engagement party, I get a call from Laura Davidson. The voluptuous woman oozes sex appeal from every pore in her curvaceous body. She makes no excuse,

"I was waiting for you to call me. But since you didn't, I did away with my feminine demureness."

Laura enjoys talking to a handsome and intelligent man like me and feels tired of eating, watching her favorite TV series, and sleeping alone. I am about to decline her invitation because "he who avoids temptation, avoids sin." The business of fidelity remains a new subject for me. In my other life, I went to bed with any woman who crossed my path regardless of status, color, or creed. Different worlds, different rules. I like Laura's straightforward approach, free of reservation and hypocrisy. I tell her that I cannot promise her anything except I will never hurt her, deceive her, or get in bed with her for the sake of sex alone. I am not ready to start a romantic relationship with anyone. She remarks,

"Your ex made her choice."

I accept her invitation to come over for dinner. Laura lives on the fourth floor of a glass building overlooking the Kennedy Expressway near the Loop. I knock on the door. She greets me with a smile.

"I thought we could talk better in my condo. Restaurants get too noisy."

She wears an apron with a pear-and-apple motif and rushes to her kitchen where she digs out several sweet potatoes from the oven. A vegetable stir-fry sizzles in a pan and releases a fragrance that whets my appetite. Two pieces of salmon lie on a plate ready for grilling. Laura cooks like a gourmet chef. The furniture and adornments in her cozy two-bedroom apartment convey her exquisite feminine taste—carmine sofas and love chair, cabinets with glassware, golden frames with excellent copies of classic painters, Rembrandt, Velazquez, Tintoretto. She watches me and remarks,

"I studied art in college. I prefer classical painting."

Next to a French window, a large table sits on one side of the combined dining and living room. A burnished counter separates it from the kitchenette. Golden dinner plates, golden silverware, a red tablecloth with gilded fringe emphasize the host's sophistication. Twilight floods the rooms with intimacy. We sit and, for the first time, I look her in the eye. I tell her what I observe and express my wonder she has never married.

"Men see my body, and that is all they want. An excess of beauty is as much of a handicap as ugliness."

Laura confesses to having sometimes felt so lonely in the past that she called some of her attractive acquaintances and shared her bed with them. This invitation has a different purpose. She never cooked for anyone of those lusty jerks and preempts my question about her altered behavior today,

"At the party, you talked about Marlene's happiness, and I admired your fortitude."

Laura gave up her sexual solace for a long time, but as a sensual young woman, her desire remains strong. A roll on her bed with an attractive and challenging mate like me would be gratifying. But sex no longer satisfies her needs. She wishes she were like Marlene, who uses her strong religious mind to restrain her impulses and stay away from sex with a handsome man like Michael. Laura recounts one of Marlene's confidences. On one occasion, Michael found his girlfriend stripped down to panties and a bra at home. He covered her with kisses, threw himself on top of her, and tried to remove her garments. But she froze like a statue of ice and resisted his attempts until he left the apartment in frustration. I ask Laura,

"Did he come to you to release himself?"

"Yes, I help Marlene keep him."

"Does Marlene know?"

"No."

Three months have passed since the last conversation, but Laura keeps calling me. I tell her, I need not release myself with her or anyone else. I wouldn't like to follow Michael Rosen's example. She laughs it off and wonders whether I will reject her for her blunt honesty and obligation to a close lady friend. Besides, her straightforwardness qualifies her as a potential soulmate. She hasn't engaged in sex with Michael or anyone else since she fell in love with me at the engagement party. Love and faithfulness must be bundled together—no love, no fidelity. Marlene's beau is now consoling himself with expensive prostitutes. I once more caution her against falling in love with me.

My head brims with Laura's intimations about Marlene's state of mind. I haven't conversed with Daniel's ex since the birth of Thomas seven months ago. She comes to my apartment during work hours and spends time with our grandson. Emmanuelle recounts the details of her visit. Her mother crawled on all fours and played with attentive and curious Thomas, enjoying herself and laughing a lot. On one occasion, Marlene lamented the loss of family unity that had turned Thanksgiving and Christmas into lonely celebrations. Everyone fended for themselves.

Marlene reminisced about the prayers to God for their blessings before long dinners with almond turkey, her mom's specialty. Marlene missed her children, her mom, and Lorna. In the past, the French ceramic tableware, refined silverware, and crystal glassware had graced a beautiful table. But these place settings now sat idle in a glass cabinet. In boxes inside a closet lay her Nativity set: a manger, Our Lady, St. Joseph, the Three Kings, shepherds, a glorious star, Christmas ornaments, and a silk tablecloth with turkeys and Santa motifs. Her decision to donate them to the Salvation Army never materialized. She couldn't force herself to do it. Michael didn't want to spend these festivities alone and counted on her. Her list of regrets didn't include Daniel. He might have been the first one who came to mind since people left out the estranged loved ones that they longed for. Perhaps, her recall of him was too painful or evoked uncontrollable anger for the damage he had inflicted on her.

Today, I have received a letter from the Metropolitan Ecclesiastical Tribunal of Chicago. It lets me know of Marlene's "Petition for Declaration of Invalid Marriage." I thought I was ready for it, but I must go out for a walk to calm my nerves. Popular lore teaches that people must search around to find comfort in others who fare worse than them. I watch a disabled young man drag along State Street. His body stands bent forward with his head closer to the sidewalk than his waist, his legs curved in, and his thighs spread out at the hips to maintain balance, his long arms almost touching the ground. He resembles a spider more than a human. Over and over, he shouts blasphemies,

"God, what sin have I committed for You to jail me in this horrendous body? You are cruel!"

Amid cries, he utters even worse insults between his teeth, his feet struggling to plod along. He blames God for a condition that humans have caused with their careless behavior. The Supreme Being granted Mankind a healthy earth and didn't create a deformed human. It was up to terrestrials to keep these blessings and correct anything that could endanger them.

On earth, divinity matters are out of hand. The letter I received from the Church discloses no reason for Marlene's request. It asks me to take part in the proceedings because it will facilitate and expedite the "spiritual process and reach a just resolution." A hearing for my interview will be scheduled. I may cosign her petition or appoint an advocate to defend my opposition to it if I so wish. An appointed priest will investigate Daniel's early background, his courtship of Marlene, their marriage and marital life. He will search for any concealment of essential facts before the wedding ceremony: criminal records, sexually transmitted diseases, infertility. None of those applies to Daniel. Psychological aspects loom large. Bride and groom must show sound minds and maturity to accept a lifelong commitment—the so-called proper internal disposition. People lack a clear understanding of what lies ahead because everyone thinks about the roll in the hay. By the criteria of the Church, most Catholic marriages are invalid. Religion embraces false arguments and disrespects its own principles. Thank goodness for the civil ceremony; otherwise, the situation would turn into chaos for all partners.

Tonight, a dream flows through the pathways of my imagination. I am a guest at Buckingham Palace in London. From my room window, I can see Victoria Memorial with its golden angels crowning a pedestal where the queen sits on her throne. It is early morning, and the place is deserted. Immobile, the guards pose in their red attire in front of sentry boxes. I am going for a walk with the royal family. The queen and Prince Phillip look forward to meeting me. Their grandchildren knock on their doors all excited. I begin to dress and regard the boxers I must wear. The bottom of the garment is made of cardboard. I am surprised. I didn't know English noblemen needed such a heavy material to support their intimate parts. The surface has a left round hole to introduce my leg. But the tailor missed the marked orifice on the right side and kept its lid intact. I push against it with my right foot, and it gives way with resistance. The result disappoints me. A large gap stares at me with rugged borders. I decide to go back into my dream and start again from scratch. No sooner do I attempt this than I hear Daniel's voice,

"No, you cannot do that. In dreams, like most of the time in real life, once you screw something up, you don't get a chance to take a step back and correct it."

Daniel explains he has stayed away from me to let me carve my destiny. But now he refuses to remain idle and watch me wreck what he built on earth. My decision to agree to the annulment of his marriage to Marlene represents an offense against his integrity. Any argument in her favor will denigrate his former union and affect their children. I point out he enjoys his bliss with Julie while his ex tries to rebuild her life. A technicality shouldn't stand in her way.

"Technicality! Stop the annulment! You, idiot."

"Why would you care? You have Julie."

"Stop this marriage. You have my body. Try harder. Remarry Marlene!"

"She hates you. And why did you write long poems to Julie and never scribble even a single verse to Marlene?"

"I didn't need to. It was a different love. Not all loves are the same."

"Maybe you didn't care for her enough."

"You know I did. I loved her with all my heart. She changed, I changed. Our relationship foundered. It often happens."

"She still has the right to pursue happiness and make her own mistakes."

This afternoon, I left Stroger Hospital early. There were several cancellations due to a heat wave with July temperatures topping 108 degrees F. I ease open the door to my apartment to avoid waking Thomas. I find Marlene on all fours in the middle of the living room while the baby crawls to get a large red plastic ball. Thomas stops, looks at me, and lifts his arms. Marlene turns her head, and her eyes flash with the pure blue of seawater. She raises her head, blinks, and sits as her loose blond hair swings on her shoulders. I proffer my hand to her, but she holds on to a love seat and stands up. Happy to have his grandparents together, the baby stops, babbles a few sounds, and then keeps moving toward the ball. Little ones have a sixth sense, so he probably realizes the awkwardness of our encounter and detects tension between us.

"I thought you'd get out of work much later. Emmanuelle went on an errand. I must leave."

I ask her to talk for a few minutes so that we can discuss the annulment. I again express my sincere wishes for her future happiness with Michael Rosen. Unsure of what to make of my words, she sits down, looks at me, and says,

"How did you change so much?"

I regard her surprised expression and worry her intuition may discover my identity.

"French, dancing, poems," she adds.

"People can rebuild their own personalities."

"Why didn't you do it when we were married? You were sensitive and polite with your patients, but you never extended that courtesy to your loved ones."

"We learn with time."

"Thank you for convincing your mother to be one of my witnesses."

"She wanted to kill me but spared my life."

"I'd have never expected that from you," Marlene says, as my clumsy attempt to make a joke fails to draw even a subtle smile on her face.

"A new life, a new personality. If you love Michael, you must also change, Marlene."

"Michael is not your business," she glares at me.

"You asked me to help you with the annulment."

"That has nothing to do with it."

"Yes, it does. I'll help you. I'll back up any excuse your advocate makes up. I want to contribute to your happiness. Please, don't let your extreme religiosity get you in trouble."

"I am not a religious fanatic."

"Maybe not, but the formalities you are requesting take time. If you love Michael and you don't want to lose him, liberate yourself from so many Catholic constraints. You can choke your relationship."

"What are you insinuating?"

A pause follows. The silence looms before us, revealing her enduring unfathomable pressure. Her sobs prompt Thomas to sit and stare at his grandparents. He attempts a grin and stops cold. Tears swell up in her eyes, rush down her cheeks, and trace long wakes of black mascara. Her reaction unsettles me. The room walls close in on me, and my breathing quickens. Moisture in my eyes distorts the reflected images of Marlene and Thomas in a large mirror over the sofa where she sits. Their heads grow disproportionate eyes and noses, their limbs become plump, and their garments bloat like French beignets. Mist seems to fog the windowpanes. An overwhelming desire to embrace Marlene and kiss her encircles my mind. I proffer her my square handkerchief. She dabs at her eyes with it and hands it back. Time moves in slow motion. I let the piece of cloth rest in my palm, hold her fingers for a long pause, and deposit a soft kiss on the back of her hand. She withholds it and says,

"It's easy for you. You must be enjoying your new love for Laura."

Her remark made with an intonation of jealousy catches me unprepared. A few embers left from her former affection for Daniel must have caught fire, or a new feeling for me might have just sprung up in her chest. I tell her my heart brims with love for her. There is no space for anyone else. She turns her head to the side, skips my eyes, and screams,

"Liar! Have you ever apologized for the divorce and what you did to me?"

A painful silence ensues. I have overlooked this act of reparation. In the recent past, I expressed my apologies to Steve when I misjudged him. But in her case, I neglected to put myself in Daniel's shoes. Pride besieged my donor all his life and restrained him from uttering any remorse. Perhaps, I share some degree of the same deficiency since he and I have developed from the same template of a human being. Daniel discovered every human was born from one, each containing a unique mixture of inherent virtues and potential vices. As the individual grew up on earth, society's influence eliminated some of those virtues and brought some of the vices afloat. Meanwhile, the same human template idled in the dream world free of external contamination in full possession of its native attributes. Everyone ended up with two distinct personalities, the real world's and the dream world's. Each resided in a separate entity with identical external appearance. But, while the real one—the physical look—aged until death at a regular pace, the other—

the dream image—lagged one or more decades and could even revert to childhood in some nighttime scenes.

Daniel never suspected he would bump into an exchange procedure that would give birth to the entity that housed his dream world's personality—myself, Sonie. I have now lived on this planet for more than two years and have preserved my virtues and kept my vices dormant. I must remain vigilant to avoid imperfections. Was the omission of my regret a case of absentmindedness? I wake up from my reverie and say,

"Marlene, I am sorry for all the suffering the divorce caused you."

I apologize for my pride and insensitivity and express my hope she will find in her heart the strength to pardon the inflicted hardships. She rushes out, wipes her tears with her arm, turns around, and says,

"I can forgive you, but I cannot forget."

Thomas issues a forceful cry of neglect and reaches for us. I lift him in my arms, hug him, and watch Marlene slam the door shut.

A few weeks later, I receive a letter—a Citation of Respondent—from the Archdiocese of Chicago with the time and date of my interview: September 9, 2011, at 10 A.M. When the date arrives, I walk into a Spartan white waiting room and sit at a dark pedestal table with four wooden chairs and a white linen tablecloth. A water jug and two glasses rest on it. A Crucifix of ebony hangs on the wall next to a dark oak framed picture of Pope Benedict XVI. The pontiff wears a red chasuble, a golden yellow stole, and a strained smile under frowning eyebrows, his little beady eyes staring at me. I feel like a snake in a wicker basket. The lanky figure of Father Mendieta shuffles in, his black cassock rustling on the purple tile floor as his ascetic face manages a stiff grin. He proffers his arachnid arm and sits next to me as though ready to officiate at a confession. He must have arrived from Mass because an intense smell of incense wafts from him. It is beyond me why clerics use this irritating fragrance to evoke the clean and odorless Heavens.

"Mother Church thanks you for your cooperation."

A sarcastic thought crosses my mind: I was born without a mother, and I now have two. And why do priests believe their peculiar vocal intonation brings them near to God or makes them resemble saints? Only the sound of rippling water or waterfalls speaks of eternity. The priest adds,

"Marlene Brandon affirms that you didn't intend to marry her until death did you part."

"Whatever she says is correct."

"And you fell in love with a ghost. "He crossed himself three times as if in front of the Devil."

"Let's not waste our time with the long questionnaire. I intend to cosign Marlene's petition."

Father Mendieta provides the name of three judges who will review the case. He also explains my right to name a canon-law priest as the defender of the bond. I waive it.

Lorna calls me a month later. She was interviewed as a witness, and the interrogatory upset her. She grumbles on,

"And you admitted you married Marlene because she was submissive and would let you do whatever you wished. Besides, she didn't have a behind big enough to render you captive of her physical attraction. What the heck is that? Did you plan to break the matrimonial bond because she didn't feed your lusty fancy? Preposterous! And why did you have to mention your father often escaped through windows when jealous husbands broke into their unfaithful spouses' bedchambers? Why did you even talk about his sexual feasts? You even dared criticize me, your mother. You told the priest I indoctrinated you and raised you like a monkey. That I followed the principles of Professor Proskish, the director of Lincoln Park Zoo and an expert in Comparative Psychology. Do you think you would have succeeded in your career without my help? You would have turned out an imbecile like your father."

"You married him."

She hangs up on me.

Eighteen

LOVE STORY

The dream begins with poetry, five or six short stanzas that re-count a love story. My memory catches two lines,

Why would I gaze down if I can look up
And watch the stars twinkle in your eyes?

A young blond woman with a svelte figure declaims this poem ad-dressed to her beloved. After their long separation, her face shines with sadness and expectancy. Her red Volkswagen beetle drives into a car yard with a few empty spaces. She parks the vehicle in one, repeats the verses over and over, and waits for him as she presses different buttons to clean the engine. Nothing happens until a handle on the armrest prompts it, and the wash begins. After so many years, the girlfriend now rejoices. How will he look? How will he find her?

Neither Daniel nor I was the protagonist of this dream. But in the oneiric world, the dreamer was always the main character. Why did I place myself in Marlene's shoes? What did I perceive in her eyes that triggered these verses? Hope for love? The young woman cleansed her engine, her soul, and prepared herself for this high emotion as a de-voted Catholic would for Sunday communion. Her beloved had been away for so long. She wondered how the passage of time had changed him and her. What do these scenes mean? Marlene's divorce from Daniel just happened two-and-a-half years ago. The dream may deal with my love for her and the hope she will find in me a different Daniel, her better half, someone she has expected for quite a few years. I would rather pick an optimistic interpretation. Perhaps, I am wrong, and she waits for Michael Rosen whom she might have loved for a long time.

A few weeks later, on March 15, 2012, Lorna calls with the news of the death of Celine, Marlene's mother. She died of uterine cancer in a hospital in Milwaukee, WI. My donor had a tumultuous relationship with the deceased. Celine was a joker, and Daniel lacked a sense of humor—let alone an understanding of French comedy. One evening, while dining at Marlene and Daniel's, she made fun of her son-in-law's laconicism,

"Marlene, maybe you should serve your husband abecedary soup?"

Her daughter reacted with guffaws. Frequently, my donor had expressed concerns to his mother about his relationship with Celine. Lorna had advised him well,

"Sons-in-law must conquer their mothers-in-law too, not only their daughters. Bring her some flowers, a gift for her birthday, a little dog, some token."

Daniel tried without success. Now I won't have to put up with the banter of the departed but must confront a new experience on earth—a funeral. I hearken back to my donor's memory files and discover Daniel attended two wakes. At the wake of Daniel's dad, mourners told jokes and laughed in a hall next to the chapel where the remains lay in repose. A few even attempted to seduce the deceased's former girl-friends. The funeral of Marlene's father was different. A heavy silence reigned, and she suffered from uncontrollable crying.

In my short time on earth, I have also learned of two remarkable funerals. The first was Michael Jackson's. It took place two and a half months after my birth. The pop star enjoyed so many fans that over three billion mourners witnessed his burial, the most attended one ever. He died of severe insomnia. No other case pinpoints one of the greatest flagrant defects in the development of the human body. People lack a voluntary mechanism to achieve an essential function since our brain has assigned it to unforeseeable luck and chance. Michael Jackson hired an anesthesiologist to induce his nightly rest at will. But one day, the doctor made a mistake, and the brilliant singer and composer died. The second was the burial of a terrorist, Osama bin Laden, who killed thousands of innocent people in God's name— a ghastly sacrilege. His remains were thrown into the sea under several government officials' watchful eyes a few hours after his death on May 2, 2011.

On our way to the Wisconsin, I drive my car with Emmanuelle and Thomas in the backseat. Lorna sits next to me. She looks like a raven inside a cage, a black dress, black leather shoes, and a black hat that lets a black veil fall over her face. Her sharp admonition of my attire breaks out again,

"I know you never liked Lady Anuscat, but you shouldn't flaunt your spitefulness for the deceased and her daughter."

Lorna uses the nickname that Daniel branded his mother-in-law with because whenever she talked, she pursed her mouth excessively and let air escape between her lips. I don't reply. I wear gray pants, a dark blue jacket with an embroidered fleur-de-lis on the left sleeve, and a light blue tie with several smaller versions of the French symbol. Lorna continues her onslaught,

"And why do you dare bring a piece of ceramic instead of a flower wreath?"

She fumes over my nonchalant attitude because I don't react like Daniel. He would have argued with her, and she would have prevailed. I ignore her. An embossed copy of the Blue Nude by Picasso adorns the white French ceramic vase. The painting shows the sadness of mortality and the resignation of Mankind to the loss of human life. It is an appropriate container for the ashes of Marlene's mother. My mind drifts to the Other Dimension, where death didn't exist. The dream world again harbored its idiosyncratic contradiction. There was an afterlife, but it consisted of changing your abode. Some who were bored with their eternal existence moved to scenic forests bathed in lovely music. Some submerged themselves in glass-covered swimming pools. Others crammed into single-occupant spaceships and traveled throughout the universe. Wanderers could still communicate with their loved ones.

Here on earth, I figure dying must feel like diving into cold water on a beach. You fear in anticipation as you wade into the sea, and the cold sensation inches up until it reaches your groin. Then, you jump into the water and feel fine. As in the Other Dimension, this earthly world enjoys an afterlife that provides humans with another abode. Other than one must die, I don't know of any other condition to reach it. Nor do I have any insight about different locations and arrangements. It might be the greatest gift God has granted humans, at least to some of them. But no one has confirmed it because there is no communication between the departed and the living. This subject remains a matter of speculation that serves as the basis of man-devised religions.

The wake of Celine takes place in a funeral home on the outskirts of Milwaukee. The place lies surrounded by a small garden and a spacious parking lot. Upon entering, I smell an incense-like, flowery perfume that permeates the air. An usher shows us into a lounge where relatives and friends of the deceased gather to converse. Coffee is being served. The women rest on one side and the men on the other, most wearing dark dresses and suits. I stand at the entrance of the chapel that holds Celine's remains. People are crying. The scene unsettles me, and sorrow weighs me down. I breathe, sense, and walk in a cloud of sadness. My thoughts rebel against reality: no, this cannot be the truth; humans shouldn't have to suffer this pain. I observe a plain white wall, round golden lamps on the ceiling, and rows of black wooden pews with red cushions. Some mourners talk in low voices or whisper. Ladies' perfume mixes with cloying flowery scents of wreaths and floral arrangements. Nausea overcomes me.

I compose myself and venture into the chapel where Marlene sits in the first row, her mother's coffin looming up in front of her. I kiss her on the cheek and offer her my sympathy. She thanks me for coming. I nod my acknowledgment because a lump in my throat thickens my voice. Tears well up in my eyes. I hand her the ceramic vase. She places it on her seat, hugs me, and rests her head on my right shoulder. I wonder whether her somber eyes also express tenderness for me. I hold her hand and tell her she can count on my unconditional friendship. Marlene signals me to join her. We kneel before her mother's casket and share a spiritual moment before returning to our seats. I excuse myself, take my leave, and explain my reservations about standing in for Michael Rosen.

"He is fine. He cannot tolerate funerals," she says.

I walk to the opposite corner of the chapel. My wandering steps end in a red armchair in a corner of the lounge. I observe everyone. Emmanuelle passes by with Thomas holding on to her dress. He giggles, stops before stern-looking adults, gazes at them and his mother, probably wondering why everyone looks serious. He escapes from her and trots to the adjacent funeral room where he stops near the prie-dieu and glances at the deceased stranger. Death and fresh life partake of a causal moment. The child makes no distinction as if everyone in the building were part of the same family, shared the same sorrow, and prayed to the same God. Perhaps, adults are not tapping into their hearts to express their true feelings. Children are more observant than their elders because, as people age, they lose the ability to determine the real meaning of what goes on around them.

I espy Michael Rosen sitting alone in another corner of the lounge. He slams the book on his lap shut and hides its title when I proffer my hand. He frowns at me and refuses it. His animadversion doesn't bother me. I wander around and come across a board with memorial photos. An elderly woman in her early eighties strolls around, admiring the display. I observe old photographs with the Seine River in the background. She turns to look at me and says,

"They made a wonderful couple, didn't they?"

She points to a picture where two teenagers, a boy and a girl, hold hands. I recognize the adolescent facial features of Marlene. Her young beau stands half a head taller and bears a gallant demeanor. Arms hang next to a tilted body to emphasize his svelteness as a handsome smile crosses his face.

"He is my son Matthew. He is the priest who will officiate at Celine's funeral."

She introduces herself as Amelie, the deceased's closest friend. She recounts how the two youngsters were very much in love and inseparable. Marlene and her boyfriend grew up in a little town in France and had known each other since childhood. A few months apart, their families moved to Chicago where the two lovebirds continued their romance. Matthew broke Marlene's heart when he entered Mundelein Seminary in the small suburb of the same name.

The conversation ends with the arrival of Father Matthew Courtier, who arouses a cloud of whispers. His slouched figure shuffles into the chapel where Celine's body lies. Steve and I sit next to Marlene who kisses her son and welcomes me back with a pat on my shoulder. Father Matthew stands in front of the casket, opens a black Gospel, and begins the service without further ado.

"I am the resurrection and the life. He who believes in Me, though he may die, he shall live."

He speaks about death, his voice firm and cheerful,

"We should consider our departure from this world as a reward... the time for us to leave behind the worries and vicissitudes of this mortal life and enjoy the presence of God."

He regards everyone in the audience, pausing and gazing at someone at the end of every sentence to elicit a reaction. His eyes now set on mine. Those are the windows to the soul of an upright person, someone concerned with his fellow man's welfare. A rictus of uneasiness surfaces on the priest's face, and his gaze switches to the Gospel as if trying to regain his bearing. He transfers the book to his left hand. His right hand drifts to the side of his cassock, wipes this palm and fingers one by one, and returns to hold the sacred scriptures. Marlene keeps her face down in constant prayer. Father Mathew never looks at her and seems afraid of what he might perceive or stir in her. He attends to the audience, realizing that most of the mourners won't step into a church or a chapel and listen to the holy scriptures until the next wake. This opportunity might be his only chance to convert them. The fear of death carries with it a convincing effect on the neglectful faithful. These wayward Christians turn to God and pray for at least a few hours. But as soon as they step out of the funeral home and the cold breeze slaps their faces, their moment of devotion will vanish.

The religious service over, the priest walks to the first row, grabs the arm of Amelie, and helps her get on her feet. He smooths a few gray hairs at the front of his bald head and approaches Marlene, who stands waiting. A slight smile enhances premature wrinkles around his mouth and eyes. She averts her eyes, probably afraid or disappointed not to find what she expected. He kisses her cheeks and she his hand. I feel as if I were watching a play, the casket with the floral wreaths, big candles, and a large crucifix immersed in a world of flowery perfume beyond anyone's reach. Behind me, a faceless audience murmurs a drone. I distinguish no one except the main actors Father Matthew and Marlene on the front stage and, next to them, their supporting actress Amelie, who serves as a bridge between them. He clears his throat, but his voice almost falters,

"Marle, *Je suis désolé pour ta maman.*"

"Father Marceau, *mercie beaucoup... depuis longtemps.* A long time for a friend to show up."

"*Ce n'est pas le moment pour les récriminations,*" Amelie reprimands them for the inappropriateness of the time and place for his apology and her repartee.

His face turns pale, and the grieving daughter's blush acquires the same irritated red of her eyelids. The protagonists turn around and kneel on the prie-dieu, their heads bowing to the cruel reality of mortality. Father Matthew stands up, dips an aspergillum into holy water, and sprinkles the corpse. Marlene continues her prayers as Amelie and her son walk out of the chapel, she with her head straight and proud and his bent and remorseful.

My dream of the love story anticipated these scenes. Maybe, part of my sixth sense in the Other Dimension was spared. Marlene never fell head over heels for Daniel. When love is abruptly severed—as with a priest who abandons his fiancé to embrace a religious life—the powerful affection might be irreplaceable. No chance for other men. The disdained woman attempts it but fails. Daniel could never erase his wife's memories of her first beloved because some wounds never heal. It must have been hard for Marlene to give Matthew up to a higher hierarchy. It would have been much easier if he had dumped her for another woman. I am sure she tried to get over him. The frigidity she showed in sexual intercourse was a sign that her injury was too sore to reveal to others. No wonder she never discussed her first relationship with Daniel.

The behavior reaffirms my belief that her marriage was a convenient relationship even though she tried hard to love her husband to the hilt. Daniel's personality didn't help because he never seduced her. Theirs was a matrimony of incomplete love. She might have transferred to him some of her disappointment with life. But conceited Daniel could never perceive his handicap. How could he? He was a magnificent groom for a modest bride like Marlene, wasn't he?

And now, what has she observed in her first boyfriend? His bearing showed a life of sainthood and service to his fellow man. I wonder whether reality will sink in and wake Marlene up from her stubborn dream.

Nineteen

NOCTURNAL VIBRATION

On my way back to Chicago, Lorna enlightens us with a thorough critique of Celine's funeral. She speaks of the Francophones and their snobbish attitudes. How Amelie became the center of the wake and acted like Marlene's mother even though her accent irritated most English-speaking mourners. Lorna criticized the use of a French flag for covering the casket. In her opinion, this bunch of starving immigrants came to America to enjoy their dreams to the detriment of other citizens born in the Land of the Free. And to boot, they paraded their priest who had been Marlene's beau in their school years. Lorna's words surprise me since my inherited memory files register no conversation between Marlene and Daniel broaching this subject. I ask her when she learned the story,

"Oh, my son, you are always in a cloud. Celine told me. What did you talk to Marlene about before you married her, sweet nothings?"

She goes on about the worn-out priest whose face brims with stupidity. He looked sullen and resentful and must blame his mother and everyone around her for wasting his life. Lorna doesn't believe Marlene was ever in love with that 'black beetle.' The poor girl faced her mom's funeral alone, no sister, no brother, no father, and no husband. The priest who should have been like a brother deserted her when she was a youngster.

I wonder how my donor's mother reached an opinion so different from mine. I realize Lorna played a crucial role in Daniel's decision to marry Marlene since his mother egged him on to commit to his girl-friend. Lorna seems to read my mind and lambasts me. I abandoned her ex-daughter-in-law for a ghost and exposed her to trials and tribula-tions in a hostile world. I never learned to love her. I should have been a husband and a brother to her—and sometimes even a father. I ask her to stop her divagations. But she goes on about her son's obsession with Julie. I tell her to shut up, but she continues her relentless diatribe,

"And now she is about to tie the knot with a guy weirder than you. He sat in a corner of the funeral home, reading medical books and offending old women."

I ask her to clarify her statement. Michael Rosen had a confrontation with Amelie that Lorna witnessed. The doctor must have criticized the priest because the elderly woman smiled at him with sarcasm and rep-rimanded him loud enough for Lorna to hear,

"You shouldn't badmouth clerics."

Lorna goes on to describe how Amelie said something about Mi-chael Rosen's mother that she couldn't make out. He turned livid, stood up, and headed for the bathroom without excusing himself. Lorna considers the guy a terrible husband for a magnificent woman like Marlene. As a young daughter, she witnessed her mom—may her soul rest in peace—have sex with every stupid male who happened to walk by their store. Despite this terrible upbringing, Marlene turned into an exemplary wife and mother—until her nincompoop of a hus-band screwed up the marriage.

The next morning, I blame the aphrodisiac effect of funerals for a nocturnal emission. I wake up to wet white sheets with extensive tell-tale signs of a lusty night. The pungent odor wafts through my bedroom. I hope I made love to Marlene because I wouldn't want to be unfaithful even in a dream. The event left no record in my brain. I remember the brouhaha of female voices and laughter that woke me up at 2:00 AM. It sounded like the drone of a beehive and came from the apartment of my next-door neighbor Antonietta. The noisy chicks drank wine and babbled aloud next to open windows. Mosquitos buzzed attacks against me like kamikaze aircraft, prompting swats from my hand. I slapped my ears and caused pain to spread to my face, feeling the bites of the tenacious creatures on my hands, cheeks, and forehead. The commotion surged over the sound of the powerful to-and-fro motions of waves on nearby Lake Michigan. I wanted to scream a few expletives at the revelers, but instead, I stuck earplugs in my ears and fell asleep again. The neighboring bustle of giggles, loud talk, songs, mosquitos, and surf got incorporated into a dream. I heard myself blare out a loud cry,

"Shut up, bitches!"

It sounded real, and I thought I had awakened the entire neighborhood in downtown Chicago. Maybe I had, and the offended women abducted me and took revenge on me. They must have subjected me to a thorough and lengthy sexual thrashing because I get up exhausted with soreness in all my muscles. As soon as I step out of the shower and walk into the kitchenette, Emmanuelle greets me with a mischievous smile,

"What a night, Mr. Bachelor. Time for a nice girlfriend. Your sobs woke me up and your bed vibrated longer than a car through a stretch of speed bumps."

A weeks later, Marlene arrives at my apartment with news of Celine's last testament. Emmanuelle opens the door. Her mother's face shows the fatigue and sadness of bereavement. She doffs her coat and reveals her black dress whose skirt is caught in its belt and hangs higher on the left side. The porcelain-like whiteness of her contoured thigh shines well above the knee. Her daughter releases the dress from the snag and embraces her. Green earrings mismatch Marlene's attire because her mood must have made her insensitive to the self-care she always exhibits. Even her hair looks tousled in the back. I hug her and kiss her cheek, and she places her arms around my waist. She reads the document,

The lady bequeaths her home in Wisconsin to her daughter and Daniel. I am surprised. I thought she disliked him. Celine explains her ex-son-in-law always welcomed her in his home and proved to love her daughter very much while they were together. He never went out to play golf or other leisure activities with friends and dedicated his meager leisure time to staying in his home office. There, he learned the latest developments in medicine. Daniel listened to all her health complaints and took care of her whenever he could or referred her to an appropriate specialist.

Celine names a list of guests for a funeral cruise in the Caribbean. Her invitees include Marlene and her betrothed, Michael Rosen MD, Laura Davidson, Lorna, her grandchildren and their partners, Amelie and Father Matthew, and me. Celine instructs her daughter to dispose of her ashes on the coast of Martinique. As a child, she always dreamed of vacationing on this paradisiacal French island but never fulfilled her dreams. Celine requests that Daniel take care of her six-year-old female Shih Tzu Gardenia. Celine details a daily schedule for feeding the animal, attending to her calls of Nature, trimming her hair, and visiting the vet. She realizes Daniel might need to hire a service to help him since his medical duties absorb most of his time. He must take care of the expenses with the proceeds from the sale of her home.

Celine was a joker, and the whole affair of her real estate and dog might be her final prank. Daniel had seen the animal on quite a few occasions since he and Marlene brought the small puppy to Celine as a birthday gift three years before their divorce. The little dog liked my donor and sat in his lap more than in anyone else's. Celine jested that the pet suffered from some type of complex and considered Daniel her dad and primary target of her love. Gardenia behaved as though he and his wife had been her parents, feeling more at ease with them than with her owner.

I like the elderly lady's idea of a memorial cruise. In the Other Dimension, the absence of death coexisted with the existence of funerals. Their celebration stood out as a blatant example of the contradictory nature of that world. Happy mourners wore elegant tuxedos or put on swimming suits and surrounded themselves with statuesque women in multicolor bikinis or good-looking muscular men in trunks.

Thomas issues a loud cry and Emmanuelle leaves us to attend to him. Marlene sits down in front of me and thanks me for keeping in contact with her mom while she was alive. Her words turn my mouth agape since I don't understand the reason for her remark. Emmanuelle visited Celine but I have never paid my respects to her because I would have needed Marlene's permission. My expression prompts her to comment,

"You had the same expression when Matthew Courtier officiated at my mom's wake."

"He was your first boyfriend. Did you have sex with him?"

"You have no right to ask that question."

I explain that airing the truth to loved ones could help her come to terms with a reality that haunted her for a long time. Trials and errors abound in adolescence. Some youngsters keep a bothersome secret because the outcome turns more painful than they expected. The chagrin of relationship breakups at those ages could exceed our tolerance. She crosses her legs and rests her hands over her knees, her new betrothed's ring boasting a sizable sparkling diamond surrounded by a circle of tiny rubies. Her eyes gaze at mine as her hand rises to enhance her words,

"I thought if we made love, he wouldn't leave for the seminary. But he resented it and made me feel dirty."

She whispers her confession and fidgets on the sofa as if sitting on pebbles. The fingers on her kneecap exhibit a fine tremor, and I sense her orange and jasmine perfume intensified by the anxiety of the moment. She must open up and own her mistake. Priests probably heard her sin more than once, but they don't count. I cannot look her straight in the eye because it is hard to watch her suffer. Somberness hides under her eyebrows when she stares down the slope of her nose, the pucker of sad lips halting an impending sob. My mood enhances misperceptions. Furniture and ornaments on the walls recede, daylight dims in distorted corners of the room, and the air turns more weightless and rises to the ceiling. The entire scene seems to occur within a balloon that stands ready to lift off before hearing the words I am about to utter,

"You had no right to go into a marriage without unloading that baggage."

She is not used to this kind of straight talk. Daniel handled problems by letting time pass. He ignored them and pretended they never happened. But they happened, and the scars deformed their marriage. Marlene and Daniel blamed each other. She thought he knew about Matthew because Celine had sometimes commented on her daughter's former relationship in front of her son-in-law. Marlene adds,

"As usual, you never listened."

I won't engage in the same diatribe as my donor. I show no anger and receive her words with kindness and understanding. Her mother's words don't qualify as a confession. I adopt the attitude of someone who expects his interlocutor to utter a sincere answer and unveil hidden thoughts. Time stops ticking, and silence engulfs us. The room around us comes into focus, and every trinket that Emmanuelle has placed on the furniture breathes new life—a little white owl with large black eyes of onyx, a svelte dark wooden statue, the framed pictures of Thomas. I search into her soul through her eyes. Her goodness surfaces and her words with it,

"I was afraid of your rejection."

She has just expressed part of the truth. But her feat reveals an improvement of my rating since I am now worthy of her confidence. The partial truth floats like an iceberg and hides its bulky portion. Perhaps, she realizes her large share of responsibility for the end of her marriage. There is no person blinder than the one who doesn't want to see. Marlene reproofed her husband's infidelity with a ghost while she had been unfaithful with another. The phantom of Father Matthew presided over her entire marital relationship year after year, living under the same roof and thawing her marriage into a lukewarm affair. Unless she exorcizes her feelings for him, there will be no chance for another romance to blossom. I encourage her to deal with reality,

"Your infatuation has made you unable to love another person fully."

"Not anymore. I should have confronted it a long time ago."

I admit there were ghosts on both sides of their marriage. A long pause ensues. Too many words, too many emotions surge in such a short moment. Life kept going and new people shared her path while her adolescent crush subjected her to its whims. But now the vagaries of time have defeated her prince charming. He no longer rides a white horse. Forehead folds and wrinkles around his eyes and mouth speak for the unhappiness of his fateful choice. Tears run down her face. I stand to comfort her, and she slips by the coffee table separating us and hangs from my shoulders with all her strength. I fuse with her. She now accepts her error and must take a fresh look at her suitors. Will it be easier for her to start anew with another man, or retrace her previous missteps and correct her wrongdoings? While a second husband would enjoy the lack of emotional baggage, a remarriage to the same man could reinforce the formerly forged ties. It would also retrieve bad memories and require the need to repair past mistakes. Unless corrected, these errors will behave like a ship without anchors because they render the couple adrift in the sea of life. She doesn't know that I afford her the advantages of both the new and the known. I ask whether she has told Michael about her first love.

"Not yet."

Twenty

A CANINE AFFAIR

The canine gift from Celine throws my brain into sizzling questions about this primeval friend of humans. Marlene provided me with a picture of cotton-white Gardenia. The little dog rests in her arms and faces the camera with outstretched legs, white hair dappled with a few black patches, pinkish belly, jet-black muzzle, and gleaming dark eyes. Black hair surrounds her orbits like a sleep mask and spreads to dangling ears, a narrow bridge of white hair bisecting the natural disguise. The first time I came in close contact with a dog occurred a few weeks after my birth. That day, I shared the elevator with an elderly lady and the young woman whose apartment lies two floors above mine. The junior resident held a small pram with a poodle inside and remarked,

"Robert and I don't want children. You know, they require a lot of effort and money and turn into hateful teenagers."

Perplexity rushed into the senior's eyes as she regarded the puppy that looked like a snowflake with a fluffy tail. The animal whined and rooted for endearments as its caretaker sprinkled the little dog with a flourish of compliments,

"Oh, my little nugget, do you want your mommy to snuggle you in her arms?"

Mommy wore a pink tee shirt with a large logo of a canine shelter, and so did her little animal. If I hadn't known her athletic, good-looking husband, I would have sworn she had given birth to a dog-like baby. I thought a sick affliction beset mankind when human couples forgot about the survival of their own species.

Now, my attitude must change because I might even need advice from my neighbor. Daniel had a lusty male German shepherd that fell in love with Marlene's pretty Lassie. The canine affair encouraged their owners to engage in an amorous relationship. Come to think of it, Celine's gift may hide a similar purpose. A dog got Daniel and Marlene together, and another could concoct the reconciliation of the divorced couple. Celine's last will provides plenty of opportunities. The elderly lady veiled her intention, but one could read between the lines. I wonder whether she voiced an opinion to her daughter and advocated for a repair of the failed marriage. Celine might have found out worrisome information about Marlene's betrothed. But if so, her daughter turned a deaf ear and disregarded her advice.

Tomorrow, Marlene and I plan to walk through Celine's ranch house in Paddle Lake, Wisconsin, before hiring a real estate agency. We also need to pick up Gardenia from the home of Amelie, who lives in the same small town. But tonight, a dream anticipates our meeting:

I am in a red Volkswagen beetle like the one where I saw Marlene in a dream several months ago. She now sits next to me, wearing a red dress and an emotionless smile. Her lips pucker as if popping bubbles of chewing gum, and her blue eyes look straight ahead. I wonder whether she sees anything because she seems indifferent to everything around her, including me. A short road leads to a village that sits atop a hill next to a small lake. Overhead, a splendid sun warms the landscape. The temperature light pops on the dashboard indicating overheating. I drive the car to the side of the road, stop it, and let Marlene sit on the ground. To check the engine, I remove the steering wheel and its column. The shaft works as a thermometer that reddens with the rise in temperature. I reintroduce the rod and pull it back after a few seconds. It shines hot with a carmine hue like a brilliant piece of iron just removed from a crucible. I rack my brain to find a solution to the problem, but I can't figure it out. To reach the core of the vehicle, I peel away layers of the car as if it were an onion.

Rich in imagery, this dream displays quite a few graphic pictures that call my attention. Marlene's emotional expression, the car overheating, the shaft that acts as a thermometer and taps deep in the core of the vehicle, the carmine rod, the Volkswagen beetle that can be peeled like an onion. I have no idea if these night scenes will lead me anywhere since I don't even know whether I ever resolved the incandescent issue.

I disregard any forebodings from the dream and park my car in front of Marlene's. She must feel at home in this neighborhood of cozy plazas, little cafés, florist shops, and local food markets, which render the area a French air. Her apartment is on the top floor of a four-story building at 2051 N. Sedgwick Street. The stylish façade boasts a pointed pediment that extends laterally into the parapet of a flat roof adorned with small ornaments.

Marlene leans over her balcony and beckons me to come up. Her hanging blond hair, rouged lips, and blue eyes match well with her black dress with a golden fringe. The semicircular arch and a stucco emblem above her balustrade confer on Marlene the look of a countess at a Florentine palace. We greet each other with a kiss on the cheek. Two pairs of slippers sit on a burnished box next to the door, one pink and another gray with black edges. The latter must belong to Michael Rosen. She ushers me into a luminous living room with a blue sofa, a loveseat, and a dark brown table covered by a glass shield etched with foliage. Behind the set of furniture hangs a broad picture of Chicago's skyline with the lighthouse on the forefront. Marlene walks toward a dining table with six chairs that sit in a corner. The table holds legal documents for me to accept the change of ownership of her mom's home. A large box lies nearby. She points at it,

"The stuff for your new dog—papers, veterinary history, instructions from my mom."

Marlene remarks that her landlord doesn't allow pets, a prohibition that explains Celine's decision. The main wall displays multiple pictures arranged like a collage. Young Marlene and her children, graduation portraits, her mom, her dad, Thomas, and an old photograph of the Brandon family with spouses, children, and mothers-in-law. A recent picture features Marlene and Michael Rosen in front of the Water Tower, his hand over her right shoulder. She waits for me to satisfy my curiosity and comments,

"You no longer have a single picture of yourself on the walls of your apartment."

"I didn't like the ties, too gloomy."

I smile, and she stares at me as though I were crazy and then breaks into hysterical guffaws. For the first time, I have cracked my first joke on earth and experienced the return of my sense of humor, which I enjoyed so much in the Other Dimension. It marks another significant milestone in my development as a human. I have studied this unique function of man in the animal kingdom. The ability to regard the funny aspects of everything around us not only decreases our stress, but it also forges links between people. The irony is that no one knows what makes something a joke, and its origin has to do with intuition. I figure that when someone launches some words with a neutral facial expression, the recipients count on the sentence to hit them within the frame of their expectancy. If it lands outside, the quip might tickle their brain and trigger their smiles or guffaws. Surprise and predisposition to laughter also play significant roles.

Marlene and I go downstairs, and I place the box and copies of documents in the trunk of my car. A lake breeze tousles her golden hair that brushes her lips and prompts them to protrude like a flower bud and blow the tuft away. The sensual image renders her an irresistible look that reminds me of that of Marilyn Monroe standing over the subway grate as her skirt flutters up in a drift of air. I open the passenger door to let her take the seat next to mine. I ask her if Michael knows we are going to Wisconsin together.

"Yes, he does."

Marlene intimates her betrothed shows no jealousy. He accepts a necessary relationship between ex-husband and ex-wife must remain in place for the welfare of their children. Our stop at Amelie's home to pick up the dog worries him. He thinks the old lady demonstrated inappropriate aggressiveness at the wake. Marlene explains her mother's friend was Michael's patient for several years and always got along with him. The French community in Chicago comprised a few immigrants and everyone knew everyone. It was logical someone would have referred her to a doctor of the same ancestry. Amelie had known about Michael Rosen's mother, but the doctor refused to talk about her with his patient because he didn't want anyone to meddle in his private affairs.

I make no comment and concentrate on the road to Wisconsin. A thin layer of snow covers the asphalt and adorns the trees with a majestic mantle. Idle cows and horses graze on the grass. Farms and silos pass by on both sides of the road with almost mathematical regularity. The repetitious monotony hypnotizes us into calm. Marlene's eyes gleam with the sadness the scenery evokes in her. It must awaken early memories of happy trips and the last heartbreaking visits to her mom. I read her thoughts, make a remark, and rest my hand on hers,

"I should have accompanied you. It is hard to suffer alone."

Marlene looks surprised at my insightful comment. She doesn't refuse my hand, but I remove it before it becomes an intrusion. Thoughts have overtaken her because her gaze focuses on the vehicles in front of us and the stretches of road that rush toward us with vertiginous speed. Marlene gazes at me, and I fight the temptation to stare at her gorgeous eyes that sparkle with curiosity. She says,

"I asked Lorna whether you had an identical twin brother."

Her voice sounds serious and profound about such an acknowledgment. I glance at her. No grin or ironic expression disturbs her face. Our eyes meet, and she regards mine, studies my reaction, and searches into them for an answer. I turn my attention to the road. Her relentless questions about the transformation of her ex-husband continue over the noise of rolling tires. Marlene repeats the words of Lorna,

"Besides Julie, my son had another ghost in his life. He named him Sonie and considered him his brother."

Lorna went into an asinine discussion—something to do with Daniel's personality at birth that deteriorated with the passage of time. Sonie lived in his dreams and possessed all the virtues her son had been born with,

"A weird mixture of President Lincoln and the comedian Jerry Lewis."

According to Lorna, Daniel strived to emulate this person but disregarded his logical mind and sense of humor. Marlene laughs at the way her ex-mother-in-law characterized the changes in her offspring. The amused passenger remarks she had firsthand experience with these peculiarities for quite a few years and adds,

"Lorna wondered how many other fictitious people your mind created."

Marlene then reasons that it doesn't matter whether the coma or something else caused the transformation. His mind had cast away the ghost of Julie and all the other phantoms. Marlene blames herself as the culprit because, after their divorce, her ex-husband has grown into a better person. Tears well up in her downcast eyes as she bends backward and rests the nape of her neck on the headrest. I set my foot on the brake to turn off the cruise control. Her anxiety threatens my concentration. My sensitivity to her emotions increases with her proximity, and a strong desire to hug her and kiss her overcomes me. I reassure her,

"I'll always be here for you. Whenever you need a friend, I'll lend you a shoulder to lean on along your path of life on earth."

I ask her not to feel guilty about events she had no control over because we are responsible for our own destiny. My words strum a calm chord in Marlene. Serenity spills out of her eyes, her lips open a bit and regain their natural carmine, and pink color tints her cheeks. After a while, paleness returns, and rigidity freezes her face. Something brews in her mind. Perhaps, qualms about a new marriage to another man bob to the surface in her agitated soul. I hope she corrects her wrong decision. But I am afraid the betrothal dinner might have put a conclusion to her hesitancy, and the signs of reversal are figments of my imagination. Marlene crosses and uncrosses her legs, her eyes twitch, and her mouth grimaces. Thoughts simmer amid silence, and my rattled mind craves for a period of tranquility. But her closeness doesn't let me disengage.

We soon reach Paddle Lake, and Amelie's neighbor, Rose, opens the door and lets Gardenia rush out to greet the visitors. The little dog jumps to Marlene, crouches on the ground, and releases a few drops of urine. The animal then turns around toward me and barks at the top of her lungs before Marlene's wondering eyes. I remark,

"These dogs forget, don't they?"

I have come ready. I toss Gardenia a treat, and she takes it to her bed to devour it. The biscuit does the trick because she lets me caress her back and flips around to expose her pink belly. I scratch it, and she shuts her eyes in instantaneous relaxation. A long pale scar in the middle of the abdomen reveals the presence of a spaying. Rose conveys the apologies of Amelie who cannot attend to her visitors because of an unexpected doctor's appointment. The gracious hostess ushers us into the living room and offers us coffee and biscuits. We decline the refreshments, and she hands us a large white box of canine food with the image of a happy poodle whose red tongue lolls under bright eyes. She adds Amelie's last recommendations,

"Gardenia needs to be groomed. You must also take her to a vet as soon as possible because her medications to prevent parasite infections are overdue."

I walk two hundred yards with Marlene and Gardenia to get to Celine's ranch-style house. The little dog stops every sixty or seventy steps to pee. I wait with the leash in my hand for her to mark her territory. Marlene's face expresses apprehension and anguish that worsen as we approach her mom's. I grab her hand to comfort her. Her facial stiffness relaxes and her countenance blossoms into pastoral beauty. Her eyes gain an aquamarine color to match the color of the picturesque lake water and cloudless sky on this sunny morning. We soon see the white façade of a home that sits atop a small hill surrounded by green grass and scattered yellow dandelions. The dog pulls away from me, and I let her go because the tight leash threatens to strangle her. Gardenia rushes toward the stoop, jumps to the door, and whines because no one answers her calls. Marlene disengages my hand and hurries toward the despairing animal, pets her, and holds her in her arms.

We step into the house, and the stale fragrance of the deceased owner greets us. The dog leaps to the floor and runs into the wide hall that leads to the bedrooms. A rustic table and six wooden chairs stand next to a counter annexed to an old kitchen. We sit on a brown sofa in front of a large television set. The eyes of Marlene well up with tears when she regards a white crocheted cloth that lies on the light-brown coffee table before us and remarks,

"It took my mom six months to make it."

I sit next to her. Her right foot repeatedly taps the area rug. Gardenia searches every corner of the house where she senses the scent of her elderly owner and returns with her tongue hanging out. Disappointed, the dog rests on a blue-and-white cushion on the loveseat next to us.

The house is in excellent condition because the owner recently repainted it. Oak-framed pictures grace the room—Gardenia with the Eiffel Tower in the background, Les Champs Élysées in the late 1800's with the Arc de Triomphe in the forefront, the Moulin Rouge with Can Can dancers. Marlene's vacant gaze reveals the emotional storms that wreak havoc in her mind. She stands up and turns around, her right foot gets caught on the rug, and her body swings sideways. I hold her right hand and correct her spin. The refrigerator in the kitchen contains two photos held in place by little magnets of Snow White and Grumpy. One shows a happy Marlene in uniform and her mom at the entrance of her primary school and the other, mother and daughter in a baseball field with their dog Polka. Marlene picks up a cookie from a jar covered in red hearts and hands me another. She takes a bite and smacks her lips,

"My mother always kept a jar full of cookies in every room at home. She baked them better than anyone else. It is a miracle I didn't become an obese child."

I grab a tissue from my pocket and dab off a tiny piece of food that hangs from the right corner of her mouth. Marlene shudders. She holds my hand for a little while and sketches an inquisitive grimace. In the guest room, a picture of Daniel and Marlene at Navy Pier sits on a nightstand. She remarks,

"After our divorce, I purged the decoration of this room. My mom must have hidden this photo somewhere."

"Your mom was a clever woman. She knew what was best for you," I say in a kidding tone.

Marlene taps me on my shoulder several times and smiles at my witticism. I grasp her hand and kiss it. She blushes and drops of perspiration burst onto her forehead. She composes herself and we walk into Celine's master bedroom.

A picture of Our Lady of the Immaculate Conception presides over dark French-styled furniture adorned with wooden flowers—a bed, a nightstand, and a dresser. The room appears impeccable, and even the blue-red-and-white quilted coverlet shows no wrinkles. The owner probably wanted to impress her sense of order on those who would walk through her home after her death. A large black and white photograph depicts little Marlene in the lap of Grandma Valentine, whose widow's weeds and stern face speak of the recent death of her husband. She holds in her hand a rosary with large beads, and a silver cross dangles from a necklace. Daniel saw this portrait on numerous occasions in Celine's old home in Chicago. It always conveyed the steadfast fusion of religion, death, and ancestry to him. The holy mixture almost crumbled under the weight of two divorces of their family in America. Yet, a wedding picture of Marlene's parents presides over the same wall as a testimony of the indestructibility of Catholic marriage and the fallacy of any subsequent unions. No trace of Celine's deceased second husband can be found anywhere in the house as though he had never existed. A small white lacquered missal book rests on a nightstand.

Marlene holds it, caresses it, and unlocks the golden clasp. A note sticks out of the golden edges of the pages. She unfolds it and then staggers out of the bedroom, crying. She lets me read it,

Ma chérie fille Marlene: Let my grandma's missal guide you through the rest of your life better than it did mine. I should have taken more care of you and your dad. But no one will love you as much as I did. Follow what your conscience dictates, continue to honor your family, and requite the affection of those who care for you. May God grant you a long and happy life. I will always be with you. Maman

Here in my hands, I hold the measure of a mother's infinite love for her children on earth. An immense abysm of orphanhood opens before me. I was born alone and miss the mighty force of maternal love. Marlene must now feel a similar emotion. I tell her how lucky she is to have been born of such an exceptional being. Many have no clue of what it means. Her eyes gaze at me with such force that I shut mine lest they discover the true meaning of those words. She perceives my distress, walks toward me, and hugs me. Her tears wet my neck, and I kiss her cheek. Gardenia whines and leaps to her legs. Marlene turns her head, and our mouths brush against each other and then fuse. I savor the texture of her lips, little by little, upper and lower, corner to corner, from the plump bottom to fleshy apex, conscious of every single furrow and crease on their sensual surfaces. Her eyes fill up with the sweet color of honey. Passion erupts, and our tongues slither into welcoming shelters. We strip off our garments and I then realize the meaning of my previous dream. We do what lovers do as I whisper sweet words in her ears, and the clock seems to stop ticking.

Cuddled into each other, we let our post orgasmic reverie melt away. Marlene becomes silent and adopts an expression of guilt. In the Other Dimension, I had intercourse with oneiric images of Marlene on several occasions, but the sexual acts reached neither the intensity of emotion nor the sublimeness of sensation I enjoyed today.

On our trip back to Chicago, her eyes absorb the scenery with a pensive look. Battles deep in her soul come to the fore, and the rouge of happiness on her face alternates with the paleness of disgust. She doesn't utter a single word all the way back to her apartment. The uneasiness of the silent an-hour-and-a-half drive has caught up with her because, when I am about to kiss her goodbye, she breaks the embrace to reproach me,

"You seduced me."

I don't reply. Marlene fumbles with the latch of her seat belt. I help her, hold her hand, and plant my lips on it. She gazes at me aghast. Her moist skin tastes of vanilla ice-cream, and I feel like a balloon floating over an immense field. Pondering, she slides her palm and fingers out of my grip, opens the car, steps out, and stands a moment with her hand on the knob. She shuts the door, bends over the rolled-down window, and regards me. Gardenia protests and barks at her because she feels ignored. Marlene turns to the side, issues an affectionate expression at the animal, and says,

"Stay with your new papa."

Marlene muses, narrows her eyes, and runs her nails over her forehead as though dispelling evil thoughts. I watch her lips quiver, and her chest frees a deep sigh. She then utters an unexpected remark,

"You don't make love like Daniel."

Her downcast gaze unveils the violet color of her eyelids, and her lips adopt a pucker that enhances her sexual attractiveness. I wish I could cover her with kisses and squeeze her in my arms. A motorcycle passes by, and the noise disturbs my reverie as an intense odor of fumes deforms the scenery. The buildings look dark and imposing, little stores shed their loveliness, and the whole atmosphere turns tainted with the ugliness of reality. Marlene averts her eyes and keeps thinking aloud, her mind churning ideas and belching them out,

"You repeat "on earth" over and over as if you came from a different planet."

An alarm goes off inside me. I shut my eyes and bend my head, afraid that she might discover a truth beyond her comprehension. The air in the car constricts my throat. I feel the doors, roof, and windshield closing in on me, suffocating me. Her perfume wafts over me, her vanilla taste still caresses my tongue, and images of her love-filled eyes during intercourse linger on, easing my anguish.

"Where is Daniel?" She asks and then reflects, murmuring to herself, "But you still have the fish on your buttock."

I smile because she refers to the beauty spot on my right gluteal area, but her expression shows the impassivity and rigidity of marble. When Daniel grew up, he often remarked he had been born under a religious sign, and Lorna never failed to mention that only his ass was Christian. Would she understand if I told her that I am the other Daniel, the person that grew inside him in the dream world?

Her ex-husband was not different from the rest of humankind. Everyone wants to be the man or woman who lives in their minds—their role model— to find a steady and durable state of happiness. This goal varies from person to person. Professional success, fame, power, excellent family, money, religious fulfillment, combination, and so on. This endeavor is what life on earth is about. The driving force is love, a divine gift shared by the real and dream worlds. People long to achieve self-love and love others who, through their efforts, will end up loving them back.

To attain stable and long-lasting joy on earth is not easy. It requires hard work, a process of self-construction. Those who succeed achieve their transformation into their ideal person with years of behavioral corrections. Their abilities and resources limit their undertaking. A few may even strive toward moral, intellectual, spiritual, and physical perfection. But Daniel bumped into a unique shortcut that led to the birth of the individual he wanted to become—me, Sonie. He realized my makeup was more advanced than his to pursue happiness and acknowledged it,

"Now a new man better than me walks upon the face of the earth."

After Marlene has finished her divagations, she impatiently frowns at me. I look her straight in the eye and repeat Julie's last words,

"Love works miracles."

"Miracles can't erase the bitter disillusion of a divorce," she says and rushes to the door of her building.

Twenty-One

RETURN TO GENESIS

I dream that I walk on deck aboard a cruise ship of several stories and numerous balconies. Ladies parade in elegant silk dresses, bell-shaped skirts that emphasize their waists, long sleeves, and deep collars. Ringlets grace their elaborate coiffures that gentlemen in dark suits admire with a bow and a tip of their top hats. The XIX Century fashion blooms on full display. I talk to several guests and point out that men love to sail on a boat that teems with beautiful women and possibilities of romance. I must have basked in public speaking because a crew member approaches me and remarks,

"You seasoned your speech."

I wonder about the subject and seasoning I used. I hope I neither offended anyone nor uttered obscene comments. I visit the casino and join Marlene, who plays poker alone. She wears a long white dress with a lacy fringe that renders her the appearance of a wealthy Parisian woman in the early 1900s. Her long hair rests on her naked shoulder and upper chest where an emerald pendant enhances her sensuality. She sits at a green velvet table in front of a dealer in a black frock who gets ready to distribute the cards. He shuffles and mixes them with sentences and phrases on pieces of thin cardboard. I read a few,

"Return to Genesis."

"You are on your own."

"We do what we can."

"To the wrath of grapes, a hearty bite."

Marlene understands them. The croupier passes the cards behind his back before handing them out and admonishes me for my lack of attention to the game. She complains,

"It must be done with dignity."

I ponder the meanings of the hidden phrases and sentences. Marlene must return to her genesis and the root of her existence in the poker game of life, reaffirm the correction of her wrong course, and bite the bullet of possible consequences.

The intrusive presence of Daniel interrupts my thoughts. He and I sit inside a floating capsule built with two plastic shells stuck together. The contraption bobs adrift in the middle of an ocean. He admonishes me,

"Yes, it must be done with dignity, something you don't understand. You have no sense of decency."

"Nothing is undignified in love."

"How dare you have sex with Marlene in the home of her mother who just died?"

"I didn't have sex with Marlene! I made love to her. The old woman would have approved of it."

"You seduced her daughter!"

"You are jealous. You could never seduce her."

"Of course, I seduced Marlene."

"No, you didn't, and your failure made your marriage boring and defective."

"Sonie, keep your ears open. Marlene never said she loved you."

"I felt it. She might be a little confused, but she will come around."

"Marlene has made up her mind. She is a tough cookie. And you are inside a cracked nutshell in the middle of the ocean."

He makes me angry. I am glad he leaves me alone. The next morning, I call Marlene, but she doesn't pick up the phone. I leave several messages on her recorder professing my love for her and asking her to withdraw the annulment request and marry me. I have my answer a week later when I arrive home to an empty apartment in the afternoon. Emmanuelle must have taken Thomas and Gardenia to a nearby park. A letter from the Archdioceses of Chicago lies on a table. Dated May 14, 2012, it informs me of the final abolition of the union of Marlene and Daniel.

At dinner, Emmanuelle hands me an invitation to Marlene's wedding on June 18, 2012. The news causes deep and uncontrollable painful jolts in my head. I don't resent my wasted efforts, but after being intimate with Marlene, my life without her looms darker than a moonless night on the high seas. My primary concern remains her happiness. I haven't been able to forestall the severe damage this marriage will cause in her mind. A lambent ray of hope still illuminates me. I won't give up until the couple exchange vows before a judge.

Emmanuelle relates an incident that occurred this morning. Marlene shambled into my apartment, her teary eyes red and her pink cheeks stained with mascara. Her daughter ushered her into a seat and held her hands to stop her sobs as Gardenia climbed on her lap to calm her down. Earlier in the day, Marlene walked into Michael Rosen's medical building to show him the printed invitations to their wedding. She found him on one side of the front counter, handing his assistant some bills from his wallet. Flustered by his betrothed's unexpected arrival, he dropped a small red item he retrieved from the floor, his face crimson like a beet. But Marlene caught sight of the bright red condom. She hid her disappointment and composed herself before providing him with the invitations they had anxiously awaited. He kissed her lips before everyone and announced their upcoming marriage.

Marlene described how her outrage worsened at home. Her boyfriend's infidelities and deception caused her disappointing doubts about his love. The unfaithfulness didn't bother her as much as the lie. She wondered about the identity of the woman who had replaced her in bed. A call to Laura Davidson confirmed her suspicion. She had performed the charitable act for a while and then referred him to a sophisticated escort service owned by a lady neighbor. Marlene was not free of sin either. She had made love with me a few weeks ago. I observe a complicit smile on Emmanuelle's face, but she ends the pause and continues her account. Marlene had earlier confessed to Michael Rosen her sexual indiscretion. She cried her eyes out and blamed her weakness on the recent death of her mom. Michael Rosen reacted with sadness but expressed his understanding,

"After all, he is still your husband in the eyes of God... you didn't even sin."

Then, Emmanuelle remarked,

"I am sorry, Mother, but you shouldn't feel guilty about Michael Rosen. He is a dishonest, cunning man with a ton of psychological damage. Mental problems run in his family."

She went on to tell Marlene what Geraldine had recounted to her that morning. Her friend traced her paternal relatives —her grandmother Martha and her aunt Brigitte. Mother and daughter moved to Quebec a few days after abandoning Michael Rosen at the orphanage. For five years, Martha worked as a waitress in several restaurants. But none of her applications ever mentioned she had left a child in the US. Martha married an older man who didn't like children but accepted Brigitte and ended up adopting her. The mother asked her daughter to keep Michael's existence a secret not to wreck their relationship with her stepfather. Martha assured her that her brother was happy with the nuns, and any change would do him more harm than good.

The stepfather died in a traffic accident and the mother two days later from injuries sustained in the same collision. This tragedy happened a few months after Brigitte turned twenty-one. She inherited a considerable fortune but did not contact her brother for fear he would contest the testament since the bequest legally came from Martha. On a cruise ship, Brigitte fell in love with a wealthy South American businessman, married him, and moved to La Paz, Bolivia. A few years later,

Brigitte eloped with another man and abandoned her husband and two children. She died on a trip to the Amazon.

Marlene did not react to the story and said that Michael had already acquainted her with the info. She realized that plenty of rumors circulated in the community of French immigrants about his family in Quebec. His sister's fate was a source of much speculation. Michael also discovered her money had ended up in her children's financial trust in Bolivia beyond any recourse.

When Michael Rosen reasoned away Marlene's infidelity, he set off a spate of remorseful feelings in his betrothed. She viewed it as a sign of his indestructible love and must have resolved to stay away from her ex until she had married Michael Rosen. Her plan frustrated my many attempts to contact her.

Early on Friday morning, May 21, 2012, Emmanuelle, Thomas and I catch a flight to Miami International Airport. We get into a taxicab and hop out at the Miami harbor terminal. Ahead of us, Marlene and Michael Rosen wait in a long line of passengers who are boarding the cruise ship. I watch them stand before a large canvas with a picture of the boat displaying the name— "Wonders of the Sea." He doffs his yacht captain cap, draws out a white comb from the back pocket, runs the row of teeth along his hair, tucks the comb back into place, and repositions his hat. He poses as for a magazine with his white shirt, light blue pants, and immaculate white shoes. Meanwhile, Marlene fidgets with the bow of her straw hat of ivory rattan. Her eyes focus on the ceramic vase with the embossed Picasso Blue Nude that rests against the bosom of her light green knit dress.

Marlene and Michael Rosen make an elegant couple. She gazes ahead and ignores the camera until a young photographer sidles toward her and voices some instructions. Marlene holds the container with the ashes straight up and forward as if checking her mom in or offering her to the Almighty like a chalice at Mass. The flash goes off. The old lady deserves this deference. She arranged every detail of this trip several months before her death—guests, staterooms, dinner seating. Celine even deposited additional money so that her guests could reserve local excursions at the various ports of call.

The mourners settle on a vast stretch of the seventh deck near the middle of the ship— staterooms 7002 to 7024, all with balconies on the port side. An atmosphere of restrained inappropriate excitement looms over the area. A Pakistani cabin steward greets us with a bow and a litany of pleasantries and condolences. Marlene and Michael Rosen accommodate themselves in the connected suites 7002 and 7004. Laura Davidson walks into 7008 with a coquettish smile, a huge straw hat with a black ribbon, a sleeveless dress with yellow daisies enhancing her voluptuous figure. Emmanuelle drags Thomas into 7012. The tired little boy cries, so I bend over and lift him in my arms. After cuddling him for a while, I plug a bottle of warm milk into his mouth. My luggage lies in front of 7010.

Marlene and Michael Rosen don't show up for dinner at our table. I find curvy Laura Davidson in a scanty bikini with a large piña colada flirting with various fellow passengers at the swimming pool. She beckons me to jump into the water with them, but I decline. I walk toward the children's pool. Emmanuelle wears a vanilla swimsuit that highlights her figure. Next to her, sitting on the edge, is Lorna in a black bikini like that of a young woman. She maintains her svelte body. The two chat while they keep an eye on Thomas, who enjoys slapping the water like a duck. I pass by a bar and take the opportunity to grab a glass of Coca Cola for Emmanuelle and another with orange juice for Lorna. As soon as I hand them over, Thomas stands up, raises his hands, and babbles at me,

"Baba, Baba, what about me?"

I cannot believe my ears. When did Thomas learn to ask questions? My grandson surprises me more and more every day, skipping all the usual developmental milestones. The little one grows fast, and uncles and aunts promenade by him to enjoy their new role. But I don't see Marlene. Michael Rosen never leaves her side and watches her like a hawk. The couple takes advantage of the large ship that propitiates areas where passengers can hide for long periods. Meals don't serve as points of encounter because of the wide choice of restaurants and hours of service.

We visit a few cozy Caribbean countries with scenic beaches. On Thursday morning, May 17, the boat docks at our main destination, Fort-de-France Cruise Harbor on Martinique. Here, our group shares an exclusive excursion to Grande Anse de Salines in Sainte Anne on the south-east of the French island. Celine must have heard about this tropical paradise when she was a child and opted for it as the repository of her ashes.

After an hour on the road, we arrive at a secluded cove and stand in awe under palm trees that bow to the beach as if in perpetual prayer. Celine must have envisioned the beauty of this seascape of breathtaking white sands and turquoise water. Her daughter removes her high-heeled shoes and walks toward the seashore. The sun sears her elegant black hat as her shrunken noon shadow projects no further than her stepping feet. A few strands of golden hair escape their confinement and swing in the breeze. Sandpipers flit away, and colonies of seagulls and brown pelicans take off with a chorus of high-pitched cries. Marlene holds the vase in her hands as her black attire submerges under the surf. Waves crowned with lacy foam reach higher and higher onto her body until half of her dress lies underwater. She uncaps the vase and pours the ashes out. A cloud of powder drops on the water and rides the ocean except for a small amount that flies in the wind and hovers over her face. The scene conjures up the image of a mother who envelopes her daughter in her last caress. Marlene dips the container into the ocean and empties it out. She rinses her face, turns around, and comes back. No one utters a single word and silence overwhelms us on our way back to the ship.

Tonight, a dream floods my mind:

I sit next to Marlene on North Avenue Beach in Chicago, both fully dressed, her face gorgeous and peaceful. We wait in a line to throw little red marbles inside small holes. We leave, return later, and as we stand in the queue again, I tell her I miss her. She looks pensive and mournful. Marlene then goes away, and I want to find her to accompany her home but cannot locate her. I forgot to let her know where to contact me if she got lost. I search on the beach but don't catch sight of her until I watch her sit at a bar counter, alone. She looks full of thoughts and minds no one. There are quite a few people around her. I notice a narrow space where I can nudge my way in and stand next to her. As I do it, a tall blond patron scrambles to stop me or displace me, but he fails.

Marlene and I then stroll through a narrow rocky path along the jetty of a turbulent Lake Michigan. Rushes of winds push her toward rough water. I proffer her my hand, and she holds on to it and says,

"You came from a new world. Where do you have what you imported? You must return it."

"It is in a bag that I have forgotten over there," I answered, pointing to the men's bathroom.

I walk into the place and pluck the sack from a redheaded boy who pees into a urinal. I sit on the grass and open it. It contains a tuna sandwich and an electric toothbrush with no brush because the youngster junked it off.

"Are you putting me off? Marlene asks. "What else did you bring?"

"Two notes that turn a musical tune into a new creation. Anyone can successfully perform a song with them. I also invented a new word, *yapage.*"

When I wake up, I don't recall the sounds that would launch composers and artists to the top of the hit parade. Losing Marlene represented the frustration I am going through with her, a theme that has often recurred in my dreams. What impresses me the most is her question about my contribution to this world. The answer in the oneiric scenes strikes my fancy and will disappoint people. Most items were intangible because no physical articles will ever satiate the earthly hunger for material things. But everything, even the insignificant ones I brought—a tuna sandwich, a toothbrush—must return to the Other Dimension.

But is this an ominous dream? Does Marlene stand ready to interrogate me with unanswerable queries? And what does *yapage* mean? It might be 'participant' because the term bears a homonymous similarity to 'pageant'—a show or exhibition with a succession of participants. Or is it related to 'yawp'—to utter a loud, harsh cry. If so, whose yelling is it?

Twenty-Two

YAPAGE

he next day, our ship puts in at St. Maarten. I push Thomas'
pram in downtown Philipsburg with Emmanuelle and Lorna
beside me. Time rolls on, and my lovely bait gets no chance to
attract his grandma as I expected. Marlene shows up nowhere.
Back on the ship, we will cruise the high seas and reach the Port of
Miami in two and a half days, the end of our trip.

In the evening, I watch Marlene and Michael Rosen sit at the table
with Amelie and me. Father Matthew excused himself. Emmanuelle
stayed in her stateroom attending to Thomas, who lay asleep. Cups of
onion soup release a delicious fragrance that wafts through the elegant
salon adorned with international flags. Bottles of red and white wine
stand before the guests who clink their glasses and drink to everyone's
health. Amelie addresses Dr. Rosen in French and congratulates him
on the upcoming wedding. He offers her a smug smile and listens to
the lady's apologies for the incident at the wake of Celine,

"*Je suis desolée.* I didn't mean to arouse your anger. I appreciate the
help you provided me for quite a few years."

"I did my best." His face shows indifference and his voice an insouciant tone as he sips a glass of water with a slice of lemon.

"I never adjusted to the new neurologist you referred me to."

"He is well trained in headaches."

"Dr. Rosen, you controlled them well. The doctor wondered why you sent me to him because he didn't speak French."

"I thought you'd get along with him."

"Perhaps, I should never have mentioned the story of your mother and your sister in Quebec."

"My referral had nothing to do with that," his angry voice booms with an upward inflection.

Marlene makes a gesture of discomfort and gazes at me with an entreating look. Michael Rosen flaps his napkin against the table, excuses himself, and attempts to stand up. But Marlene holds him down and whispers some words. I come to her rescue. I lift my glass of red wine and propose a toast to the life of Celine, whose generosity allows us to share this intimate moment in her memory. Marlene's eyes drift around and, for a moment, rest on mine, her face blushing because of a thought I wish I could read. I feel my skin crawl, and Michael Rosen seems uneasy. He either dodges Cupid's arrows that hiss from side to side of the table or dwells in lingering displeasure from the previous conversation.

My words evoke reminiscences in the senior guest. Amelie opens her purse and passes around a small black-and-white picture. It shows two novices inside the blooming garden of a convent. She points to the taller Celine who holds a rosary of thick beads in her hand and a large cross on her chest. I find a marked resemblance with Marlene when Daniel first met her. Mother and daughter radiate the same peaceful beauty and innocence, but the mom's lips are thinner and her forehead wider.

"We had this photograph taken a few months before we left the order," Amelie explains.

She smiles and recounts the day Celine fell in love with Marlene's dad. Every month, the two novices went to visit their parents in a little village in the French Provencal flatlands. One day, they trekked home by the fields of fruit trees and vines and spied a youngster swimming in a river that further down its course embraced their hometown. Their neighbor Vincent was nude, and his clothes lay in a small pile on the grass near the bank. Playful Celine couldn't resist subjecting others to funny pranks. The youngsters slunk from bush to bush, seized the booty, and took to their heels, laughing. Vincent rushed out of the water with a piece of bark covering his genitals, screaming from the top of his lungs.

"Thieves! I will tell the mother superior on you!"

That evening, Stripper, as they called him from then on, waited at the central plaza and shouted names at them. Celine was Sister Rapine and Amelie was Sister Underpants since his underwear had hung from her hand when they ran away. The novices kept going back to their hometown, and Stripper kept waiting in the village square to carry out his vengeance until they pleaded for a truce. The butt of the prank and the pranksters sat over vanilla ice-cream at a cafeteria. He accepted their apologies. Amelie noticed how Vincent and Celine exchanged glances that betrayed an intense attraction. A few months later, he approached Celine and whispered in her ear,

"You won't take the vows, will you? That would break my heart forever."

Amelie then knew her friend wouldn't become a nun at the ceremony scheduled one year away. They both left the convent. Celine and Vincent eventually got divorced, and his heart survived the split because, despite popular beliefs, no one dies of lovesickness. I review my memory files. I find no conversation between Daniel and Marlene about the anecdote of her parents' falling in love, nor any mention of Celine's novitiate as a youngster. Marlene might have felt embarrassed to reveal her progenitors' auspicious romance after the terrible end of their marriage and the ordeal they had put her through. Besides, she seldom reminisced of their years in France as if their lives and her own had begun when the family arrived in this country. Shortly before his divorce, Daniel regretted his lack of acquaintance with his wife's childhood. He wondered whether he would have understood her better if he had known more.

I wonder whether Michael Rosen had learned this information before he wooed Marlene because his face shows no surprise. He must have heard it from Amelie or any other confidant in the circle of the French community in Chicago. His vendetta could be an insane way of punishing his mother and his sister. If so, it should endanger not only Francophone female members or ex-members of religious orders but also their daughters. Marlene might become the next victim. I place an urgent call to private detective Mr. O'Connor but cannot locate him. Nor can I the next morning. His answering machine repeats over and over that his office will open on Monday at 8.00 AM. I leave several messages.

The next evening, the celebration of Celine's life blazes with the music of Ravel's Boléro. The French classical music mesmerizes the guests, lulling them into nostalgia of memories of times past. I watch Marlene mingle with the attendees in the chapel. Waiters and waitresses in livery distribute cheese and wine among mourners whose happy faces belie the purpose of the fete. Three violinists entertain the audience. Pictures of Celine hang from the ceiling on multicolor strings—at the Eiffel Tower as a child with her parents, behind a desk at the primary school in her little village, in the convent with a group of nuns. In a gorgeous dress at her wedding, as a newlywed in a lovely hat in front of a blooming almond tree. Celine and Vincent with little Marlene by the Seine River, the family on a boat with the Statue of Liberty in the background.

The entrance of the captain of the ship into this venue interrupts my review of the display. He walks toward Michael Rosen, expresses his condolences, and engages in a conversation. Marlene lounges next to Steve, Marie, and Lorna. Their faces reflect the somberness of bereavement and, perhaps, their apprehension about the upcoming wedding. I greet them. Marlene wears a black gown with a brooch of blue topaz that enhances the color of her eyes. My olfactory sense distinguishes her unique scent from her companions' and arouses my almost unrestrained desire to hug her, snatch her to my stateroom, and make love to her until we dock in Miami.

I usher Marlene to the promenade deck to discuss a pressing matter. A full moon draws its silvery wake in the water under a starry sky while her eyes reveal love and sadness for me. She misreads the reason for my interruption and issues an erroneous explanation,

"Don't reach any conclusion from my slip at my mom's. I don't blame you alone, but I was vulnerable."

"Please, Marlene, don't complicate the situation. Michael Rosen is harming you."

"Stop it. You have been attacking us since I first went out with him."

"End the farce. It is simple. I love you and you love me."

"Please, don't pressure me. Respect my mother's memory."

"You know I do. But let's not fight. I brought you here for a different purpose. Mr. Winters called me from the bank because he couldn't reach you. You must have forgotten to erase my name as a contact in case of an alert in your account."

"What is the problem?"

"He wants to confirm that you have allowed the transfer of all your money to the account of your betrothed, Michael Rosen. He held in his hand a document he claimed you had signed. But I wasn't sure and placed the transaction on hold."

"Why would I sign that? It must be an error."

I offer to accompany her to her cabin where she keeps her phone, for she will need to confirm her identity through texting. Lividness overwhelms her face, and a greenish color taints her flawless complexion. I want her to calm down, but she rushes down the corridors immersed in her thoughts, and I cannot make a dent in her concerns. People enter and exit their cabins, lounge, and loiter throughout the ship, stewards push their carts with linens. But Marlene hurries oblivious to even my presence. She opens the door to her stateroom, and we hear Michael Rosen's angry voice through the closed door that connects both cabins,

"Why haven't you transferred my betrothed's money to my account? She signed the document."

Silence ensues, and Marlene and I can hear him snorting,

"It must be a mistake. Daniel Brandon cannot place the transaction on hold. He is no longer her husband. Their marriage was annulled as if it had never existed."

Silence lingers.

"Fine, I understand. I'll take care of it as soon as I get to Miami in a couple of days."

I warn Marlene to stay calm and raise no fuss until we reach our destination because an enraged Michael Rosen might turn violent. We will remain vigilant, but I know he will make no false move on the ship. She must keep the connecting door locked and always seek others' company whenever she goes out with him. Marlene promises to be cautious.

The next morning, Mr. O'Connor returns my calls. He says he phoned me several times but got no answer. The needed information arrived two days ago:

During the past sixteen years, Michael Rosen had numerous brief affairs, but only two long-lasting relationships. The first partner, Louise Gauthier, was a novice at the Felician Sisters Convent on Peterson Avenue in Chicago. In her early forties, the spinster and heir of a sizable fortune chaired the Gauthier's Christian Foundation, an organization dedicated to providing shelter to abused women and their children. Louise left the religious order in 2001 and engaged in a relationship with Michael Rosen for about two years. One year into his courtship, he became the foundation's president. During the following six months, Michael Rosen used several bank checks to purchase three luxurious condominiums in Puerto Vallarta, Mexico. Ms. Gauthier's lawyers initiated a legal case against him, but they dropped the suit one month later.

The second was 51-year-old Marie Blanche, a childless widow and the daughter of a novice. Her three-year liaison with Michael Rosen ended when she died from a horse-riding accident on May 12, 2008. Michael Rosen didn't witness the tragedy because he didn't join her on her journey that day. During the time Dr. Rosen was engaged to her, he bought a chateau in France whose title was only in his name. An inquiry raised doubts about whether Marie bought it for Michael Rosen as a gift, or deception had occurred. Nothing could be proven. Her two nephews didn't file a civil or criminal complaint against him. In the end, one half of her estate went to her old convent of the Sisters of Notre Dame in Paris, France, and the other half to Michael Rosen. He gracefully divided his inheritance into two halves, one for himself and the other for the two relatives.

Mr. O'Connor's update on Michael Rosen arouses terrible fears. As I expected, Marlene's profile fits well with that of Michael Rosen's victims—a wealthy and beautiful daughter of an ex-novice of French ancestry. But Marie Blanche's death adds a new danger that freezes the blood in my veins. Did her betrothed plan to throw Marlene overboard once her assets were in his possession. I try to contact her, but to no avail. I ease my fear by reassuring myself that Marlene knows of Michael Rosen's evil scheme and won't let him swindle her out of her money. If he doesn't achieve his goal, she should be safe.

On the last evening of the cruise, the atrium of the ship teems with lights and decorations, and crystal elevators rush up and down with guests in formal wear. An orchestra gathers in the middle of the space and delights the audience with romantic music. A few couples take to the floor and flaunt their dancing abilities at everyone. They belong to a club and have trained all year long for this occasion. Marlene and Michael Rosen swagger in. She looks radiant in a light blue dress that matches a necklace and a pair of earrings of resplendent sapphires. Daniel bought these jewels for her on a trip to San Diego, California. Her expression betrays no discomfort or uneasiness, and her wide smile makes me wonder whether her betrothed convinced her of his honorable intentions. They sit at a table close to where I stand. The notes of the French bolero *Je Confess* vibrate in the pianos, guitars, and violins. My feet, as though they had a mind of their own, move almost uncontrollably.

I amble toward Marlene with my eyes fixed on hers as the music gathers strength. Before Michael Rosen can react, I grab her hand, embrace her waist with my arm, and escort her to the dance floor. He stays frozen and pale like a marble statue, his face contorted with hatred. I ignore him, and we glide over the vinyl tiles as the glorious music lifts us in a cloud of joy. Her heart palpitates next to mine, and her lips bloom like a rosebud, and I am again fighting my desire. Michael stands up and paces back and forth, waiting for us to end the dance. I sneak her out to the deck before the song ends.

Outside, the night blossoms with the fresh fragrance of sea breeze. Some passengers sit on lounge chairs, gather in small groups to chat, stroll by, or watch small waves caress the ship. Stars twinkle as the moonlight bathes everyone in peaceful splendor that evokes the pleasure of romance. I inform Marlene of Michael Rosen's previous long-lasting relationships and the outcome of these liaisons. She listens but shrugs and doesn't comment, not even when I voice my fears about Marie Blanche's death or reveal the victims' profile. Marlene must have figured it out herself and sensed her impending danger. A thought seems to loom large in her mind, for an enigmatic smile surfaces on her face. I embrace her and whisper in her ear,

"*Ma cherie* Marlene, you don't deserve even a shadow of pain over your eyes. Marry me."

She hesitates, looks me straight in the eye, and answers,

"Tell me who you are. Even Gardenia didn't recognize you. Your voice, your expression, the way you make love. You can sing, you can dance. Daniel couldn't do those things. He stood on the floor like a dizzy duck and lacked musical sense. Your mole on the upper lip."

The scenes of my last dream rush through my mind. Her knowledge of my true identity, her harsh interrogation about my contribution to my fellow human beings' lives on earth, including hers, my answers to her straightforward questions. In the other dimension, the human mind does not object to contradictory responses because weird, logical, or illogical reasoning becomes permissible. But here on earth, I have a hard time with her question and utter the first thought that crosses my mind,

"I love you, Marlene, you know I love you more than anyone in this world."

"Please answer my question. Or I must then conclude that I was married to you for many years, and I already know what is to be married to you."

"No, you don't! You are correct. I don't want to live the rest of my life with a secret."

"Who are you?"

"I am Sonie, the other Daniel, the person who lived in his dreams. I traded places with him so Daniel could stay in the World of Dreams with his beloved Julie, the ghost how you call her. I took over his body."

"You are scaring me! What did you do to Daniel?"

"Nothing, my love, Daniel lives in the Other Dimension. His experiment succeeded. Our exchange happened when his body was in a coma."

"You are crazy!"

Marlene runs away with an astonished expression on her face, her dress and hair fluttering in the wind and the air that rushes into the void the ship has abandoned in its wake.

"Wait, Marlene, let me explain to you!"

"Leave me alone!"

I dash after her, and when I am about to overtake her, a hand grabs my right arm. The figure of Michael looms before me. I watch his fist charge against me, and his expletive scratches the already disturbed quietness of the evening,

"Get the hell away from my betrothed!"

I skirt the blow and hear the captain's voice boom behind us,

"Gentlemen, there will be no fights aboard this ship."

He instructs three corpulent crew members to escort us to our staterooms. Michael Rosen pounds Marlene's door for a while and finally ceases. I wait for a few minutes and follow suit. Whispering, I beg and tap with my knuckles for Marlene to let me in over and over, but she doesn't answer.

The next day, we bask in a radiant sun, and huge cotton-like cumulus clouds rest on the horizon. Under them, seagulls and pelicans circle around and seem to utter cries of welcome. Only a stench of gasoline breaks the spell of the morning as if auguring distress. Some crew members already get busy polishing the shiny wooden handrails of the magnificent floating palace. Passengers sit next to their carry-on luggage, waiting to disembark. I see Marlene and Lorna on the promenade deck, their expression stern and somber. I don't understand the reason for their emotions until I stand next to them and notice how two officers handcuff Michael Rosen and push him into a squad car. I hear Marlene's comments,

"The police searched his condo and found evidence of his crimes in the safe—threatening letters, nude pictures, falsified documents."

I observe an ambulance next to the police car. The officers must have expected a physical confrontation, but the detainee didn't resist arrest. I thought passengers would leave the ship by the same bridge that had connected it with the port facility when we boarded it. But on this occasion, the gangway descends to the harbor grounds. Lorna looks at Marlene and then me and says,

"The cops left. Let's go down."

I offer my hand to Marlene, but she looks me straight in the eye and wipes off her tears on the sleeve of her dress. My beloved gazes at her feet to avoid falling, but I can no longer wait and begin to explain my situation. She shakes her head, and Lorna reprimands me because of the inappropriateness of the place and time. I step off the ship, and two enormous paramedics tramp toward me, pin me down to the floor, and slip a straitjacket on me under the watchful eyes of my companions. As my assailants lift me and push me into the ambulance, I shout my *yapage*,

"Marlene, I am not crazy! I told you the truth!"

I hear how an impassive Lorna consoles Marlene,

"Don't cry, my daughter. He'll get well soon."

"I hope so."

Twenty-Three

THE CHAMBER

I wake up in a semidark room. My arms are tied to the sides of the bed, and an aromatic smell of antiseptic fills my room. The closed door has a small glass window at the top. A green blanket covers me. The mismatch of this color with the bright white on the walls rasps my nerves. On the right wall hangs a little picture of Lake Michigan with skyscrapers in the background. I don't know who undressed me and donned me this flowery robe that doesn't conceal my nudity. I hear distant noises of elevators and male voices. I can barely distinguish what they are saying,

"Where did you hide your pills?"

"I didn't hide anything. I've taken them."

The last thing I remember is an injection into my right arm. It must have been phenothiazine because my mouth is dry, and an intense headache concentrates on my forehead. My muscles are tense and stiff from the induced artificial sleep. Not a single dream with sweet night scenes comforts my terrible life here. I hear a key, and the door opens with a screech. A black security guard of colossal size appears at the doorstep. His large bulging eyes have darkened whites and brown

212

pupils that glow with the indifference of someone who bears a drab job. He addresses me with a hoarse voice,

"Daniel Brandon?"

"Yes. what do you want?"

"If you promise me that you won't try to escape, I'll release your hands. I don't want to crush you down."

"Crush me down?"

"Last night, we had to tie you to the bed. You tried to get away several times."

"Why do you detain me here? I did nothing."

The security guard doesn't answer, but he frowns as his eyes scrutinize me,

"You were delirious all night, 'Daniel, help me. I love you, Marlene. I am not crazy. Daniel is with Julie in the Other Dimension. Lorna, it is Sonie; let me go home.' We had to inject you with another tranquilizer."

"Where am I?"

"I can't answer any more questions. Dr. Leroy Mansfield, your psychiatrist, is waiting. You never met him, did you?"

"No."

"He is new here. Does the wound on your scalp hurt?"

"What wound?"

"You hit a bed side rail. The resident doctor sewed the cut with three stitches and stopped the bleeding."

"I don't remember."

The sun sneaks in through small top windows and illuminates the hall. I spot a grayish sky with white clouds. An older man pushes an empty wheelchair and turns his head to stare beyond me. Large, swollen eyelids cover half of his eyes. He stands still when we overtake him. His right hand has dark spots and trembles on the handlebar. A well-groomed lady in a pink suit and a black pearl necklace sits in a little room. Next to her, a thin young woman wears a black dress and holds an unlit cigarette between her narrow lips. The young woman's face bears more wrinkles than that of the older woman. When we pass by them, they stop their conversation and regard us without blinking or making gestures. My companion breaks the silence,

"You must recognize Lake Michigan Psychiatric Pavilion. It is two blocks from Riverfront Hospital. You made several neurological consultations here a few years ago."

"I don't remember."

I've got a lot of difficulties accessing my memory files. Daniel might have come here, and I guess he must have brought a key to get out. The thought makes me smile. This place looks more like a prison than a mental health facility. The security guard closes my gown so that passersby won't see my bottom. But if he hadn't, no one would have noticed it, anyway.

We enter a spacious and bright office. My warden left, and Dr. Leroy Mansfield gets up to say hello. A bang of black hair rises along with him and falls on his right temple. His lanky body pulls the white lab coat's front, which appears to hang crooked on his left shoulder. The doctor sits behind a wide semicircular wooden desk. The back of his chair almost touches the wall where a large diploma presides over the room. He fiddles with a ballpen, lifts his accusatory eyes, and addresses me.

"Dr. Brandon, nice to meet you. It is an honor to be your doctor. How did you wake up this morning?"

"I don't know. You'll tell me why I am here."

"I think you know why you are here, don't you?"

"No, I don't."

"Well, that confirms my suspicion. You are a physician. You realize that quite a few patients with mental illnesses are not aware of their conditions."

"I am fine. Please let me go home."

"I can't. You suffer from a grave multiple personality disorder. I don't want to be responsible for your death or serious injury. I reviewed your records. I think you tried to commit suicide twice and almost died the second time."

"I am not suicidal."

"I talked with your mother. She denied you had any abuse in your childhood, which is often the case in your condition. Your parents divorced when you were young, but your mother didn't report any depressive reaction on your part."

"Dr. Mansfield, I am not depressed. Let me go home."

"Who are you? What is your name?"

"I see an identification tag on my wrist. It reads Daniel Brandon."

"I will not put up with your sarcasm!"

"You cannot keep me here against my will. I will call my lawyer."

"Yes, Dr. Brandon, I can. You may not call any lawyer. I admitted you against your will. I've got your mother's signature and legal authorization."

"I signed nothing."

Dr. Mansfield stands up, scowls, and shouts out,

"Mr. Zedekiah, Dr. Brandon is not cooperating. Please restrain him!"

The giant guard and an assistant—a bald white man with humongous biceps covered in cobra tattoos—dart through the door. I try to get up, but they grab me, beat me to the ground, drag my hands behind my back, and handcuff me. The bald guy lifts me like a sack of potatoes and seats me in a wheelchair. The psychiatrist doesn't even gaze at me, he regards various papers, and when he hears the squeaking wheels, he raises his head and addresses my jailer,

"Mr. Zedekiah, please take Dr. Brandon back to the ward and apply the Promethazine-injection protocol."

"Yes, doctor, I'll let the nurse know."

"Sleep well, Dr. Brandon. You'll rest all day. Tomorrow, you will feel better and be able to answer questions."

I can't send Dr. Mansfield to hell because his giant hireling pokes a handkerchief into my mouth and seals it with duct tape. The women in the little room watch me go by but don't flinch. In this institution, one must expect a patient to enter an office with his legs and leave bound to a wheelchair and gagged. A nurse walks by and greets my evil-spirited black bear with a smile. She looks at me like a piece of wood in a cart.

I don't know how many days I have slept. My head hurts. Next to my bed lies a bouquet of roses. Marlene saw me. She left a note headed by 'My beloved Daniel.' She cried because I see tear marks on the envelope. It is hard for me to read. My vision gets blurry, and every few seconds, my neck rotates and stretches to either side despite my attempts to control it. My tongue crawls across the bottom and ceiling of my mouth as if a reptile. It is dry and bears a bitter taste that worsens my headache. Marlene sympathizes with my predicament and cheers me up. She says I'll be all right, and we'll soon start our lives together. She ends it with, "I love you with all my heart." I would have liked to see her and ask for help. Marlene does not understand what the psychiatrist and his mercenaries are doing to me. She doesn't believe me. I hope she realizes the truth before it is too late.

I don't think Lorna came with her. Daniel's mother was never credulous, even when her son explained who Sonie was over and over. To her, my existence meant madness that needed to be tackled. Lorna won't visit me until the treatment has accomplished the changes she wants. Now, I understand why Daniel told me that I couldn't survive life on earth without imperfections; that I had to learn to lie. I can avoid questions or try to deflect them but cannot compromise my integrity and lie. I haven't seen Daniel in a while because these medications keep blocking my dreams. He and Julie must be worried.

A blond nurse interrupts my thoughts. She holds a syringe in her hand and grins with big red lips and large white teeth, her voice high-pitched and screechy.

"Dr. Brandon, I am Lydia Fuentes, a nurse anesthetist. I've brought you a remedy for your spasms, a mixture of Pentothal and Midazolam."

"That is not effective. Please don't inject me with any more drugs."

"Stand still."

"Don't do it, please. Tell Dr. Mansfield I'll answer all his questions. I don't need any truth serum. I always tell the truth."

She injects me. I cannot do anything because the security guard immobilizes my hands and feet. Half asleep, I wake up on a stretcher in the middle of a bright room with white walls and a marbled floor. It is as silent as a refrigerating chamber. I feel my feet and hands cold, and everything appears bathed in a dense fog. Dr. Mansfield sits on a chair next to the nurse. Their faces and figures grow blurry, and their white lab coats swell like inflatable Santa Clauses. The echo of the psychiatrist's voice roars,

"What is your name?"

"Sonie. Daniel named me Sonie."

"Then, Daniel knows you exist."

"Yes, of course."

The doctor mutters a few words to the nurse, and I make out some, "Weird... an exception... condition... he shouldn't know him."

Dr. Mansfield shows experience. He knows that one identity is unaware of the other in the cases of double personality syndrome. The first does not recall any of the acts of the second and vice versa. They may notice gaps in their memories, but nothing else. Their personalities also display opposite traits. With Daniel and me, we are different but not opposite. We share several qualities: hard workers, intellectual, courageous, and responsible. He and I love our family, respect others, abstain from alcohol and drugs. We are not envious, nor do we wish ill to anyone.

The doctor's voice resonates in my ears,

"When were you born?"

"July 15, 2009."

"Then, you are almost three years old. Aren't you?"

"Yes, I am."

I answer all his methodical questions. I detail to Dr. Mansfield how I instilled life into Daniel's body. That I exchanged my eternal existence in the Other dimension with this brief mortal life so he could stay with his beloved Julie. It makes no sense to the psychiatrist. He thinks I am lying and maybe covering a crime. He asks me several times where Daniel is, and I always reply the same answer: in the Other Dimension, in the world of dreams. I tell him I must correct Daniel's mistakes on earth and secure the long-term happiness of Marlene. I love her more than anything in this world. The doctor shrugs his shoulders and grimaces a gesture of disgust.

After the truth-serum interrogatory, the psychiatrist adds Clozapine, an antipsychotic drug, to my treatment. This medication enhances my headache. It now extends beyond my temples and forehead and causes nausea. I still bear the leather restraints, but the nurses have loosened them, and the bruises on my wrists are fading. I cannot phone anyone. I ask my caregivers to call Lorna so she can help me, but they won't. I wish the police would question me.

Marlene will come to see me today. I have already been here for a month. This hospital doesn't recommend visits more than once a week because psychiatrists believe these interactions hinder patients' improvement. But I think they just want to conceal the primitive state of their knowledge and unscientific methods. These doctors hide behind bombastic words that mean nothing. They articulate them with a solemn, deceitful appearance and lack any understanding of homo sapiens' mind.

The door opens, and Marlene looms before me in a light-blue suit that enhances her eyes' brightness. She walks toward me with a smile as a blush illuminates her face. His hips sway in a curvy body with graceful promontories that seem sculpted by Michael Angelo. Marlene bends down and kisses my lips. Her heat brings gooseflesh upon my skin.

"You're better, aren't you?"

I shrug. She doesn't realize my suffering—bruises, a head wound, marks from the leather restraints on my wrists, and a numb glow in my eyes. I've had headaches during the past few months but not as severe as those I now suffer. A dry throat makes my pronunciation falter because my tongue sticks to my mouth's ceiling. My neck cranes to either side like that of an ostrich. I try to disguise it.

"Dr. Mansfield said you are now cooperating with the treatment. But your delirium has yet to subside."

"My delirium? What delirium? I told you the truth. Daniel separated his spirit from his body and reached the Other Dimension. I grew up in his dreams. I love him like a brother. That is why I saved the body he'd abandoned in the ICU bed. If I hadn't, Daniel would have died. He didn't want to come back and separate from Julie. "

"Honey, get rid of those ideas."

"The human mind cannot understand them. But they are true. Please, Marlene, call my lawyer and explain that I need help. Don't you realize what the psychiatrist and his assistants are doing to me?"

A voice crosses the door threshold,

"Leave him alone, Marlene. He won't listen to you. Daniel is very stubborn."

"Lorna! Don't hide. I am also your son. Help me. Why did you sign to commit me here? Which lawyer did you manipulate?"

There's no answer, just a few steps fading away in the hallway.

"Daniel, honey, I love you with all my heart. As soon as your treatment ends, and you get well, we'll get married again. "

"You're blind, Marlene."

"Our children will be happy to know. Father Roche already helped me file an appeal to reverse our recent marriage's annulment."

"Marlene, listen to me. I am not getting out of here alive."

"Don't say that. I won't be able to come next week. My menopause arrived," and she adds, smiling. "My old age has begun."

"Your old age?"

"Yes. I haven't had my period this month. I made an appointment with my gynecologist."

"Are you getting hot flashes?"

"No, not yet."

The psychiatrist informed me that I didn't respond to Clozapine. The next step would be electroshock. He assured me of this procedure's success because a multiple personality disorder with depression and delirium should respond to this therapy. The cruel technique seems more in accord with the Spanish Inquisition's olden times than those of the new scientific revolution. It consists of placing electrodes on the temples or the forehead and the back of the head and discharging 70 to 100 volts of electricity for up to six seconds. The stimulus will unleash a direct current of 800 milliamperes through the entire brain.

I wonder whether I'll resist the seizure or wake up after the convulsion. I also worry about the aftermath. I may lose memory and not even recognize Marlene. After begging for a while, a nurse pities me and releases my right hand so that I can write a letter to Marlene. My Good Samaritan will give it to her when she visits me.

The day has arrived. Lydia Fuentes, the nurse anesthetist, walks into my room with a wheelchair. Her overdone perfume increases my headache and clouds my eyesight as she shakes her hair, which has gotten blonder because of an excess of peroxide.

"Good morning, Dr. Brandon. Are you going to cooperate, or should I call security?"

"You shouldn't give me electroshock. It is not indicated."

"Dr. Mansfield and I have a lot of experience with the electroconvulsive technique. We get excellent results."

"I don't need it. Let me go home."

The giant security guard rushes into my room like a whirlwind. Ms. Fuentes plants a syringe into my right arm. I fell asleep for a while, but I now watch Dr. Mansfield enter the refrigerating chamber. Dr. Mark Loeffler, a freckly young redheaded anesthesiologist, stands next to him. An oxygen mask covers my face. Several monitors loom nearby—electrocardiograph, electroencephalograph, oximeter, blood pressure. Ms. Fuentes inserts an intravenous catheter into my left arm to infuse a general anesthetic and other drugs. Then, she wraps a blood-pressure cuff around my left ankle. In this way, Dr. Mansfield wants to prevent the injected muscle relaxant from reaching my foot and paralyzing its muscles. He needs to watch the seizure. The muscular contractions won't affect the rest of my body because the drug will mask...

I don't know how long I have been out. From the ceiling where I find myself, I see my pale body atop an operating table. Tubes and machines torture my poor anatomy, the one Daniel donated to me, the depository of my immense love for Marlene. The split of my spirit from my living body renders me free to go back to the World of Dreams. As my last dream forewarned me: everything that came from the Other Dimension must return. Until then, I thought I had given up my eternal existence. It would have been wonderful to share terrestrial life with Marlene for several years, but my heart won't beat again. Besides, I completed my task on earth when I planted a seed of happiness in my beloved. This joyful saga will go on. I must leave and inform Daniel and Julie.

A big commotion rages in the room. Dr. Loeffler removes my oxygen mask, and Dr. Mansfield jolts my chest with a defibrillator over and over. Terror grows on their faces as they wait for a response. A flat line crosses the cardiac monitor as an alarm wails a plaintive beep. Dr. Mansfield yells at the nurse,

"Code blue! Code blue!"

Ms. Fuentes stands paralyzed, her legs tremble, and her eyes gape at the doctors. Dr. Loeffler screams,

"Hurry up! Call intensive care. He is leaving us! He is leaving us!"

Twenty-Four

THE SEED

Une grande souffrance me aflige. It causes me immense pain to see my beloved Daniel's inert body in the open coffin. Lorna is devastated. She doesn't even cry anymore because her tears have run out. I cannot comprehend his death. It pains me so much. Even the surprising result of the autopsy doesn't give me a shred of relief. The pathologist's words still hurt,

"We found a malignant tumor in the frontal lobe of the brain. It grew slowly but expanded quickly as of late. It affected the two brain hemispheres. Dr. Brandon had very little time left to live: a month or maybe two. We reviewed his medical records and found that the MRI done in July 2009 shows a tiny suspicious lesion in the area. But the neuroradiologist cannot be certain."

Those lost weeks hurt a lot since we would have enjoyed our love. Even a few minutes to seal our moment with a kiss would have been a magnificent gift. I should have listened to Daniel. I approach his body many times and ask him for forgiveness. Daniel appears as if he were asleep in the black-lacquered wooden casket adorned with carved floral designs. Wreaths of white lilies surround him. A subtle smile graces his cold and silky-smooth face as his skin reflects the light of two chandeliers with giant red candles.

All our children are here. Immeasurable sadness crops upon them because, after so many years, he conquered their hearts just as he did mine. My grandson Thomas doesn't grasp the grieving around him and shuffles in the hall. He looks everywhere as if he waited for Daniel to wake up, hold him in his arms, and cover him with kisses. The child approaches the coffin and tries to understand why his grandfather does not wake up. He cries when his mother cries and stops weeping when Emmanuelle does.

Many people attend the funeral service, among them several doctors from Riverfront and Stroger Hospitals. Most brought floral wreaths. Everyone has already expressed condolences. Daniel has done quite a bit of good for more than thirty years. I don't know how his patients heard about the bad news, but I see quite a few of them. Some are well-dressed, and some less well-dressed. They all bear grief on their faces as they sit on the magenta-cushioned chairs in the chapel. I watch a nurse trudge toward me,

"Mrs. Marlene Brandon?"

"Yes."

"I am sorry about Dr. Brandon's death. My deepest sympathy. Before he received the electroconvulsive therapy, your ex-husband left me a letter for you. I couldn't hand it to you before."

My hands are shaking. As I open the envelope, I feel like my beloved has sent me a message from the afterlife. His words overwhelm me,

Dear Marlene,

I don't think my heart will resist the electroshock. If so, please don't cry for me. I would have returned to the Other Dimension—the place where I came from. Finding and experiencing love with you made my brief life on earth worth it. By now, you should also know the good news of your pregnancy. Our baby will always be a constant reminder of our love and provide us with boundless happiness. I will always be in his dreams and protect you both. Please find yourself a loving husband who cares for our offspring.

Forever yours,

Sonie

I don't know what to say. My gynecologist, Dr. Robert Osler, called me this morning to break the news. I wonder how Daniel knew a week ago. Did Daniel's brain tumor create a delusion? Or does Sonie exist and live in the Other Dimension?

Time passes by, and today, I hold seven-year-old Daniel Brandon Jr.'s hand as we walk into Lincoln Park Zoo. It is a sunny morning, and children's joyful sounds cheer the place. They romp around as their mothers rush behind them, and their fathers stand before little shops to buy candies, balloons, and stuffed animals. An aroma of popcorn reaches us, a sea lion barks and jumps into a pond, and a tiger roars nearby. Little Daniel then asks,

"Mom, who is Sonie?"

I look at my son in awe and watch his eyes burst with the honey color and loving expression I observed in Daniel's so many times during the last three years of his life.

"Where did you hear that name? At Lorna's?"

"No. I asked him. He is in my dreams every night."

"It was true... Sonie lives. My God!"

My scream makes people around us turn their heads and look at me as if something horrible had occurred. But my expression of amazement and joy reassures them. My child now gazes at my astonished face and waits for me to answer his question with impatient curiosity.

"My son, it is a long story..."

ABOUT THE AUTHOR

Louis Villalba was born in Spain in 1945 and has resided in the US since 1970. He completed his neurology training at Chicago Medical School, where he became a clinical professor and taught for more than thirty years. He has authored several literary works of fiction and non-fiction:

The Silver Teacup: Tales of Cadiz (Createspace, 2012) contains short stories. The accounts take place in his hometown, Cadiz, Spain, shuttling the reader to a world full of historical fiction, human drama, and fantasy.

La Tacita de Plata: Cuentos de Cádiz (Createspace, 2012). Villalba rewrites the stories of his first book in Spanish.

The Stranger's Enigma (Createspace, 2014) features the first book of a two-part series. Kirkus praises it as "a provocative character study of a man facing a personal and professional crisis."

Afterlife Tracks: Glimpses of the Occult (Createspace, 2015). The author reports the paranormal events that occurred in his thirty-four-year neurology practice.

Cuban Seeds (Floricanto Press, December 2016) narrates the memoir of a widow who pursues her children's American dream after defying the Cuban tyranny.

The Series of Tales of Cadiz (Gades Books, 2017) re-edits and publishes ten stories about his hometown in Kindle format.

Uprooted Agave (Gades Books, 2018) recounts Latino Immi-grants' struggle to achieve the American dream.

The Series of Hispanic Immigrants' Stories (Gades Books, 2020.) Eight short stories in Kindle format.

Please visit www. TheClassicWriter. com, www.LouisVillalba.com, or www.GadesBooks.com for further information.

AUTHOR'S NOTE

Dear Reader,

Thank you for taking the time to read "Born of Dreams." If you enjoyed it, please post a brief review on www.Amazon.com—a few sentences describing what you liked about the story. Your words will help others discover the book.

Thank you again,
Louis Villalba

OTHER BOOKS BY LOUIS VILLALBA

The Silver Teacup
La Tacita de Plata
Afterlife Tracks
Cuban Seeds
The Series of the Tales of Cádiz
Uprooted Agave
The Stranger's Enigma
The Series of Hispanic Immigrants' Stories